The Wife of His Youth and Other Stories of the Color-Line

The Wife of His Youth and Other Stories of the Color-Line

Charles W. Chesnutt

MINT EDITIONS

The Wife of His Youth and Other Stories of the Color-Line was first published in 1899.

This edition published by Mint Editions 2021.

ISBN 9781513269313 | E-ISBN 9781513274317

Published by Mint Editions®

 MINT
EDITIONS

minteditionbooks.com

Publishing Director: Jennifer Newens
Design & Production: Rachel Lopez Metzger
Typesetting: Westchester Publishing Services

Contents

The Wife of His Youth

I

Mr. Ryder was going to give a ball. There were several reasons why this was an opportune time for such an event.

Mr. Ryder might aptly be called the dean of the Blue Veins. The original Blue Veins were a little society of colored persons organized in a certain Northern city shortly after the war. Its purpose was to establish and maintain correct social standards among a people whose social condition presented almost unlimited room for improvement. By accident, combined perhaps with some natural affinity, the society consisted of individuals who were, generally speaking, more white than black. Some envious outsider made the suggestion that no one was eligible for membership who was not white enough to show blue veins. The suggestion was readily adopted by those who were not of the favored few, and since that time the society, though possessing a longer and more pretentious name, had been known far and wide as the "Blue Vein Society," and its members as the "Blue Veins."

The Blue Veins did not allow that any such requirement existed for admission to their circle, but, on the contrary, declared that character and culture were the only things considered; and that if most of their members were light-colored, it was because such persons, as a rule, had had better opportunities to qualify themselves for membership. Opinions differed, too, as to the usefulness of the society. There were those who had been known to assail it violently as a glaring example of the very prejudice from which the colored race had suffered most; and later, when such critics had succeeded in getting on the inside, they had been heard to maintain with zeal and earnestness that the society was a lifeboat, an anchor, a bulwark and a shield,—a pillar of cloud by day and of fire by night, to guide their people through the social wilderness. Another alleged prerequisite for Blue Vein membership was that of free birth; and while there was really no such requirement, it is doubtless true that very few of the members would have been unable to meet it if there had been. If there were one or two of the older members who had come up from the South and from slavery, their history presented enough romantic circumstances to rob their servile origin of its grosser aspects.

While there were no such tests of eligibility, it is true that the Blue Veins had their notions on these subjects, and that not all of them were equally liberal in regard to the things they collectively disclaimed. Mr. Ryder was one of the most conservative. Though he had not been among the founders of the society, but had come in some years later, his genius for social leadership was such that he had speedily become its recognized adviser and head, the custodian of its standards, and the preserver of its traditions. He shaped its social policy, was active in providing for its entertainment, and when the interest fell off, as it sometimes did, he fanned the embers until they burst again into a cheerful flame.

There were still other reasons for his popularity. While he was not as white as some of the Blue Veins, his appearance was such as to confer distinction upon them. His features were of a refined type, his hair was almost straight; he was always neatly dressed; his manners were irreproachable, and his morals above suspicion. He had come to Groveland a young man, and obtaining employment in the office of a railroad company as messenger had in time worked himself up to the position of stationery clerk, having charge of the distribution of the office supplies for the whole company. Although the lack of early training had hindered the orderly development of a naturally fine mind, it had not prevented him from doing a great deal of reading or from forming decidedly literary tastes. Poetry was his passion. He could repeat whole pages of the great English poets; and if his pronunciation was sometimes faulty, his eye, his voice, his gestures, would respond to the changing sentiment with a precision that revealed a poetic soul and disarmed criticism. He was economical, and had saved money; he owned and occupied a very comfortable house on a respectable street. His residence was handsomely furnished, containing among other things a good library, especially rich in poetry, a piano, and some choice engravings. He generally shared his house with some young couple, who looked after his wants and were company for him; for Mr. Ryder was a single man. In the early days of his connection with the Blue Veins he had been regarded as quite a catch, and young ladies and their mothers had manoeuvred with much ingenuity to capture him. Not, however, until Mrs. Molly Dixon visited Groveland had any woman ever made him wish to change his condition to that of a married man.

Mrs. Dixon had come to Groveland from Washington in the spring, and before the summer was over she had won Mr. Ryder's heart. She possessed many attractive qualities. She was much younger than he; in fact, he was old enough to have been her father, though no one knew exactly how old he was. She was whiter than he, and better educated. She had moved in the best colored society of the country, at Washington, and had taught in the schools of that city. Such a superior person had been eagerly welcomed to the Blue Vein Society, and had taken a leading part in its activities. Mr. Ryder had at first been attracted by her charms of person, for she was very good looking and not over twenty-five; then by her refined manners and the vivacity of her wit. Her husband had been a government clerk, and at his death had left a considerable life insurance. She was visiting friends in Groveland, and, finding the town and the people to her liking, had prolonged her stay indefinitely. She had not seemed displeased at Mr. Ryder's attentions, but on the contrary had given him every proper encouragement; indeed, a younger and less cautious man would long since have spoken. But he had made up his mind, and had only to determine the time when he would ask her to be his wife. He decided to give a ball in her honor, and at some time during the evening of the ball to offer her his heart and hand. He had no special fears about the outcome, but, with a little touch of romance, he wanted the surroundings to be in harmony with his own feelings when he should have received the answer he expected.

Mr. Ryder resolved that this ball should mark an epoch in the social history of Groveland. He knew, of course,—no one could know better,— the entertainments that had taken place in past years, and what must be done to surpass them. His ball must be worthy of the lady in whose honor it was to be given, and must, by the quality of its guests, set an example for the future. He had observed of late a growing liberality, almost a laxity, in social matters, even among members of his own set, and had several times been forced to meet in a social way persons whose complexions and callings in life were hardly up to the standard which he considered proper for the society to maintain. He had a theory of his own.

"I have no race prejudice," he would say, "but we people of mixed blood are ground between the upper and the nether millstone. Our fate lies between absorption by the white race and extinction in the black. The one doesn't want us yet, but may take us in time. The other would welcome us, but it would be for us a backward step. 'With malice towards none, with charity for all,' we must do the best we can for ourselves and those who are to follow us. Self-preservation is the first law of nature."

His ball would serve by its exclusiveness to counteract leveling tendencies, and his marriage with Mrs. Dixon would help to further the upward process of absorption he had been wishing and waiting for.

II

THE BALL WAS TO TAKE place on Friday night. The house had been put in order, the carpets covered with canvas, the halls and stairs decorated with palms and potted plants; and in the afternoon Mr. Ryder sat on his front porch, which the shade of a vine running up over a wire netting made a cool and pleasant lounging place. He expected to respond to the toast "The Ladies" at the supper, and from a volume of Tennyson—his favorite poet—was fortifying himself with apt quotations. The volume was open at "A Dream of Fair Women." His eyes fell on these lines, and he read them aloud to judge better of their effect:—

> *"At length I saw a lady within call,*
> *Stiller than chisell'd marble, standing there;*
> *A daughter of the gods, divinely tall,*
> *And most divinely fair."*

He marked the verse, and turning the page read the stanza beginning,—

> *"O sweet pale Margaret,*
> *O rare pale Margaret."*

He weighed the passage a moment, and decided that it would not do. Mrs. Dixon was the palest lady he expected at the ball, and she was of a rather ruddy complexion, and of lively disposition and buxom build. So he ran over the leaves until his eye rested on the description of Queen Guinevere:—

> *"She seem'd a part of joyous Spring;*
> *A gown of grass-green silk she wore,*
> *Buckled with golden clasps before;*
> *A light-green tuft of plumes she bore*
> *Closed in a golden ring.*

CHARLES W. CHESNUTT

> *"She look'd so lovely, as she sway'd*
> *The rein with dainty finger-tips,*
> *A man had given all other bliss,*
> *And all his worldly worth for this,*
> *To waste his whole heart in one kiss*
> *Upon her perfect lips."*

As Mr. Ryder murmured these words audibly, with an appreciative thrill, he heard the latch of his gate click, and a light footfall sounding on the steps. He turned his head, and saw a woman standing before his door.

She was a little woman, not five feet tall, and proportioned to her height. Although she stood erect, and looked around her with very bright and restless eyes, she seemed quite old; for her face was crossed and recrossed with a hundred wrinkles, and around the edges of her bonnet could be seen protruding here and there a tuft of short gray wool. She wore a blue calico gown of ancient cut, a little red shawl fastened around her shoulders with an old-fashioned brass brooch, and a large bonnet profusely ornamented with faded red and yellow artificial flowers. And she was very black,—so black that her toothless gums, revealed when she opened her mouth to speak, were not red, but blue. She looked like a bit of the old plantation life, summoned up from the past by the wave of a magician's wand, as the poet's fancy had called into being the gracious shapes of which Mr. Ryder had just been reading.

He rose from his chair and came over to where she stood.

"Good-afternoon, madam," he said.

"Good-evenin', suh," she answered, ducking suddenly with a quaint curtsy. Her voice was shrill and piping, but softened somewhat by age. "Is dis yere whar Mistuh Ryduh lib, suh?" she asked, looking around her doubtfully, and glancing into the open windows, through which some of the preparations for the evening were visible.

"Yes," he replied, with an air of kindly patronage, unconsciously flattered by her manner, "I am Mr. Ryder. Did you want to see me?"

"Yas, suh, ef I ain't 'sturbin' of you too much."

"Not at all. Have a seat over here behind the vine, where it is cool. What can I do for you?"

"'Scuse me, suh," she continued, when she had sat down on the edge of a chair, "'scuse me, suh, I 's lookin' for my husban'. I heerd you wuz a big man an' had libbed heah a long time, an' I 'lowed you would n't min' ef I 'd come roun' an' ax you ef you 'd ever heerd of a merlatter man by de name er Sam Taylor 'quirin' roun' in de chu'ches ermongs' de people fer his wife 'Liza Jane?"

Mr. Ryder seemed to think for a moment.

"There used to be many such cases right after the war," he said, "but it has been so long that I have forgotten them. There are very few now. But tell me your story, and it may refresh my memory."

She sat back farther in her chair so as to be more comfortable, and folded her withered hands in her lap.

"My name 's 'Liza," she began, "'Liza Jane. W'en I wuz young I us'ter b'long ter Marse Bob Smif, down in ole Missoura. I wuz bawn down dere. Wen I wuz a gal I wuz married ter a man named Jim. But Jim died, an' after dat I married a merlatter man named Sam Taylor. Sam wuz free-bawn, but his mammy and daddy died, an' de w'ite folks 'prenticed him ter my marster fer ter work fer 'im 'tel he wuz growed up. Sam worked in de fiel', an' I wuz de cook. One day Ma'y Ann, ole miss's maid, came rushin' out ter de kitchen, an' says she, "'Liza Jane, ole marse gwine sell yo' Sam down de ribber."

"'Go way f'm yere,' says I; 'my husban' 's free!'

"'Don' make no diff'ence. I heerd ole marse tell ole miss he wuz gwine take yo' Sam 'way wid 'im ter-morrow, fer he needed money, an' he knowed whar he could git a t'ousan' dollars fer Sam an' no questions axed.'

"W'en Sam come home f'm de fiel' dat night, I tole him 'bout ole marse gwine steal 'im, an' Sam run erway. His time wuz mos' up, an' he swo' dat w'en he wuz twenty-one he would come back an' he'p me run erway, er else save up de money ter buy my freedom. An' I know he 'd 'a' done it, fer he thought a heap er me, Sam did. But w'en he come back he didn' fin' me, fer I wuzn' dere. Ole marse had heerd dat I warned Sam, so he had me whip' an' sol' down de ribber.

"Den de wah broke out, an' w'en it wuz ober de cullud folks wuz scattered. I went back ter de ole home; but Sam wuzn' dere, an' I could n' l'arn nuffin' 'bout 'im. But I knowed he 'd be'n dere to look fer me an' had n' foun' me, an' had gone erway ter hunt fer me.

"I 's be'n lookin' fer 'im eber sence," she added simply, as though twenty-five years were but a couple of weeks, "an' I knows he 's be'n lookin' fer me. Fer he sot a heap er sto' by me, Sam did, an' I know he 's be'n huntin' fer me all dese years,—'less'n he 's be'n sick er sump'n, so he could n' work, er out'n his head, so he could n' 'member his promise. I went back down de ribber, fer I 'lowed he 'd gone down dere lookin' fer me. I 's be'n ter Noo Orleans, an' Atlanty, an' Charleston, an' Richmon'; an' w'en I 'd be'n all ober de Souf I come ter de Norf. Fer I knows I 'll fin' 'im some er dese days," she added softly, "er he 'll fin' me, an' den we 'll bofe be as happy in freedom as we wuz in de ole days befo' de wah." A smile stole over her withered countenance as she paused a moment, and her bright eyes softened into a far-away look.

This was the substance of the old woman's story. She had wandered a little here and there. Mr. Ryder was looking at her curiously when she finished.

"How have you lived all these years?" he asked.

"Cookin', suh. I 's a good cook. Does you know anybody w'at needs a good cook, suh? I 's stoppin' wid a cullud fam'ly roun' de corner yonder 'tel I kin git a place."

"Do you really expect to find your husband? He may be dead long ago."

She shook her head emphatically. "Oh no, he ain' dead. De signs an' de tokens tells me. I dremp three nights runnin' on'y dis las' week dat I foun' him."

"He may have married another woman. Your slave marriage would not have prevented him, for you never lived with him after the war, and without that your marriage does n't count."

"Would n' make no diff'ence wid Sam. He would n' marry no yuther 'ooman 'tel he foun' out 'bout me. I knows it," she added. "Sump'n 's be'n tellin' me all dese years dat I 's gwine fin' Sam 'fo' I dies."

"Perhaps he 's outgrown you, and climbed up in the world where he would n't care to have you find him."

"No, indeed, suh," she replied, "Sam ain' dat kin' er man. He wuz good ter me, Sam wuz, but he wuz n' much good ter nobody e'se, fer he wuz one er de triflin'es' han's on de plantation. I 'spec's ter haf ter suppo't 'im w'en I fin' 'im, fer he nebber would work 'less'n he had ter. But den he wuz free, an' he did n' git no pay fer his work, an' I don' blame 'im much. Mebbe he 's done better sence he run erway, but I ain' 'spectin' much."

"You may have passed him on the street a hundred times during the twenty-five years, and not have known him; time works great changes."

She smiled incredulously. "I 'd know 'im 'mongs' a hund'ed men. Fer dey wuz n' no yuther merlatter man like my man Sam, an' I could n' be mistook. I 's toted his picture roun' wid me twenty-five years."

"May I see it?" asked Mr. Ryder. "It might help me to remember whether I have seen the original."

As she drew a small parcel from her bosom he saw that it was fastened to a string that went around her neck. Removing several wrappers, she brought to light an old-fashioned daguerreotype in a black case. He looked long and intently at the portrait. It was faded with time, but the features were still distinct, and it was easy to see what manner of man it had represented.

He closed the case, and with a slow movement handed it back to her.

"I don't know of any man in town who goes by that name," he said, "nor have I heard of any one making such inquiries. But if you will leave me your address, I will give the matter some attention, and if I find out anything I will let you know."

She gave him the number of a house in the neighborhood, and went away, after thanking him warmly.

He wrote the address on the fly-leaf of the volume of Tennyson, and, when she had gone, rose to his feet and stood looking after her curiously. As she walked down the street with mincing step, he saw several persons whom she passed turn and look back at her with a smile of kindly amusement. When she had turned the corner, he went upstairs to his bedroom, and stood for a long time before the mirror of his dressing-case, gazing thoughtfully at the reflection of his own face.

III

At eight o'clock the ballroom was a blaze of light and the guests had begun to assemble; for there was a literary programme and some routine business of the society to be gone through with before the dancing. A black servant in evening dress waited at the door and directed the guests to the dressing-rooms.

The occasion was long memorable among the colored people of the city; not alone for the dress and display, but for the high average of intelligence and culture that distinguished the gathering as a whole. There were a number of school-teachers, several young doctors, three or four lawyers, some professional singers, an editor, a lieutenant in the United States army spending his furlough in the city, and others in various polite callings; these were colored, though most of them would not have attracted even a casual glance because of any marked difference from white people. Most of the ladies were in evening costume, and dress coats and dancing pumps were the rule among the men. A band of string music, stationed in an alcove behind a row of palms, played popular airs while the guests were gathering.

The dancing began at half past nine. At eleven o'clock supper was served. Mr. Ryder had left the ballroom some little time before the intermission, but reappeared at the supper-table. The spread was worthy of the occasion, and the guests did full justice to it. When the coffee had been served, the toast-master, Mr. Solomon Sadler, rapped for order. He made a brief introductory speech, complimenting host and guests, and then presented in their order the toasts of the evening. They were responded to with a very fair display of after-dinner wit.

"The last toast," said the toast-master, when he reached the end of the list, "is one which must appeal to us all. There is no one of us of the sterner sex who is not at some time dependent upon woman,—in infancy for protection, in manhood for companionship, in old age for care and comforting. Our good host has been trying to live alone, but the fair faces I see around me to-night prove that he too is largely dependent upon the gentler sex for most that makes life worth living,—the society and love of friends,—and rumor is at fault if he does not soon yield entire subjection to one of them. Mr. Ryder will now respond to the toast,—The Ladies."

There was a pensive look in Mr. Ryder's eyes as he took the floor and adjusted his eyeglasses. He began by speaking of woman as the gift of Heaven to man, and after some general observations on the relations of the sexes he said: "But perhaps the quality which most distinguishes woman is her fidelity and devotion to those she loves. History is full of examples, but has recorded none more striking than one which only to-day came under my notice."

He then related, simply but effectively, the story told by his visitor of the afternoon. He gave it in the same soft dialect, which came readily to his lips, while the company listened attentively and sympathetically. For the story had awakened a responsive thrill in many hearts. There were some present who had seen, and others who had heard their fathers and grandfathers tell, the wrongs and sufferings of this past generation, and all of them still felt, in their darker moments, the shadow hanging over them. Mr. Ryder went on:—

"Such devotion and confidence are rare even among women. There are many who would have searched a year, some who would have waited five years, a few who might have hoped ten years; but for twenty-five years this woman has retained her affection for and her faith in a man she has not seen or heard of in all that time.

"She came to me to-day in the hope that I might be able to help her find this long-lost husband. And when she was gone I gave my fancy rein, and imagined a case I will put to you.

"Suppose that this husband, soon after his escape, had learned that his wife had been sold away, and that such inquiries as he could make brought no information of her whereabouts. Suppose that he was young, and she much older than he; that he was light, and she was black; that their marriage was a slave marriage, and legally binding only if they chose to make it so after the war. Suppose, too, that he made his way to the North, as some of us have done, and there, where he had larger opportunities, had improved them, and had in the course of all these years grown to be as different from the ignorant boy who ran away from fear of slavery as the day is from the night. Suppose, even, that he had qualified himself, by industry, by thrift, and by study, to win the friendship and be considered worthy the society of such people as these I see around me to-night, gracing my board and filling my heart with gladness; for I am old enough to remember the day when such a gathering would not have been possible in this land. Suppose, too, that, as the years went by, this man's memory of the past grew more and more indistinct, until at last it was rarely, except in his dreams, that any image of this bygone period rose before his mind. And then suppose that accident should bring to his knowledge the fact that the wife of his youth, the wife he had left behind him,—not one who had walked by his side and kept pace with him in his upward struggle, but one upon whom advancing years and a laborious life had set their mark,—was alive and seeking him, but that he was absolutely safe from recognition or discovery, unless he chose to reveal himself. My friends, what would the man do? I will presume that he was one who loved honor, and tried to deal justly with all men. I will even carry the case further, and suppose that perhaps he had set his heart upon another, whom he had hoped to call his own. What would he do, or rather what ought he to do, in such a crisis of a lifetime?

"It seemed to me that he might hesitate, and I imagined that I was an old friend, a near friend, and that he had come to me for advice; and I argued the case with him. I tried to discuss it impartially. After we had looked upon the matter from every point of view, I said to him, in words that we all know:—

> *"'This above all: to thine own self be true,*
> *And it must follow, as the night the day,*
> *Thou canst not then be false to any man.'*

"Then, finally, I put the question to him, 'Shall you acknowledge her?'

"And now, ladies and gentlemen, friends and companions, I ask you, what should he have done?"

There was something in Mr. Ryder's voice that stirred the hearts of those who sat around him. It suggested more than mere sympathy with an imaginary situation; it seemed rather in the nature of a personal appeal. It was observed, too, that his look rested more especially upon Mrs. Dixon, with a mingled expression of renunciation and inquiry.

She had listened, with parted lips and streaming eyes. She was the first to speak: "He should have acknowledged her."

"Yes," they all echoed, "he should have acknowledged her."

"My friends and companions," responded Mr. Ryder, "I thank you, one and all. It is the answer I expected, for I knew your hearts."

He turned and walked toward the closed door of an adjoining room, while every eye followed him in wondering curiosity. He came back in a moment, leading by the hand his visitor of the afternoon, who stood startled and trembling at the sudden plunge into this scene of brilliant gayety. She was neatly dressed in gray, and wore the white cap of an elderly woman.

"Ladies and gentlemen," he said, "this is the woman, and I am the man, whose story I have told you. Permit me to introduce to you the wife of my youth."

HER VIRGINIA MAMMY

I

THE PIANIST HAD STRUCK UP a lively two-step, and soon the floor was covered with couples, each turning on its own axis, and all revolving around a common centre, in obedience perhaps to the same law of motion that governs the planetary systems. The dancing-hall was a long room, with a waxed floor that glistened with the reflection of the lights from the chandeliers. The walls were hung in paper of blue and white, above a varnished hard wood wainscoting; the monotony of surface being broken by numerous windows draped with curtains of dotted muslin, and by occasional engravings and colored pictures representing the dances of various nations, judiciously selected. The rows of chairs along the two sides of the room were left unoccupied by the time the music was well under way, for the pianist, a tall colored woman with long fingers and a muscular wrist, played with a verve and a swing that set the feet of the listeners involuntarily in motion.

The dance was sure to occupy the class for a quarter of an hour at least, and the little dancing-mistress took the opportunity to slip away to her own sitting-room, which was on the same floor of the block, for a few minutes of rest. Her day had been a hard one. There had been a matinee at two o'clock, a children's class at four, and at eight o'clock the class now on the floor had assembled.

When she reached the sitting-room she gave a start of pleasure. A young man rose at her entrance, and advanced with both hands extended—a tall, broad-shouldered, fair-haired young man, with a frank and kindly countenance, now lit up with the animation of pleasure. He seemed about twenty-six or twenty-seven years old. His face was of the type one instinctively associates with intellect and character, and it gave the impression, besides, of that intangible something which we call race. He was neatly and carefully dressed, though his clothing was not without indications that he found it necessary or expedient to practice economy.

"Good-evening, Clara," he said, taking her hands in his; "I've been waiting for you five minutes. I supposed you would be in, but if you had been a moment later I was going to the hall to look you up. You seem tired to-night," he added, drawing her nearer to him and scanning her features at short range. "This work is too hard; you are not fitted for it. When are you going to give it up?"

"The season is almost over," she answered, "and then I shall stop for the summer."

He drew her closer still and kissed her lovingly. "Tell me, Clara," he said, looking down into her face,—he was at least a foot taller than she,—"when I am to have my answer."

"Will you take the answer you can get to-night?" she asked with a wan smile.

"I will take but one answer, Clara. But do not make me wait too long for that. Why, just think of it! I have known you for six months."

"That is an extremely long time," said Clara, as they sat down side by side.

"It has been an age," he rejoined. "For a fortnight of it, too, which seems longer than all the rest, I have been waiting for my answer. I am turning gray under the suspense. Seriously, Clara dear, what shall it be? or rather, when shall it be? for to the other question there is but one answer possible."

He looked into her eyes, which slowly filled with tears. She repulsed him gently as he bent over to kiss them away.

"You know I love you, John, and why I do not say what you wish. You must give me a little more time to make up my mind before I can consent to burden you with a nameless wife, one who does not know who her mother was"—

"She was a good woman, and beautiful, if you are at all like her."

"Or her father"—

"He was a gentleman and a scholar, if you inherited from him your mind or your manners."

"It is good of you to say that, and I try to believe it. But it is a serious matter; it is a dreadful thing to have no name."

"You are known by a worthy one, which was freely given you, and is legally yours."

"I know—and I am grateful for it. After all, though, it is not my real name; and since I have learned that it was not, it seems like a garment—something external, accessory, and not a part of myself. It does not mean what one's own name would signify."

"Take mine, Clara, and make it yours; I lay it at your feet. Some honored men have borne it."

"Ah yes, and that is what makes my position the harder. Your great-grandfather was governor of Connecticut."

"I have heard my mother say so."

"And one of your ancestors came over in the Mayflower."

"In some capacity—I have never been quite clear whether as ship's cook or before the mast."

"Now you are insincere, John; but you cannot deceive me. You never spoke in that way about your ancestors until you learned that I had none. I know you are proud of them, and that the memory of the governor and the judge and the Harvard professor and the Mayflower pilgrim makes you strive to excel, in order to prove yourself worthy of them."

"It did until I met you, Clara. Now the one inspiration of my life is the hope to make you mine."

"And your profession?"

"It will furnish me the means to take you out of this; you are not fit for toil."

"And your book—your treatise that is to make you famous?"

"I have worked twice as hard on it and accomplished twice as much since I have hoped that you might share my success."

"Oh! if I but knew the truth!" she sighed, "or could find it out! I realize that I am absurd, that I ought to be happy. I love my parents—my foster-parents—dearly. I owe them everything. Mother—poor, dear mother!—could not have loved me better or cared for me more faithfully had I been her own child. Yet—I am ashamed to say it—I always felt that I was not like them, that there was a subtle difference between us. They were contented in prosperity, resigned in misfortune; I was ever restless, and filled with vague ambitions. They were good, but dull. They loved me, but they never said so. I feel that there is warmer, richer blood coursing in my veins than the placid stream that crept through theirs."

"There will never be any such people to me as they were," said her lover, "for they took you and brought you up for me."

"Sometimes," she went on dreamily, "I feel sure that I am of good family, and the blood of my ancestors seems to call to me in clear and certain tones. Then again when my mood changes, I am all at sea—I feel that even if I had but simply to turn my hand to learn who I am and whence I came, I should shrink from taking the step, for fear that what I might learn would leave me forever unhappy."

"Dearest," he said, taking her in his arms, while from the hall and down the corridor came the softened strains of music, "put aside these unwholesome fancies. Your past is shrouded in mystery. Take my name, as you have taken my love, and I'll make your future so happy that you won't have time to think of the past. What are a lot of musty, mouldy old grandfathers, compared with life and love and happiness? It's hardly good form to mention one's ancestors nowadays, and what's the use of them at all if one can't boast of them?"

"It's all very well of you to talk that way," she rejoined. "But suppose you should marry me, and when you become famous and rich, and patients flock to your office, and fashionable people to your home, and every one wants to know who you are and whence you came, you'll be obliged to bring out the governor, and the judge, and the rest of them. If you should refrain, in order to forestall embarrassing inquiries about *my* ancestry, I should have deprived you of something you are entitled to, something which has a real social value. And when people found out all about you, as they eventually would from some source, they would want to know—we Americans are a curious people—who your wife was, and you could only say"—

"The best and sweetest woman on earth, whom I love unspeakably."

"You know that is not what I mean. You could only say—a Miss Nobody, from Nowhere."

"A Miss Hohlfelder, from Cincinnati, the only child of worthy German parents, who fled from their own country in '49 to escape political persecution—an ancestry that one surely need not be ashamed of."

"No; but the consciousness that it was not true would be always with me, poisoning my mind, and darkening my life and yours."

"Your views of life are entirely too tragic, Clara," the young man argued soothingly. "We are all worms of the dust, and if we go back far enough, each of us has had millions of ancestors; peasants and serfs, most of them; thieves, murderers, and vagabonds, many of them, no doubt; and therefore the best of us have but little to boast of. Yet we are all made after God's own image, and formed by his hand, for his ends; and therefore not to be lightly despised, even the humblest of us, least of all by ourselves. For the past we can claim no credit, for those who made it died with it. Our destiny lies in the future."

"Yes," she sighed, "I know all that. But I am not like you. A woman is not like a man; she cannot lose herself in theories and generalizations. And there are tests that even all your philosophy could not endure. Suppose you should marry me, and then some time, by the merest accident, you should learn that my origin was the worst it could be— that I not only had no name, but was not entitled to one."

"I cannot believe it," he said, "and from what we do know of your history it is hardly possible. If I learned it, I should forget it, unless, perchance, it should enhance your value in my eyes, by stamping you as a rare work of nature, an exception to the law of heredity, a triumph of pure beauty and goodness over the grosser limitations of matter. I cannot imagine, now that I know you, anything that could make me love you less. I would marry you just the same—even if you were one of your dancing-class to-night."

"I must go back to them," said Clara, as the music ceased.

"My answer," he urged, "give me my answer!"

"Not to-night, John," she pleaded. "Grant me a little longer time to make up my mind—for your sake."

"Not for my sake, Clara, no."

"Well—for mine." She let him take her in his arms and kiss her again.

"I have a patient yet to see to-night," he said as he went out. "If I am not detained too long, I may come back this way—if I see the lights in the hall still burning. Do not wonder if I ask you again for my answer, for I shall be unhappy until I get it."

II

A STRANGER ENTERING THE HALL with Miss Hohlfelder would have seen, at first glance, only a company of well-dressed people, with nothing to specially distinguish them from ordinary humanity in temperate climates. After the eye had rested for a moment and begun to separate the mass into its component parts, one or two dark faces would have arrested its attention; and with the suggestion thus offered, a closer inspection would have revealed that they were nearly all a little less than white. With most of them this fact would not have been noticed, while they were alone or in company with one another, though if a fair white person had gone among them it would perhaps have been more apparent. From the few who were undistinguishable from pure white, the colors ran down the scale by minute gradations to the two or three brown faces at the other extremity.

It was Miss Hohlfelder's first colored class. She had been somewhat startled when first asked to take it. No person of color had ever applied to her for lessons; and while a woman of that race had played the piano for her for several months, she had never thought of colored people as possible pupils. So when she was asked if she would take a class of twenty or thirty, she had hesitated, and begged for time to consider the application. She knew that several of the more fashionable dancing-schools tabooed all pupils, singly or in classes, who labored under social disabilities—and this included the people of at least one other race who were vastly farther along in the world than the colored people of the community where Miss Hohlfelder lived. Personally she had no such prejudice, except perhaps a little shrinking at the thought of personal contact with the dark faces of whom Americans always think when "colored people" are spoken of. Again, a class of forty pupils was not to be despised, for she taught for money, which was equally current and desirable, regardless of its color. She had consulted her foster-parents, and after them her lover. Her foster-parents, who were German-born, and had never become thoroughly Americanized, saw no objection. As for her lover, he was indifferent.

"Do as you please," he said. "It may drive away some other pupils. If it should break up the business entirely, perhaps you might be willing to give me a chance so much the sooner."

She mentioned the matter to one or two other friends, who expressed conflicting opinions. She decided at length to take the class, and take the consequences.

"I don't think it would be either right or kind to refuse them for any such reason, and I don't believe I shall lose anything by it."

She was somewhat surprised, and pleasantly so, when her class came together for their first lesson, at not finding them darker and more uncouth. Her pupils were mostly people whom she would have passed on the street without a second glance, and among them were several whom she had known by sight for years, but had never dreamed of as being colored people. Their manners were good, they dressed quietly and as a rule with good taste, avoiding rather than choosing bright colors and striking combinations—whether from natural preference, or because of a slightly morbid shrinking from criticism, of course she could not say. Among them, the dancing-mistress soon learned, there were lawyers and doctors, teachers, telegraph operators, clerks, milliners and dressmakers, students of the local college and scientific school, and, somewhat to her awe at the first meeting, even a member of the legislature. They were mostly young, although a few light-hearted older people joined the class, as much for company as for the dancing.

"Of course, Miss Hohlfelder," explained Mr. Solomon Sadler, to whom the teacher had paid a compliment on the quality of the class, "the more advanced of us are not numerous enough to make the fine distinctions that are possible among white people; and of course as we rise in life we can't get entirely away from our brothers and our sisters and our cousins, who don't always keep abreast of us. We do, however, draw certain lines of character and manners and occupation. You see the sort of people we are. Of course we have no prejudice against color, and we regard all labor as honorable, provided a man does the best he can. But we must have standards that will give our people something to aspire to."

The class was not a difficult one, as many of the members were already fairly good dancers. Indeed the class had been formed as much for pleasure as for instruction. Music and hall rent and a knowledge of the latest dances could be obtained cheaper in this way than in any other. The pupils had made rapid progress, displaying in fact a natural aptitude for rhythmic motion, and a keen susceptibility to musical sounds. As their race had never been criticised for these characteristics, they gave them full play, and soon developed, most of them, into graceful and indefatigable dancers. They were now almost at the end of their course, and this was the evening of the last lesson but one.

Miss Hohlfelder had remarked to her lover more than once that it was a pleasure to teach them. "They enter into the spirit of it so thoroughly, and they seem to enjoy themselves so much."

"One would think," he suggested, "that the whitest of them would find their position painful and more or less pathetic; to be so white and yet to be classed as black—so near and yet so far."

"They don't accept our classification blindly. They do not acknowledge any inferiority; they think they are a great deal better than any but the best white people," replied Miss Hohlfelder. "And since they have been coming here, do you know," she went on, "I hardly think of them as any different from other people. I feel perfectly at home among them."

"It is a great thing to have faith in one's self," he replied. "It is a fine thing, too, to be able to enjoy the passing moment. One of your greatest charms in my eyes, Clara, is that in your lighter moods you have this faculty. You sing because you love to sing. You find pleasure in dancing, even by way of work. You feel the *joie de vivre*—the joy of living. You are not always so, but when you are so I think you most delightful."

Miss Hohlfelder, upon entering the hall, spoke to the pianist and then exchanged a few words with various members of the class. The pianist began to play a dreamy Strauss waltz. When the dance was well

CHARLES W. CHESNUTT

under way Miss Hohlfelder left the hall again and stepped into the ladies' dressing-room. There was a woman seated quietly on a couch in a corner, her hands folded on her lap.

"Good-evening, Miss Hohlfelder. You do not seem as bright as usual to-night."

Miss Hohlfelder felt a sudden yearning for sympathy. Perhaps it was the gentle tones of the greeting; perhaps the kindly expression of the soft though faded eyes that were scanning Miss Hohlfelder's features. The woman was of the indefinite age between forty and fifty. There were lines on her face which, if due to years, might have carried her even past the half-century mark, but if caused by trouble or ill health might leave her somewhat below it. She was quietly dressed in black, and wore her slightly wavy hair low over her ears, where it lay naturally in the ripples which some others of her sex so sedulously seek by art. A little woman, of clear olive complexion and regular features, her face was almost a perfect oval, except as time had marred its outline. She had been in the habit of coming to the class with some young women of the family she lived with, part boarder, part seamstress and friend of the family. Sometimes, while waiting for her young charges, the music would jar her nerves, and she would seek the comparative quiet of the dressing-room.

"Oh, I'm all right, Mrs. Harper," replied the dancing-mistress, with a brave attempt at cheerfulness,—"just a little tired, after a hard day's work."

She sat down on the couch by the elder woman's side. Mrs. Harper took her hand and stroked it gently, and Clara felt soothed and quieted by her touch.

"There are tears in your eyes and trouble in your face. I know it, for I have shed the one and known the other. Tell me, child, what ails you? I am older than you, and perhaps I have learned some things in the hard school of life that may be of comfort or service to you."

Such a request, coming from a comparative stranger, might very properly have been resented or lightly parried. But Clara was not what would be called self-contained. Her griefs seemed lighter when they were shared with others, even in spirit. There was in her nature a childish strain that craved sympathy and comforting. She had never known—or if so it was only in a dim and dreamlike past—the tender, brooding care that was her conception of a mother's love. Mrs. Hohlfelder had been fond of her in a placid way, and had given her every comfort and luxury her means permitted. Clara's ideal of maternal love had been of another and more romantic type; she had thought of a fond, impulsive mother, to whose bosom she could fly when in trouble or distress, and to whom she could communicate her sorrows and trials; who would dry her tears and soothe her with caresses. Now, when even her kind foster-mother was gone, she felt still more the need of sympathy and companionship with her own sex; and when this little Mrs. Harper spoke to her so gently, she felt her heart respond instinctively.

"Yes, Mrs. Harper," replied Clara with a sigh, "I am in trouble, but it is trouble that you nor any one else can heal."

"You do not know, child. A simple remedy can sometimes cure a very grave complaint. Tell me your trouble, if it is something you are at liberty to tell."

"I have a story," said Clara, "and it is a strange one,—a story I have told to but one other person, one very dear to me."

"He must be dear to you indeed, from the tone in which you speak of him. Your very accents breathe love."

"Yes, I love him, and if you saw him—perhaps you have seen him, for he has looked in here once or twice during the dancing-lessons— you would know why I love him. He is handsome, he is learned, he is ambitious, he is brave, he is good; he is poor, but he will not always be so; and he loves me, oh, so much!"

The other woman smiled. "It is not so strange to love, nor yet to be loved. And all lovers are handsome and brave and fond."

"That is not all of my story. He wants to marry me." Clara paused, as if to let this statement impress itself upon the other.

"True lovers always do," said the elder woman.

"But sometimes, you know, there are circumstances which prevent them."

"Ah yes," murmured the other reflectively, and looking at the girl with deeper interest, "circumstances which prevent them. I have known of such a case."

"The circumstance which prevents us from marrying is my story."

"Tell me your story, child, and perhaps, if I cannot help you otherwise, I can tell you one that will make yours seem less sad."

"You know me," said the young woman, "as Miss Hohlfelder; but that is not actually my name. In fact I do not know my real name, for I am not the daughter of Mr. and Mrs. Hohlfelder, but only an adopted child. While Mrs. Hohlfelder lived, I never knew that I was not her child. I knew I was very different from her and father,—I mean Mr. Hohlfelder. I knew they were fair and I was dark; they were stout and I was slender; they were slow and I was quick. But of course I never dreamed of the true reason of this difference. When mother—Mrs. Hohlfelder—died, I found among her things one day a little packet, carefully wrapped up, containing a child's slip and some trinkets. The paper wrapper of the packet bore an inscription that awakened my curiosity. I asked father Hohlfelder whose the things had been, and then for the first time I learned my real story.

"I was not their own daughter, he stated, but an adopted child. Twenty-three years ago, when he had lived in St. Louis, a steamboat explosion had occurred up the river, and on a piece of wreckage floating down stream, a girl baby had been found. There was nothing on the child to give a hint of its home or parentage; and no one came to claim it, though the fact that a child had been found was advertised all along the river. It was believed that the infant's parents must have perished in the wreck, and certainly no one of those who were saved could identify the child. There had been a passenger list on board the steamer, but the list, with the officer who kept it, had been lost in the accident. The child was turned over to an orphan asylum, from which within a year it was adopted by the two kind-hearted and childless German people who brought it up as their own. I was that child."

The woman seated by Clara's side had listened with strained attention. "Did you learn the name of the steamboat?" she asked quietly, but quickly, when Clara paused.

"The Pride of St. Louis," answered Clara. She did not look at Mrs. Harper, but was gazing dreamily toward the front, and therefore did not see the expression that sprang into the other's face,—a look in which hope struggled with fear, and yearning love with both,—nor the strong effort with which Mrs. Harper controlled herself and moved not one muscle while the other went on.

"I was never sought," Clara continued, "and the good people who brought me up gave me every care. Father and mother—I can never train my tongue to call them anything else—were very good to me. When they adopted me they were poor; he was a pharmacist with a small shop. Later on he moved to Cincinnati, where he made and sold a popular 'patent' medicine and amassed a fortune. Then I went to a fashionable school, was taught French, and deportment, and dancing. Father Hohlfelder made some bad investments, and lost most of his money. The patent medicine fell off in popularity. A year or two ago we came to this city to live. Father bought this block and opened the little drug store below. We moved into the rooms upstairs. The business was poor, and I felt that I ought to do something to earn money and help support the family. I could dance; we had this hall, and it was not rented all the time, so I opened a dancing-school."

"Tell me, child," said the other woman, with restrained eagerness, "what were the things found upon you when you were taken from the river?"

"Yes," answered the girl, "I will. But I have not told you all my story, for this is but the prelude. About a year ago a young doctor rented an office in our block. We met each other, at first only now and then, and afterwards oftener; and six months ago he told me that he loved me."

She paused, and sat with half opened lips and dreamy eyes, looking back into the past six months.

"And the things found upon you"—

"Yes, I will show them to you when you have heard all my story. He wanted to marry me, and has asked me every week since. I have told him that I love him, but I have not said I would marry him. I don't think it would be right for me to do so, unless I could clear up this mystery. I believe he is going to be great and rich and famous, and there might come a time when he would be ashamed of me. I don't say that I shall never marry him; for I have hoped—I have a presentiment that in some strange way I shall find out who I am, and who my parents were. It may be mere imagination on my part, but somehow I believe it is more than that."

"Are you sure there was no mark on the things that were found upon you?" said the elder woman.

"Ah yes," sighed Clara, "I am sure, for I have looked at them a hundred times. They tell me nothing, and yet they suggest to me many things. Come," she said, taking the other by the hand, "and I will show them to you."

She led the way along the hall to her sitting-room, and to her bedchamber beyond. It was a small room hung with paper showing a pattern of morning-glories on a light ground, with dotted muslin curtains, a white iron bedstead, a few prints on the wall, a rocking-chair—a very dainty room. She went to the maple dressing-case, and opened one of the drawers.

As they stood for a moment, the mirror reflecting and framing

CHARLES W. CHESNUTT

their image, more than one point of resemblance between them was emphasized. There was something of the same oval face, and in Clara's hair a faint suggestion of the wave in the older woman's; and though Clara was fairer of complexion, and her eyes were gray and the other's black, there was visible, under the influence of the momentary excitement, one of those indefinable likenesses which are at times encountered,—sometimes marking blood relationship, sometimes the impress of a common training; in one case perhaps a mere earmark of temperament, and in another the index of a type. Except for the difference in color, one might imagine that if the younger woman were twenty years older the resemblance would be still more apparent.

Clara reached her hand into the drawer and drew out a folded packet, which she unwrapped, Mrs. Harper following her movements meanwhile with a suppressed intensity of interest which Clara, had she not been absorbed in her own thoughts, could not have failed to observe.

When the last fold of paper was removed there lay revealed a child's muslin slip. Clara lifted it and shook it gently until it was unfolded before their eyes. The lower half was delicately worked in a lacelike pattern, revealing an immense amount of patient labor.

The elder woman seized the slip with hands which could not disguise their trembling. Scanning the garment carefully, she seemed to be noting the pattern of the needlework, and then, pointing to a certain spot, exclaimed:—

"I thought so! I was sure of it! Do you not see the letters—M.S.?"

"Oh, how wonderful!" Clara seized the slip in turn and scanned the monogram. "How strange that you should see that at once and that I should not have discovered it, who have looked at it a hundred times! And here," she added, opening a small package which had been inclosed in the other, "is my coral necklace. Perhaps your keen eyes can find something in that."

It was a simple trinket, at which the older woman gave but a glance—a glance that added to her emotion.

"Listen, child," she said, laying her trembling hand on the other's arm. "It is all very strange and wonderful, for that slip and necklace, and, now that I have seen them, your face and your voice and your ways, all tell me who you are. Your eyes are your father's eyes, your voice is your father's voice. The slip was worked by your mother's hand."

"Oh!" cried Clara, and for a moment the whole world swam before her eyes.

"I was on the Pride of St. Louis, and I knew your father—and your mother."

Clara, pale with excitement, burst into tears, and would have fallen had not the other woman caught her in her arms. Mrs. Harper placed her on the couch, and, seated by her side, supported her head on her shoulder. Her hands seemed to caress the young woman with every touch.

"Tell me, oh, tell me all!" Clara demanded, when the first wave of emotion had subsided. "Who were my father and my mother, and who am I?"

The elder woman restrained her emotion with an effort, and answered as composedly as she could,—

"There were several hundred passengers on the Pride of St. Louis when she left Cincinnati on that fateful day, on her regular trip to New Orleans. Your father and mother were on the boat—and I was on the boat. We were going down the river, to take ship at New Orleans for France, a country which your father loved."

"Who was my father?" asked Clara. The woman's words fell upon her ear like water on a thirsty soil.

"Your father was a Virginia gentleman, and belonged to one of the first families, the Staffords, of Melton County."

Clara drew herself up unconsciously, and into her face there came a frank expression of pride which became it wonderfully, setting off a beauty that needed only this to make it all but perfect of its type.

"I knew it must be so," she murmured. "I have often felt it. Blood will always tell. And my mother?"

"Your mother—also belonged to one of the first families of Virginia, and in her veins flowed some of the best blood of the Old Dominion."

"What was her maiden name?"

"Mary Fairfax. As I was saying, your father was a Virginia gentleman. He was as handsome a man as ever lived, and proud, oh, so proud!—and good, and kind. He was a graduate of the University and had studied abroad."

"My mother—was she beautiful?"

"She was much admired, and your father loved her from the moment he first saw her. Your father came back from Europe, upon his father's sudden death, and entered upon his inheritance. But he had been away from Virginia so long, and had read so many books, that he had outgrown his home. He did not believe that slavery was right, and one of the first things he did was to free his slaves. His views were not popular, and he sold out his lands a year before the war, with the intention of moving to Europe."

"In the mean time he had met and loved and married my mother?"

"In the mean time he had met and loved your mother."

"My mother was a Virginia belle, was she not?"

"The Fairfaxes," answered Mrs. Harper, "were the first of the first families, the bluest of the blue-bloods. The Miss Fairfaxes were all beautiful and all social favorites."

"What did my father do then, when he had sold out in Virginia?"

"He went with your mother and you—you were then just a year old—to Cincinnati, to settle up some business connected with his estate. When he had completed his business, he embarked on the Pride of St. Louis with you and your mother and a colored nurse."

"And how did you know about them?" asked Clara.

"I was one of the party. I was"—

"You were the colored nurse?—my 'mammy,' they would have called you in my old Virginia home?"

"Yes, child, I was—your mammy. Upon my bosom you have rested; my breasts once gave you nourishment; my hands once ministered to you; my arms sheltered you, and my heart loved you and mourned you like a mother loves and mourns her firstborn."

"Oh, how strange, how delightful!" exclaimed Clara. "Now I understand why you clasped me so tightly, and were so agitated when I told you my story. It is too good for me to believe. I am of good blood, of an old and aristocratic family. My presentiment has come true. I can marry my lover, and I shall owe all my happiness to you. How can I ever repay you?"

"You can kiss me, child, kiss your mammy."

Their lips met, and they were clasped in each other's arms. One put into the embrace all of her new-found joy, the other all the suppressed feeling of the last half hour, which in turn embodied the unsatisfied yearning of many years.

The music had ceased and the pupils had left the hall. Mrs. Harper's charges had supposed her gone, and had left for home without her. But the two women, sitting in Clara's chamber, hand in hand, were oblivious to external things and noticed neither the hour nor the cessation of the music.

"Why, dear mammy," said the young woman musingly, "did you not find me, and restore me to my people?"

"Alas, child! I was not white, and when I was picked up from the water, after floating miles down the river, the man who found me kept me prisoner for a time, and, there being no inquiry for me, pretended not to believe that I was free, and took me down to New Orleans and sold me as a slave. A few years later the war set me free. I went to St. Louis but could find no trace of you. I had hardly dared to hope that a child had been saved, when so many grown men and women had lost their lives. I made such inquiries as I could, but all in vain."

"Did you go to the orphan asylum?"

"The orphan asylum had been burned and with it all the records. The war had scattered the people so that I could find no one who knew about a lost child saved from a river wreck. There were many orphans in those days, and one more or less was not likely to dwell in the public mind."

"Did you tell my people in Virginia?"

"They, too, were scattered by the war. Your uncles lost their lives on the battlefield. The family mansion was burned to the ground. Your father's remaining relatives were reduced to poverty, and moved away from Virginia."

"What of my mother's people?"

"They are all dead. God punished them. They did not love your father, and did not wish him to marry your mother. They helped to drive him to his death."

"I am alone in the world, then, without kith or kin," murmured Clara, "and yet, strange to say, I am happy. If I had known my people and lost them, I should be sad. They are gone, but they have left me their name and their blood. I would weep for my poor father and mother if I were not so glad."

Just then some one struck a chord upon the piano in the hall, and the sudden breaking of the stillness recalled Clara's attention to the lateness of the hour.

"I had forgotten about the class," she exclaimed. "I must go and attend to them."

They walked along the corridor and entered the hall. Dr. Winthrop was seated at the piano, drumming idly on the keys.

"I did not know where you had gone," he said. "I knew you would be around, of course, since the lights were not out, and so I came in here to wait for you."

"Listen, John, I have a wonderful story to tell you."

CHARLES W. CHESNUTT

Then she told him Mrs. Harper's story. He listened attentively and sympathetically, at certain points taking his eyes from Clara's face and glancing keenly at Mrs. Harper, who was listening intently. As he looked from one to the other he noticed the resemblance between them, and something in his expression caused Mrs. Harper's eyes to fall, and then glance up appealingly.

"And now," said Clara, "I am happy. I know my name. I am a Virginia Stafford. I belong to one, yes, to two of what were the first families of Virginia. John, my family is as good as yours. If I remember my history correctly, the Cavaliers looked down upon the Roundheads."

"I admit my inferiority," he replied. "If you are happy I am glad."

"Clara Stafford," mused the girl. "It is a pretty name."

"You will never have to use it," her lover declared, "for now you will take mine."

"Then I shall have nothing left of all that I have found"—

"Except your husband," asserted Dr. Winthrop, putting his arm around her, with an air of assured possession.

Mrs. Harper was looking at them with moistened eyes in which joy and sorrow, love and gratitude, were strangely blended. Clara put out her hand to her impulsively.

"And my mammy," she cried, "my dear Virginia mammy."

THE SHERIFF'S CHILDREN

B ranson County, North Carolina, is in a sequestered district of one of the staidest and most conservative States of the Union. Society in Branson County is almost primitive in its simplicity. Most of the white people own the farms they till, and even before the war there were no very wealthy families to force their neighbors, by comparison, into the category of "poor whites."

To Branson County, as to most rural communities in the South, the war is the one historical event that overshadows all others. It is the era from which all local chronicles are dated,—births, deaths, marriages, storms, freshets. No description of the life of any Southern community would be perfect that failed to emphasize the all pervading influence of the great conflict.

Yet the fierce tide of war that had rushed through the cities and along the great highways of the country had comparatively speaking but slightly disturbed the sluggish current of life in this region, remote from railroads and navigable streams. To the north in Virginia, to the west in Tennessee, and all along the seaboard the war had raged; but the thunder of its cannon had not disturbed the echoes of Branson County, where the loudest sounds heard were the crack of some hunter's rifle, the baying of some deep-mouthed hound, or the yodel of some tuneful negro on his way through the pine forest. To the east, Sherman's army had passed on its march to the sea; but no straggling band of "bummers" had penetrated the confines of Branson County. The war, it is true, had robbed the county of the flower of its young manhood; but the burden of taxation, the doubt and uncertainty of the conflict, and the sting of ultimate defeat, had been borne by the people with an apathy that robbed misfortune of half its sharpness.

The nearest approach to town life afforded by Branson County is found in the little village of Troy, the county seat, a hamlet with a population of four or five hundred.

Ten years make little difference in the appearance of these remote Southern towns. If a railroad is built through one of them, it infuses some enterprise; the social corpse is galvanized by the fresh blood of civilization that pulses along the farthest ramifications of our great system of commercial highways. At the period of which I write, no railroad had come to Troy. If a traveler, accustomed to the bustling life of cities, could have ridden through Troy on a summer day, he might easily have fancied himself in a deserted village. Around him he would have seen weather-beaten houses, innocent of paint, the shingled roofs in many instances covered with a rich growth of moss. Here and there he would have met a razor-backed hog lazily rooting his way along the principal thoroughfare; and more than once he would probably have had to disturb the slumbers of some yellow dog, dozing away the hours in the ardent sunshine, and reluctantly yielding up his place in the middle of the dusty road.

On Saturdays the village presented a somewhat livelier appearance, and the shade trees around the court house square and along Front Street served as hitching-posts for a goodly number of horses and mules and stunted oxen, belonging to the farmer-folk who had come in to trade at the two or three local stores.

A murder was a rare event in Branson County. Every well-informed citizen could tell the number of homicides committed in the county for fifty years back, and whether the slayer, in any given instance, had escaped, either by flight or acquittal, or had suffered the penalty of the law. So, when it became known in Troy early one Friday morning in summer, about ten years after the war, that old Captain Walker, who had served in Mexico under Scott, and had left an arm on the field of Gettysburg, had been foully murdered during the night, there was intense excitement in the village. Business was practically suspended, and the citizens gathered in little groups to discuss the murder, and speculate upon the identity of the murderer. It transpired from testimony at the coroner's inquest, held during the morning, that a strange mulatto had been seen going in the direction of Captain Walker's house the night before, and had been met going away from Troy early Friday morning, by a farmer on his way to town. Other circumstances seemed to connect the stranger with the crime. The sheriff organized a posse to search for him, and early in the evening, when most of the citizens of Troy were at supper, the suspected man was brought in and lodged in the county jail.

By the following morning the news of the capture had spread to the farthest limits of the county. A much larger number of people than usual came to town that Saturday,—bearded men in straw hats and blue homespun shirts, and butternut trousers of great amplitude of material and vagueness of outline; women in homespun frocks and slat-bonnets, with faces as expressionless as the dreary sandhills which gave them a meagre sustenance.

The murder was almost the sole topic of conversation. A steady stream of curious observers visited the house of mourning, and gazed upon the rugged face of the old veteran, now stiff and cold in death; and more than one eye dropped a tear at the remembrance of the cheery smile, and the joke—sometimes superannuated, generally feeble, but always good-natured—with which the captain had been wont to greet his acquaintances. There was a growing sentiment of anger among these stern men, toward the murderer who had thus cut down their friend, and a strong feeling that ordinary justice was too slight a punishment for such a crime.

Toward noon there was an informal gathering of citizens in Dan Tyson's store.

"I hear it 'lowed that Square Kyahtah's too sick ter hol' co'te this evenin'," said one, "an' that the purlim'nary hearin' 'll haf ter go over 'tel nex' week."

A look of disappointment went round the crowd.

"Hit 's the durndes', meanes' murder ever committed in this caounty," said another, with moody emphasis.

"I s'pose the nigger 'lowed the Cap'n had some green-backs," observed a third speaker.

"The Cap'n," said another, with an air of superior information, "has left two bairls of Confedrit money, which he 'spected 'ud be good some day er nuther."

This statement gave rise to a discussion of the speculative value of Confederate money; but in a little while the conversation returned to the murder.

"Hangin' air too good fer the murderer," said one; "he oughter be burnt, stidier bein' hung."

There was an impressive pause at this point, during which a jug of moonlight whiskey went the round of the crowd.

"Well," said a round-shouldered farmer, who, in spite of his peaceable expression and faded gray eye, was known to have been one of the most daring followers of a rebel guerrilla chieftain, "what air yer gwine ter do about it? Ef you fellers air gwine ter set down an' let a wuthless nigger kill the bes' white man in Branson, an' not say nuthin' ner do nuthin', *I* '*ll* move outen the caounty."

This speech gave tone and direction to the rest of the conversation. Whether the fear of losing the round-shouldered farmer operated to bring about the result or not is immaterial to this narrative; but, at all

CHARLES W. CHESNUTT

events, the crowd decided to lynch the negro. They agreed that this was the least that could be done to avenge the death of their murdered friend, and that it was a becoming way in which to honor his memory. They had some vague notions of the majesty of the law and the rights of the citizen, but in the passion of the moment these sunk into oblivion; a white man had been killed by a negro.

"The Cap'n was an ole sodger," said one of his friends solemnly. "He 'll sleep better when he knows that a co'te-martial has be'n hilt an' jestice done."

By agreement the lynchers were to meet at Tyson's store at five o'clock in the afternoon, and proceed thence to the jail, which was situated down the Lumberton Dirt Road (as the old turnpike antedating the plank-road was called), about half a mile south of the court-house. When the preliminaries of the lynching had been arranged, and a committee appointed to manage the affair, the crowd dispersed, some to go to their dinners, and some to secure recruits for the lynching party.

It was twenty minutes to five o'clock, when an excited negro, panting and perspiring, rushed up to the back door of Sheriff Campbell's dwelling, which stood at a little distance from the jail and somewhat farther than the latter building from the court-house. A turbaned colored woman came to the door in response to the negro's knock.

"Hoddy, Sis' Nance."

"Hoddy, Brer Sam."

"Is de shurff in," inquired the negro.

"Yas, Brer Sam, he 's eatin' his dinner," was the answer.

"Will yer ax 'im ter step ter de do' a minute, Sis' Nance?"

The woman went into the dining-room, and a moment later the sheriff came to the door. He was a tall, muscular man, of a ruddier complexion than is usual among Southerners. A pair of keen, deep-set gray eyes looked out from under bushy eyebrows, and about his mouth was a masterful expression, which a full beard, once sandy in color, but now profusely sprinkled with gray, could not entirely conceal. The day was hot; the sheriff had discarded his coat and vest, and had his white shirt open at the throat.

"What do you want, Sam?" he inquired of the negro, who stood hat in hand, wiping the moisture from his face with a ragged shirt-sleeve.

"Shurff, dey gwine ter hang de pris'ner w'at 's lock' up in de jail. Dey 're comin' dis a-way now. I wuz layin' down on a sack er corn down at de sto', behine a pile er flour-bairls, w'en I hearn Doc' Cain en Kunnel Wright talkin' erbout it. I slip' outen de back do', en run here as fas' as I could. I hearn you say down ter de sto' once't dat you would n't let nobody take a pris'ner 'way fum you widout walkin' over yo' dead body, en I thought I 'd let you know 'fo' dey come, so yer could pertec' de pris'ner."

The sheriff listened calmly, but his face grew firmer, and a determined gleam lit up his gray eyes. His frame grew more erect, and he unconsciously assumed the attitude of a soldier who momentarily expects to meet the enemy face to face.

"Much obliged, Sam," he answered. "I 'll protect the prisoner. Who 's coming?"

"I dunno who-all *is* comin'," replied the negro. "Dere 's Mistah McSwayne, en Doc' Cain, en Maje' McDonal', en Kunnel Wright, en a heap er yuthers. I wuz so skeered I done furgot mo' d'n half un em. I spec' dey mus' be mos' here by dis time, so I 'll git outen de way, fer I don' want nobody fer ter think I wuz mix' up in dis business." The negro glanced nervously down the road toward the town, and made a movement as if to go away.

"Won't you have some dinner first?" asked the sheriff.

The negro looked longingly in at the open door, and sniffed the appetizing odor of boiled pork and collards.

"I ain't got no time fer ter tarry, Shurff," he said, "but Sis' Nance mought gin me sump'n I could kyar in my han' en eat on de way."

A moment later Nancy brought him a huge sandwich of split corn-pone, with a thick slice of fat bacon inserted between the halves, and a couple of baked yams. The negro hastily replaced his ragged hat on his head, dropped the yams in the pocket of his capacious trousers, and, taking the sandwich in his hand, hurried across the road and disappeared in the woods beyond.

The sheriff reëntered the house, and put on his coat and hat. He then took down a double-barreled shotgun and loaded it with buckshot. Filling the chambers of a revolver with fresh cartridges, he slipped it into the pocket of the sack-coat which he wore.

A comely young woman in a calico dress watched these proceedings with anxious surprise.

"Where are you going, father?" she asked. She had not heard the conversation with the negro.

"I am goin' over to the jail," responded the sheriff. "There 's a mob comin' this way to lynch the nigger we 've got locked up. But they won't do it," he added, with emphasis.

"Oh, father! don't go!" pleaded the girl, clinging to his arm; "they'll shoot you if you don't give him up."

"You never mind me, Polly," said her father reassuringly, as he gently unclasped her hands from his arm. "I'll take care of myself and the prisoner, too. There ain't a man in Branson County that would shoot me. Besides, I have faced fire too often to be scared away from my duty. You keep close in the house," he continued, "and if any one disturbs you just use the old horse-pistol in the top bureau drawer. It's a little old-fashioned, but it did good work a few years ago."

The young girl shuddered at this sanguinary allusion, but made no further objection to her father's departure.

The sheriff of Branson was a man far above the average of the community in wealth, education, and social position. His had been one of the few families in the county that before the war had owned large estates and numerous slaves. He had graduated at the State University at Chapel Hill, and had kept up some acquaintance with current literature and advanced thought. He had traveled some in his youth, and was looked up to in the county as an authority on all subjects connected with the outer world. At first an ardent supporter of the Union, he had opposed the secession movement in his native State as long as opposition availed to stem the tide of public opinion. Yielding at last to the force of circumstances, he had entered the Confederate service rather late in the war, and served with distinction through several campaigns, rising in time to the rank of colonel. After the war he had taken the oath of allegiance, and had been chosen by the people as the most available candidate for the office of sheriff, to which he had been elected without opposition. He had filled the office for several terms, and was universally popular with his constituents.

Colonel or Sheriff Campbell, as he was indifferently called, as the military or civil title happened to be most important in the opinion of the person addressing him, had a high sense of the responsibility attaching to his office. He had sworn to do his duty faithfully, and he knew what his duty was, as sheriff, perhaps more clearly than he had apprehended it in other passages of his life. It was, therefore, with no uncertainty in regard to his course that he prepared his weapons and went over to the jail. He had no fears for Polly's safety.

The sheriff had just locked the heavy front door of the jail behind him when a half dozen horsemen, followed by a crowd of men on foot, came round a bend in the road and drew near the jail. They halted in front of the picket fence that surrounded the building, while several of the committee of arrangements rode on a few rods farther to the sheriff's house. One of them dismounted and rapped on the door with his riding-whip.

"Is the sheriff at home?" he inquired.

"No, he has just gone out," replied Polly, who had come to the door.

"We want the jail keys," he continued.

"They are not here," said Polly. "The sheriff has them himself." Then she added, with assumed indifference, "He is at the jail now."

The man turned away, and Polly went into the front room, from which she peered anxiously between the slats of the green blinds of a window that looked toward the jail. Meanwhile the messenger returned to his companions and announced his discovery. It looked as though the sheriff had learned of their design and was preparing to resist it.

One of them stepped forward and rapped on the jail door.

"Well, what is it?" said the sheriff, from within.

"We want to talk to you, Sheriff," replied the spokesman.

There was a little wicket in the door; this the sheriff opened, and answered through it.

"All right, boys, talk away. You are all strangers to me, and I don't know what business you can have." The sheriff did not think it necessary to recognize anybody in particular on such an occasion; the question of identity sometimes comes up in the investigation of these extra-judicial executions.

"We're a committee of citizens and we want to get into the jail."

"What for? It ain't much trouble to get into jail. Most people want to keep out."

The mob was in no humor to appreciate a joke, and the sheriff's witticism fell dead upon an unresponsive audience.

"We want to have a talk with the nigger that killed Cap'n Walker."

"You can talk to that nigger in the court-house, when he's brought out for trial. Court will be in session here next week. I know what you fellows want, but you can't get my prisoner to-day. Do you want to take the bread out of a poor man's mouth? I get seventy-five cents a day for keeping this prisoner, and he's the only one in jail. I can't have my family suffer just to please you fellows."

One or two young men in the crowd laughed at the idea of Sheriff Campbell's suffering for want of seventy-five cents a day; but they were frowned into silence by those who stood near them.

CHARLES W. CHESNUTT

"Ef yer don't let us in," cried a voice, "we 'll bu's' the do' open."

"Bust away," answered the sheriff, raising his voice so that all could hear. "But I give you fair warning. The first man that tries it will be filled with buckshot. I 'm sheriff of this county; I know my duty, and I mean to do it."

"What's the use of kicking, Sheriff," argued one of the leaders of the mob. "The nigger is sure to hang anyhow; he richly deserves it; and we 've got to do something to teach the niggers their places, or white people won't be able to live in the county."

"There 's no use talking, boys," responded the sheriff. "I 'm a white man outside, but in this jail I 'm sheriff; and if this nigger 's to be hung in this county, I propose to do the hanging. So you fellows might as well right-about-face, and march back to Troy. You 've had a pleasant trip, and the exercise will be good for you. You know *me*. I 've got powder and ball, and I 've faced fire before now, with nothing between me and the enemy, and I don't mean to surrender this jail while I 'm able to shoot." Having thus announced his determination, the sheriff closed and fastened the wicket, and looked around for the best position from which to defend the building.

The crowd drew off a little, and the leaders conversed together in low tones.

The Branson County jail was a small, two-story brick building, strongly constructed, with no attempt at architectural ornamentation. Each story was divided into two large cells by a passage running from front to rear. A grated iron door gave entrance from the passage to each of the four cells. The jail seldom had many prisoners in it, and the lower windows had been boarded up. When the sheriff had closed the wicket, he ascended the steep wooden stairs to the upper floor. There was no window at the front of the upper passage, and the most available position from which to watch the movements of the crowd below was the front window of the cell occupied by the solitary prisoner.

The sheriff unlocked the door and entered the cell. The prisoner was crouched in a corner, his yellow face, blanched with terror, looking ghastly in the semi-darkness of the room. A cold perspiration had gathered on his forehead, and his teeth were chattering with affright.

"For God's sake, Sheriff," he murmured hoarsely, "don't let 'em lynch me; I did n't kill the old man."

The sheriff glanced at the cowering wretch with a look of mingled contempt and loathing.

"Get up," he said sharply. "You will probably be hung sooner or later, but it shall not be to-day, if I can help it. I 'll unlock your fetters, and if I can't hold the jail, you 'll have to make the best fight you can. If I 'm shot, I 'll consider my responsibility at an end."

There were iron fetters on the prisoner's ankles, and handcuffs on his wrists. These the sheriff unlocked, and they fell clanking to the floor.

"Keep back from the window," said the sheriff. "They might shoot if they saw you."

The sheriff drew toward the window a pine bench which formed a part of the scanty furniture of the cell, and laid his revolver upon it. Then he took his gun in hand, and took his stand at the side of the window where he could with least exposure of himself watch the movements of the crowd below.

The lynchers had not anticipated any determined resistance. Of course they had looked for a formal protest, and perhaps a sufficient show of opposition to excuse the sheriff in the eye of any stickler for legal formalities. They had not however come prepared to fight a battle, and no one of them seemed willing to lead an attack upon the jail. The leaders of the party conferred together with a good deal of animated gesticulation, which was visible to the sheriff from his outlook, though the distance was too great for him to hear what was said. At length one of them broke away from the group, and rode back to the main body of the lynchers, who were restlessly awaiting orders.

"Well, boys," said the messenger, "we 'll have to let it go for the present. The sheriff says he 'll shoot, and he 's got the drop on us this time. There ain't any of us that want to follow Cap'n Walker jest yet. Besides, the sheriff is a good fellow, and we don't want to hurt 'im. But," he added, as if to reassure the crowd, which began to show signs of disappointment, "the nigger might as well say his prayers, for he ain't got long to live."

There was a murmur of dissent from the mob, and several voices insisted that an attack be made on the jail. But pacific counsels finally prevailed, and the mob sullenly withdrew.

The sheriff stood at the window until they had disappeared around the bend in the road. He did not relax his watchfulness when the last one was out of sight. Their withdrawal might be a mere feint, to be followed by a further attempt. So closely, indeed, was his attention drawn to the outside, that he neither saw nor heard the prisoner creep stealthily across the floor, reach out his hand and secure the revolver which lay on the bench behind the sheriff, and creep as noiselessly back to his place in the corner of the room.

A moment after the last of the lynching party had disappeared there was a shot fired from the woods across the road; a bullet whistled by the window and buried itself in the wooden casing a few inches from where the sheriff was standing. Quick as thought, with the instinct born of a semi-guerrilla army experience, he raised his gun and fired twice at the point from which a faint puff of smoke showed the hostile bullet to have been sent. He stood a moment watching, and then rested his gun against the window, and reached behind him mechanically for the other weapon. It was not on the bench. As the sheriff realized this fact, he turned his head and looked into the muzzle of the revolver.

"Stay where you are, Sheriff," said the prisoner, his eyes glistening, his face almost ruddy with excitement.

The sheriff mentally cursed his own carelessness for allowing him to be caught in such a predicament. He had not expected anything of the kind. He had relied on the negro's cowardice and subordination in the presence of an armed white man as a matter of course. The sheriff was a brave man, but realized that the prisoner had him at an immense disadvantage. The two men stood thus for a moment, fighting a harmless duel with their eyes.

"Well, what do you mean to do?" asked the sheriff with apparent calmness.

"To get away, of course," said the prisoner, in a tone which caused the sheriff to look at him more closely, and with an involuntary feeling of apprehension; if the man was not mad, he was in a state of mind akin to madness, and quite as dangerous. The sheriff felt that he must speak the prisoner fair, and watch for a chance to turn the tables on him. The keen-eyed, desperate man before him was a different being altogether from the groveling wretch who had begged so piteously for life a few minutes before.

At length the sheriff spoke:—

"Is this your gratitude to me for saving your life at the risk of my own? If I had not done so, you would now be swinging from the limb of some neighboring tree."

"True," said the prisoner, "you saved my life, but for how long? When you came in, you said Court would sit next week. When the crowd went away they said I had not long to live. It is merely a choice of two ropes."

"While there's life there's hope," replied the sheriff. He uttered this commonplace mechanically, while his brain was busy in trying to think out some way of escape. "If you are innocent you can prove it."

The mulatto kept his eye upon the sheriff. "I did n't kill the old man," he replied; "but I shall never be able to clear myself. I was at his house at nine o'clock. I stole from it the coat that was on my back when I was taken. I would be convicted, even with a fair trial, unless the real murderer were discovered beforehand."

The sheriff knew this only too well. While he was thinking what argument next to use, the prisoner continued:—

"Throw me the keys—no, unlock the door."

The sheriff stood a moment irresolute. The mulatto's eye glittered ominously. The sheriff crossed the room and unlocked the door leading into the passage.

"Now go down and unlock the outside door."

The heart of the sheriff leaped within him. Perhaps he might make a dash for liberty, and gain the outside. He descended the narrow stairs, the prisoner keeping close behind him.

The sheriff inserted the huge iron key into the lock. The rusty bolt yielded slowly. It still remained for him to pull the door open.

"Stop!" thundered the mulatto, who seemed to divine the sheriff's purpose. "Move a muscle, and I 'll blow your brains out."

The sheriff obeyed; he realized that his chance had not yet come.

"Now keep on that side of the passage, and go back upstairs."

Keeping the sheriff under cover of the revolver, the mulatto followed him up the stairs. The sheriff expected the prisoner to lock him into the cell and make his own escape. He had about come to the conclusion that the best thing he could do under the circumstances was to submit quietly, and take his chances of recapturing the prisoner after the alarm had been given. The sheriff had faced death more than once upon the battlefield. A few minutes before, well armed, and with a brick wall between him and them he had dared a hundred men to fight; but he felt instinctively that the desperate man confronting him was not to be trifled with, and he was too prudent a man to risk his life against such heavy odds. He had Polly to look after, and there was a limit beyond which devotion to duty would be quixotic and even foolish.

"I want to get away," said the prisoner, "and I don't want to be captured; for if I am I know I will be hung on the spot. I am afraid," he added somewhat reflectively, "that in order to save myself I shall have to kill you."

"Good God!" exclaimed the sheriff in involuntary terror; "you would not kill the man to whom you owe your own life."

"You speak more truly than you know," replied the mulatto. "I indeed owe my life to you."

The sheriff started, he was capable of surprise, even in that moment of extreme peril. "Who are you?" he asked in amazement.

"Tom, Cicely's son," returned the other. He had closed the door and stood talking to the sheriff through the grated opening. "Don't you remember Cicely—Cicely whom you sold, with her child, to the speculator on his way to Alabama?"

The sheriff did remember. He had been sorry for it many a time since. It had been the old story of debts, mortgages, and bad crops. He had quarreled with the mother. The price offered for her and her child had been unusually large, and he had yielded to the combination of anger and pecuniary stress.

"Good God!" he gasped, "you would not murder your own father?"

"My father?" replied the mulatto. "It were well enough for me to claim the relationship, but it comes with poor grace from you to ask anything by reason of it. What father's duty have you ever performed for me? Did you give me your name, or even your protection? Other white men gave their colored sons freedom and money, and sent them to the free States. *You* sold *me* to the rice swamps."

"I at least gave you the life you cling to," murmured the sheriff.

"Life?" said the prisoner, with a sarcastic laugh. "What kind of a life? You gave me your own blood, your own features,—no man need look at us together twice to see that,—and you gave me a black mother. Poor wretch! She died under the lash, because she had enough womanhood to call her soul her own. You gave me a white man's spirit, and you made me a slave, and crushed it out."

"But you are free now," said the sheriff. He had not doubted, could not doubt, the mulatto's word. He knew whose passions coursed beneath that swarthy skin and burned in the black eyes opposite his own. He saw in this mulatto what he himself might have become had not the safeguards of parental restraint and public opinion been thrown around him.

"Free to do what?" replied the mulatto. "Free in name, but despised and scorned and set aside by the people to whose race I belong far more than to my mother's."

"There are schools," said the sheriff. "You have been to school." He had noticed that the mulatto spoke more eloquently and used better language than most Branson County people.

"I have been to school, and dreamed when I went that it would work some marvelous change in my condition. But what did I learn? I learned to feel that no degree of learning or wisdom will change the color of my skin and that I shall always wear what in my own country is a badge of degradation. When I think about it seriously I do not care particularly for such a life. It is the animal in me, not the man, that flees the gallows. I owe you nothing," he went on, "and expect nothing of you; and it would be no more than justice if I should avenge upon you my mother's wrongs and my own. But still I hate to shoot you; I have never yet taken human life—for I did *not* kill the old captain. Will you promise to give no alarm and make no attempt to capture me until morning, if I do not shoot?"

So absorbed were the two men in their colloquy and their own tumultuous thoughts that neither of them had heard the door below move upon its hinges. Neither of them had heard a light step come stealthily up the stairs, nor seen a slender form creep along the darkening passage toward the mulatto.

The sheriff hesitated. The struggle between his love of life and his sense of duty was a terrific one. It may seem strange that a man who could sell his own child into slavery should hesitate at such a moment, when his life was trembling in the balance. But the baleful influence of human slavery poisoned the very fountains of life, and created new standards of right. The sheriff was conscientious; his conscience had merely been warped by his environment. Let no one ask what his answer would have been; he was spared the necessity of a decision.

"Stop," said the mulatto, "you need not promise. I could not trust you if you did. It is your life for mine; there is but one safe way for me; you must die."

He raised his arm to fire, when there was a flash—a report from the passage behind him. His arm fell heavily at his side, and the pistol dropped at his feet.

The sheriff recovered first from his surprise, and throwing open the door secured the fallen weapon. Then seizing the prisoner he thrust him into the cell and locked the door upon him; after which he turned to Polly, who leaned half-fainting against the wall, her hands clasped over her heart.

"Oh, father, I was just in time!" she cried hysterically, and, wildly sobbing, threw herself into her father's arms.

"I watched until they all went away," she said. "I heard the shot from the woods and I saw you shoot. Then when you did not come out I feared something had happened, that perhaps you had been wounded. I got out the other pistol and ran over here. When I found the door open, I knew something was wrong, and when I heard voices I crept upstairs, and reached the top just in time to hear him say he would kill you. Oh, it was a narrow escape!"

When she had grown somewhat calmer, the sheriff left her standing there and went back into the cell. The prisoner's arm was bleeding from a flesh wound. His bravado had given place to a stony apathy. There was no sign in his face of fear or disappointment or feeling of any kind. The sheriff sent Polly to the house for cloth, and bound up the prisoner's wound with a rude skill acquired during his army life.

"I 'll have a doctor come and dress the wound in the morning," he said to the prisoner. "It will do very well until then, if you will keep quiet. If the doctor asks you how the wound was caused, you can say that you were struck by the bullet fired from the woods. It would do you no good to have it known that you were shot while attempting to escape."

The prisoner uttered no word of thanks or apology, but sat in sullen silence. When the wounded arm had been bandaged, Polly and her father returned to the house.

The sheriff was in an unusually thoughtful mood that evening. He put salt in his coffee at supper, and poured vinegar over his pancakes. To many of Polly's questions he returned random answers. When he had gone to bed he lay awake for several hours.

In the silent watches of the night, when he was alone with God, there came into his mind a flood of unaccustomed thoughts. An hour or two before, standing face to face with death, he had experienced a sensation similar to that which drowning men are said to feel—a kind of clarifying of the moral faculty, in which the veil of the flesh, with its obscuring passions and prejudices, is pushed aside for a moment, and all the acts of one's life stand out, in the clear light of truth, in their correct proportions and relations,—a state of mind in which one sees himself as God may be supposed to see him. In the reaction following his rescue, this feeling had given place for a time to far different emotions. But now, in the silence of midnight, something of this clearness of spirit returned to the sheriff. He saw that he had owed some duty to this son of his,—that neither law nor custom could destroy a responsibility inherent in the nature of mankind. He could not thus, in the eyes of God at least, shake off the consequences of his sin. Had he never sinned, this wayward spirit would never have come back from the vanished past to haunt him. As these thoughts came, his anger against the mulatto died away, and in its place there sprang up a great pity. The hand of parental authority might have restrained the passions he had seen burning in the prisoner's eyes when the desperate man spoke the words which had seemed to doom his father to death. The sheriff felt that he might have saved this fiery spirit from the slough of slavery; that he might have sent him to the free North, and given him there, or in some other land, an opportunity to turn to usefulness and honorable pursuits the talents that had run to crime, perhaps to madness; he might, still less, have given this son of his the poor simulacrum of liberty which men of his caste could possess in a slave-holding community; or least of all, but still something, he might have kept the boy on the plantation, where the burdens of slavery would have fallen lightly upon him.

The sheriff recalled his own youth. He had inherited an honored name to keep untarnished; he had had a future to make; the picture of a fair young bride had beckoned him on to happiness. The poor wretch now stretched upon a pallet of straw between the brick walls of the jail had had none of these things,—no name, no father, no mother—in the true meaning of motherhood,—and until the past few years no possible future, and then one vague and shadowy in its outline, and dependent for form and substance upon the slow solution of a problem in which there were many unknown quantities.

From what he might have done to what he might yet do was an easy transition for the awakened conscience of the sheriff. It occurred to him, purely as a hypothesis, that he might permit his prisoner to escape; but his oath of office, his duty as sheriff, stood in the way of such a course, and the sheriff dismissed the idea from his mind. He could, however, investigate the circumstances of the murder, and move Heaven and earth to discover the real criminal, for he no longer doubted the prisoner's innocence; he could employ counsel for the accused, and perhaps influence public opinion in his favor. An acquittal once secured, some plan could be devised by which the sheriff might in some degree atone for his crime against this son of his—against society—against God.

When the sheriff had reached this conclusion he fell into an unquiet slumber, from which he awoke late the next morning.

He went over to the jail before breakfast and found the prisoner lying on his pallet, his face turned to the wall; he did not move when the sheriff rattled the door.

"Good-morning," said the latter, in a tone intended to waken the prisoner.

There was no response. The sheriff looked more keenly at the recumbent figure; there was an unnatural rigidity about its attitude.

He hastily unlocked the door and, entering the cell, bent over the prostrate form. There was no sound of breathing; he turned the body over—it was cold and stiff. The prisoner had torn the bandage from his wound and bled to death during the night. He had evidently been dead several hours.

A Matter of Principle

I

"WHAT OUR COUNTRY NEEDS MOST in its treatment of the race problem," observed Mr. Cicero Clayton at one of the monthly meetings of the Blue Vein Society, of which he was a prominent member, "is a clearer conception of the brotherhood of man."

The same sentiment in much the same words had often fallen from Mr. Clayton's lips,—so often, in fact, that the younger members of the society sometimes spoke of him—among themselves of course—as "Brotherhood Clayton." The sobriquet derived its point from the application he made of the principle involved in this oft-repeated proposition.

The fundamental article of Mr. Clayton's social creed was that he himself was not a negro.

"I know," he would say, "that the white people lump us all together as negroes, and condemn us all to the same social ostracism. But I don't accept this classification, for my part, and I imagine that, as the chief party in interest, I have a right to my opinion. People who belong by half or more of their blood to the most virile and progressive race of modern times have as much right to call themselves white as others have to call them negroes."

Mr. Clayton spoke warmly, for he was well informed, and had thought much upon the subject; too much, indeed, for he had not been able to escape entirely the tendency of too much concentration upon one subject to make even the clearest minds morbid.

"Of course we can't enforce our claims, or protect ourselves from being robbed of our birthright; but we can at least have principles, and try to live up to them the best we can. If we are not accepted as white, we can at any rate make it clear that we object to being called black. Our protest cannot fail in time to impress itself upon the better class of white people; for the Anglo-Saxon race loves justice, and will eventually do it, where it does not conflict with their own interests."

Whether or not the fact that Mr. Clayton meant no sarcasm, and was conscious of no inconsistency in this eulogy, tended to establish the racial identity he claimed may safely be left to the discerning reader.

In living up to his creed Mr. Clayton declined to associate to any considerable extent with black people. This was sometimes a little inconvenient, and occasionally involved a sacrifice of some pleasure for himself and his family, because they would not attend entertainments where many black people were likely to be present. But they had a social refuge in a little society of people like themselves; they attended, too, a church, of which nearly all the members were white, and they were connected with a number of the religious and benevolent associations open to all good citizens, where they came into contact with the better class of white people, and were treated, in their capacity of members, with a courtesy and consideration scarcely different from that accorded to other citizens.

Mr. Clayton's racial theory was not only logical enough, but was in his own case backed up by substantial arguments. He had begun life with a small patrimony, and had invested his money in a restaurant, which by careful and judicious attention had grown from a cheap eating-house into the most popular and successful confectionery and catering establishment in Groveland. His business occupied a double store on Oakwood Avenue. He owned houses and lots, and stocks and bonds, had good credit at the banks, and lived in a style befitting his income and business standing. In person he was of olive complexion, with slightly curly hair. His features approached the Cuban or Latin-American type rather than the familiar broad characteristics of the mulatto, this suggestion of something foreign being heightened by a Vandyke beard and a carefully waxed and pointed mustache. When he walked to church on Sunday mornings with his daughter Alice, they were a couple of such striking appearance as surely to attract attention.

Miss Alice Clayton was queen of her social set. She was young, she was handsome. She was nearly white; she frankly confessed her sorrow that she was not entirely so. She was accomplished and amiable, dressed in good taste, and had for her father by all odds the richest colored man—the term is used with apologies to Mr. Clayton, explaining that it does not necessarily mean a negro—in Groveland. So pronounced was her superiority that really she had but one social rival worthy of the name,—Miss Lura Watkins, whose father kept a prosperous livery stable and lived in almost as good style as the Claytons. Miss Watkins, while good-looking enough, was not so young nor quite so white as Miss Clayton. She was popular, however, among their mutual acquaintances, and there was a good-natured race between the two as to which should make the first and best marriage.

Marriages among Miss Clayton's set were serious affairs. Of course marriage is always a serious matter, whether it be a success or a failure, and there are those who believe that any marriage is better than no marriage. But among Miss Clayton's friends and associates matrimony took on an added seriousness because of the very narrow limits within which it could take place. Miss Clayton and her friends, by reason of their assumed superiority to black people, or perhaps as much by reason of a somewhat morbid shrinking from the curiosity manifested toward married people of strongly contrasting colors, would not marry black men, and except in rare instances white men would not marry them. They were therefore restricted for a choice to the young men of their own complexion. But these, unfortunately for the girls, had a wider choice. In any State where the laws permit freedom of the marriage contract, a man, by virtue of his sex, can find a wife of whatever complexion he prefers; of course he must not always ask too much in other respects, for most women like to better their social position when they marry. To the number thus lost by "going on the other side," as the phrase went, add the worthless contingent whom no self-respecting woman would marry, and the choice was still further restricted; so that it had become fashionable, when the supply of eligible men ran short, for those of Miss Clayton's set who could afford it to go traveling, ostensibly for pleasure, but with the serious hope that they might meet their fate away from home.

Miss Clayton had perhaps a larger option than any of her associates. Among such men as there were she could have taken her choice. Her beauty, her position, her accomplishments, her father's wealth, all made her eminently desirable. But, on the other hand, the same things rendered her more difficult to reach, and harder to please. To get access to her heart, too, it was necessary to run the gauntlet of her parents, which, until she had reached the age of twenty-three, no one had succeeded in doing safely. Many had called, but none had been chosen.

There was, however, one spot left unguarded, and through it Cupid, a veteran sharpshooter, sent a dart. Mr. Clayton had taken into his service and into his household a poor relation, a sort of cousin several times removed. This boy—his name was Jack—had gone into Mr. Clayton's service at a very youthful age,—twelve or thirteen. He had helped about the housework, washed the dishes, swept the floors, taken care of the lawn and the stable for three or four years, while he attended school. His cousin had then taken him into the store, where he had swept the floor, washed the windows, and done a class of work that kept fully impressed upon him the fact that he was a poor dependent. Nevertheless he was a cheerful lad, who took what he could get and was properly grateful, but always meant to get more. By sheer force of industry and affability and shrewdness, he forced his employer to promote him in time to a position of recognized authority in the establishment. Any one outside of the family would have perceived in him a very suitable husband for Miss Clayton; he was of about the same age, or a year or two older, was as fair of complexion as she, when she was not powdered, and was passably good-looking, with a bearing of which the natural manliness had been no more warped than his training and racial status had rendered inevitable; for he had early learned the law of growth, that to bend is better than to break. He was sometimes sent to accompany Miss Clayton to places in the evening, when she had no other escort, and it is quite likely that she discovered his good points before her parents did. That they should in time perceive them was inevitable. But even then, so accustomed were they to looking down upon the object of their former bounty, that they only spoke of the matter jocularly.

"Well, Alice," her father would say in his bluff way, "you'll not be absolutely obliged to die an old maid. If we can't find anything better for you, there's always Jack. As long as he does n't take to some other girl, you can fall back on him as a last chance. He'd be glad to take you to get into the business."

Miss Alice had considered the joke a very poor one when first made, but by occasional repetition she became somewhat familiar with it. In time it got around to Jack himself, to whom it seemed no joke at all. He had long considered it a consummation devoutly to be wished, and when he became aware that the possibility of such a match had occurred to the other parties in interest, he made up his mind that the idea should in due course of time become an accomplished fact. He had even suggested as much to Alice, in a casual way, to feel his ground; and while she had treated the matter lightly, he was not without hope that she had been impressed by the suggestion. Before he had had time, however, to follow up this lead, Miss Clayton, in the spring of 187-, went away on a visit to Washington.

The occasion of her visit was a presidential inauguration. The new President owed his nomination mainly to the votes of the Southern delegates in the convention, and was believed to be correspondingly well disposed to the race from which the Southern delegates were for the most part recruited. Friends of rival and unsuccessful candidates for the nomination had more than hinted that the Southern delegates were very substantially rewarded for their support at the time when it was given; whether this was true or not the parties concerned know best. At any rate the colored politicians did not see it in that light, for they were gathered from near and far to press their claims for recognition and patronage. On the evening following the White House inaugural ball, the colored people of Washington gave an "inaugural" ball at a large public hall. It was under the management of their leading citizens, among them several high officials holding over from the last administration, and a number of professional and business men. This ball was the most noteworthy social event that colored circles up to that time had ever known. There were many visitors from various parts of the country. Miss Clayton attended the ball, the honors of which she carried away easily. She danced with several partners, and was introduced to innumerable people whom she had never seen before, and whom she hardly expected ever to meet again. She went away from the ball, at four o'clock in the morning, in a glow of triumph, and with a confused impression of senators and representatives and lawyers and doctors of all shades, who had sought an introduction, led her through the dance, and overwhelmed her with compliments. She returned home the next day but one, after the most delightful week of her life.

II

ONE AFTERNOON, ABOUT THREE WEEKS after her return from Washington, Alice received a letter through the mail. The envelope bore the words "House of Representatives" printed in one corner, and in the opposite corner, in a bold running hand, a Congressman's frank, "Hamilton M. Brown, M.C." The letter read as follows:—

> House of Representatives,
> Washington, D.C., March 30, 187-.
> Miss Alice Clayton, Groveland.
>
> Dear Friend (if I may be permitted to call you so after so brief an acquaintance),
>
> I remember with sincerest pleasure our recent meeting at the inaugural ball, and the sensation created by your beauty,

your amiable manners, and your graceful dancing. Time has so strengthened the impression I then received, that I should have felt inconsolable had I thought it impossible ever to again behold the charms which had brightened the occasion of our meeting and eclipsed by their brilliancy the leading belles of the capital. I had hoped, however, to have the pleasure of meeting you again, and circumstances have fortunately placed it in my power to do so at an early date. You have doubtless learned that the contest over the election in the Sixth Congressional District of South Carolina has been decided in my favor, and that I now have the honor of representing my native State at the national capital. I have just been appointed a member of a special committee to visit and inspect the Sault River and the Straits of Mackinac, with reference to the needs of lake navigation. I have made arrangements to start a week ahead of the other members of the committee, whom I am to meet in Detroit on the 20th. I shall leave here on the 2d, and will arrive in Groveland on the 3d, by the 7.30 evening express. I shall remain in Groveland several days, in the course of which I shall be pleased to call, and renew the acquaintance so auspiciously begun in Washington, which it is my fondest hope may ripen into a warmer friendship.

If you do not regard my visit as presumptuous, and do not write me in the mean while forbidding it, I shall do myself the pleasure of waiting on you the morning after my arrival in Groveland.

With renewed expressions of my sincere admiration and profound esteem, I remain,

Sincerely yours,
Hamilton M. Brown, M.C.

To Alice, and especially to her mother, this bold and flowery letter had very nearly the force of a formal declaration. They read it over again and again, and spent most of the afternoon discussing it. There were few young men in Groveland eligible as husbands for so superior a person as Alice Clayton, and an addition to the number would be very acceptable. But the mere fact of his being a Congressman was not sufficient to qualify him; there were other considerations.

"I 've never heard of this Honorable Hamilton M. Brown," said Mr. Clayton. The letter had been laid before him at the supper-table. "It 's strange, Alice, that you have n't said anything about him before. You must have met lots of swell folks not to recollect a Congressman."

"But he was n't a Congressman then," answered Alice; "he was only a claimant. I remember Senator Bruce, and Mr. Douglass; but there were so many doctors and lawyers and politicians that I could n't keep track of them all. Still I have a faint impression of a Mr. Brown who danced with me."

She went into the parlor and brought out the dancing programme she had used at the Washington ball. She had decorated it with a bow of blue ribbon and preserved it as a souvenir of her visit.

"Yes," she said, after examining it, "I must have danced with him. Here are the initials—'H.M.B.'"

"What color is he?" asked Mr. Clayton, as he plied his knife and fork.

"I have a notion that he was rather dark—darker than any one I had ever danced with before."

"Why did you dance with him?" asked her father. "You were n't obliged to go back on your principles because you were away from home."

"Well, father, 'when you 're in Rome'—you know the rest. Mrs. Clearweather introduced me to several dark men, to him among others. They were her friends, and common decency required me to be courteous."

"If this man is black, we don't want to encourage him. If he 's the right sort, we 'll invite him to the house."

"And make him feel at home," added Mrs. Clayton, on hospitable thoughts intent.

"We must ask Sadler about him to-morrow," said Mr. Clayton, when he had drunk his coffee and lighted his cigar. "If he 's the right man he shall have cause to remember his visit to Groveland. We 'll show him that Washington is not the only town on earth."

The uncertainty of the family with regard to Mr. Brown was soon removed. Mr. Solomon Sadler, who was supposed to know everything worth knowing concerning the colored race, and everybody of importance connected with it, dropped in after supper to make an evening call. Sadler was familiar with the history of every man of negro ancestry who had distinguished himself in any walk of life. He could give the pedigree of Alexander Pushkin, the titles of scores of Dumas's

CHARLES W. CHESNUTT

novels (even Sadler had not time to learn them all), and could recite the whole of Wendell Phillips's lecture on Toussaint l'Ouverture. He claimed a personal acquaintance with Mr. Frederick Douglass, and had been often in Washington, where he was well known and well received in good colored society.

"Let me see," he said reflectively, when asked for information about the Honorable Hamilton M. Brown. "Yes, I think I know him. He studied at Oberlin just after the war. He was about leaving there when I entered. There were two H.M. Browns there—a Hamilton M. Brown and a Henry M. Brown. One was stout and dark and the other was slim and quite light; you could scarcely tell him from a dark white man. They used to call them 'light Brown' and 'dark Brown.' I did n't know either of them except by sight, for they were there only a few weeks after I went in. As I remember them, Hamilton was the fair one—a very good-looking, gentlemanly fellow, and, as I heard, a good student and a fine speaker."

"Do you remember what kind of hair he had?" asked Mr. Clayton.

"Very good indeed; straight, as I remember it. He looked something like a Spaniard or a Portuguese."

"Now that you describe him," said Alice, "I remember quite well dancing with such a gentleman; and I 'm wrong about my 'H.M.B.' The dark man must have been some one else; there are two others on my card that I can't remember distinctly, and he was probably one of those."

"I guess he 's all right, Alice," said her father when Sadler had gone away. "He evidently means business, and we must treat him white. Of course he must stay with us; there are no hotels in Groveland while he is here. Let 's see—he 'll be here in three days. That is n't very long, but I guess we can get ready. I 'll write a letter this afternoon—or you write it, and invite him to the house, and say I 'll meet him at the depot. And you may have *carte blanche* for making the preparations."

"We must have some people to meet him."

"Certainly; a reception is the proper thing. Sit down immediately and write the letter and I 'll mail it first thing in the morning, so he 'll get it before he has time to make other arrangements. And you and your mother put your heads together and make out a list of guests, and I 'll have the invitations printed to-morrow. We will show the darkeys of Groveland how to entertain a Congressman."

It will be noted that in moments of abstraction or excitement Mr. Clayton sometimes relapsed into forms of speech not entirely consistent with his principles. But some allowance must be made for his atmosphere; he could no more escape from it than the leopard can change his spots, or the—In deference to Mr. Clayton's feelings the quotation will be left incomplete.

Alice wrote the letter on the spot and it was duly mailed, and sped on its winged way to Washington.

The preparations for the reception were made as thoroughly and elaborately as possible on so short a notice. The invitations were issued; the house was cleaned from attic to cellar; an orchestra was engaged for the evening; elaborate floral decorations were planned and the flowers ordered. Even the refreshments, which ordinarily, in the household of a caterer, would be mere matter of familiar detail, became a subject of serious consultation and study.

The approaching event was a matter of very much interest to the fortunate ones who were honored with invitations, and this for several reasons. They were anxious to meet this sole representative of their race in the—th Congress, and as he was not one of the old-line colored leaders, but a new star risen on the political horizon, there was a special curiosity to see who he was and what he looked like. Moreover, the Claytons did not often entertain a large company, but when they did, it was on a scale commensurate with their means and position, and to be present on such an occasion was a thing to remember and to talk about. And, most important consideration of all, some remarks dropped by members of the Clayton family had given rise to the rumor that the Congressman was seeking a wife. This invested his visit with a romantic interest, and gave the reception a practical value; for there were other marriageable girls besides Miss Clayton, and if one was left another might be taken.

III

On the evening of April 3d, at fifteen minutes of six o'clock, Mr. Clayton, accompanied by Jack, entered the livery carriage waiting at his gate and ordered the coachman to drive to the Union Depot. He had taken Jack along, partly for company, and partly that Jack might relieve the Congressman of any trouble about his baggage, and make himself useful in case of emergency. Jack was willing enough to go, for he had foreseen in the visitor a rival for Alice's hand,—indeed he had heard more or less of the subject for several days,—and was glad to make a reconnaissance before the enemy arrived upon the field of battle.

CHARLES W. CHESNUTT

He had made—at least he had thought so—considerable progress with Alice during the three weeks since her return from Washington, and once or twice Alice had been perilously near the tender stage. This visit had disturbed the situation and threatened to ruin his chances; but he did not mean to give up without a struggle.

Arrived at the main entrance, Mr. Clayton directed the carriage to wait, and entered the station with Jack. The Union Depot at Groveland was an immense oblong structure, covering a dozen parallel tracks and furnishing terminal passenger facilities for half a dozen railroads. The tracks ran east and west, and the depot was entered from the south, at about the middle of the building. On either side of the entrance, the waiting-rooms, refreshment rooms, baggage and express departments, and other administrative offices, extended in a row for the entire length of the building; and beyond them and parallel with them stretched a long open space, separated from the tracks by an iron fence or *grille*. There were two entrance gates in the fence, at which tickets must be shown before access could be had to trains, and two other gates, by which arriving passengers came out.

Mr. Clayton looked at the blackboard on the wall underneath the station clock, and observed that the 7.30 train from Washington was five minutes late. Accompanied by Jack he walked up and down the platform until the train, with the usual accompaniment of panting steam and clanging bell and rumbling trucks, pulled into the station, and drew up on the third or fourth track from the iron railing. Mr. Clayton stationed himself at the gate nearest the rear end of the train, reasoning that the Congressman would ride in a parlor car, and would naturally come out by the gate nearest the point at which he left the train.

"You 'd better go and stand by the other gate, Jack," he said to his companion, "and stop him if he goes out that way."

The train was well filled and a stream of passengers poured through. Mr. Clayton scanned the crowd carefully as they approached the gate, and scrutinized each passenger as he came through, without seeing any one that met the description of Congressman Brown, as given by Sadler, or any one that could in his opinion be the gentleman for whom he was looking. When the last one had passed through he was left to the conclusion that his expected guest had gone out by the other gate. Mr. Clayton hastened thither.

"Did n't he come out this way, Jack?" he asked.

"No, sir," replied the young man, "I have n't seen him."

"That 's strange," mused Mr. Clayton, somewhat anxiously. "He would hardly fail to come without giving us notice. Surely we must have missed him. We 'd better look around a little. You go that way and I 'll go this."

Mr. Clayton turned and walked several rods along the platform to the men's waiting-room, and standing near the door glanced around to see if he could find the object of his search. The only colored person in the room was a stout and very black man, wearing a broadcloth suit and a silk hat, and seated a short distance from the door. On the seat by his side stood a couple of valises. On one of them, the one nearest him, on which his arm rested, was written, in white letters, plainly legible,—

H.M. Brown, M.C.
Washington, D.C.

Mr. Clayton's feelings at this discovery can better be imagined than described. He hastily left the waiting-room, before the black gentleman, who was looking the other way, was even aware of his presence, and, walking rapidly up and down the platform, communed with himself upon what course of action the situation demanded. He had invited to his house, had come down to meet, had made elaborate preparations to entertain on the following evening, a light-colored man,—a white man by his theory, an acceptable guest, a possible husband for his daughter, an avowed suitor for her hand. If the Congressman had turned out to be brown, even dark brown, with fairly good hair, though he might not have desired him as a son-in-law, yet he could have welcomed him as a guest. But even this softening of the blow was denied him, for the man in the waiting-room was palpably, aggressively black, with pronounced African features and woolly hair, without apparently a single drop of redeeming white blood. Could he, in the face of his well-known principles, his lifelong rule of conduct, take this negro into his home and introduce him to his friends? Could he subject his wife and daughter to the rude shock of such a disappointment? It would be bad enough for them to learn of the ghastly mistake, but to have him in the house would be twisting the arrow in the wound.

Mr. Clayton had the instincts of a gentleman, and realized the delicacy of the situation. But to get out of his difficulty without wounding the feelings of the Congressman required not only diplomacy but dispatch. Whatever he did must be done promptly; for if he waited many minutes the Congressman would probably take a carriage and be driven to Mr. Clayton's residence.

A ray of hope came for a moment to illumine the gloom of the situation. Perhaps the black man was merely sitting there, and not the owner of the valise! For there were two valises, one on each side of the supposed Congressman. For obvious reasons he did not care to make the inquiry himself, so he looked around for his companion, who came up a moment later.

"Jack," he exclaimed excitedly, "I'm afraid we're in the worst kind of a hole, unless there's some mistake! Run down to the men's waiting-room and you'll see a man and a valise, and you'll understand what I mean. Ask that darkey if he is the Honorable Mr. Brown, Congressman from South Carolina. If he says yes, come back right away and let me know, without giving him time to ask any questions, and put your wits to work to help me out of the scrape."

"I wonder what's the matter?" said Jack to himself, but did as he was told. In a moment he came running back.

"Yes, sir," he announced; "he says he's the man."

"Jack," said Mr. Clayton desperately, "if you want to show your appreciation of what I've done for you, you must suggest some way out of this. I'd never dare to take that negro to my house, and yet I'm obliged to treat him like a gentleman."

Jack's eyes had worn a somewhat reflective look since he had gone to make the inquiry. Suddenly his face brightened with intelligence, and then, as a newsboy ran into the station calling his wares, hardened into determination.

"Clarion, special extry 'dition! All about de epidemic er dipt'eria!" clamored the newsboy with shrill childish treble, as he made his way toward the waiting-room. Jack darted after him, and saw the man to whom he had spoken buy a paper. He ran back to his employer, and dragged him over toward the ticket-seller's window.

"I have it, sir!" he exclaimed, seizing a telegraph blank and writing rapidly, and reading aloud as he wrote. "How's this for a way out?"—

Dear Sir,
     I write you this note here in the depot to inform you of an unfortunate event which has interfered with my plans

and those of my family for your entertainment while in Groveland. Yesterday my daughter Alice complained of a sore throat, which by this afternoon had developed into a case of malignant diphtheria. In consequence our house has been quarantined; and while I have felt myself obliged to come down to the depot, I do not feel that I ought to expose you to the possibility of infection, and I therefore send you this by another hand. The bearer will conduct you to a carriage which I have ordered placed at your service, and unless you should prefer some other hotel, you will be driven to the Forest Hill House, where I beg you will consider yourself my guest during your stay in the city, and make the fullest use of every convenience it may offer. From present indications I fear no one of our family will be able to see you, which we shall regret beyond expression, as we have made elaborate arrangements for your entertainment. I still hope, however, that you may enjoy your visit, as there are many places of interest in the city, and many friends will doubtless be glad to make your acquaintance.

> With assurances of my profound regret, I am
> Sincerely yours,
> Cicero Clayton

"Splendid!" cried Mr. Clayton. "You 've helped me out of a horrible scrape. Now, go and take him to the hotel and see him comfortably located, and tell them to charge the bill to me."

"I suspect, sir," suggested Jack, "that I 'd better not go up to the house, and you 'll have to stay in yourself for a day or two, to keep up appearances. I 'll sleep on the lounge at the store, and we can talk business over the telephone."

"All right, Jack, we 'll arrange the details later. But for Heaven's sake get him started, or he 'll be calling a hack to drive up to the house. I 'll go home on a street car."

"So far so good," sighed Mr. Clayton to himself as he escaped from the station. "Jack is a deuced clever fellow, and I 'll have to do something more for him. But the tug-of-war is yet to come. I 've got to bribe a doctor, shut up the house for a day or two, and have all the ill-humor of two disappointed women to endure until this negro leaves town. Well, I 'm sure my wife and Alice will back me up at any cost.

No sacrifice is too great to escape having to entertain him; of course I have no prejudice against his color,—he can't help that,—but it is the *principle* of the thing. If we received him it would be a concession fatal to all my views and theories. And I am really doing him a kindness, for I 'm sure that all the world could not make Alice and her mother treat him with anything but cold politeness. It 'll be a great mortification to Alice, but I don't see how else I could have got out of it."

He boarded the first car that left the depot, and soon reached home. The house was lighted up, and through the lace curtains of the parlor windows he could see his wife and daughter, elegantly dressed, waiting to receive their distinguished visitor. He rang the bell impatiently, and a servant opened the door.

"The gentleman did n't come?" asked the maid.

"No," he said as he hung up his hat. This brought the ladies to the door.

"He did n't come?" they exclaimed. "What 's the matter?"

"I 'll tell you," he said. "Mary," this to the servant, a white girl, who stood in open-eyed curiosity, "we shan't need you any more to-night."

Then he went into the parlor, and, closing the door, told his story. When he reached the point where he had discovered the color of the honorable Mr. Brown, Miss Clayton caught her breath, and was on the verge of collapse.

"That nigger," said Mrs. Clayton indignantly, "can never set foot in this house. But what did you do with him?"

Mr. Clayton quickly unfolded his plan, and described the disposition he had made of the Congressman.

"It 's an awful shame," said Mrs. Clayton. "Just think of the trouble and expense we have gone to! And poor Alice 'll never get over it, for everybody knows he came to see her and that he 's smitten with her. But you 've done just right; we never would have been able to hold up our heads again if we had introduced a black man, even a Congressman, to the people that are invited here to-morrow night, as a sweetheart of Alice. Why, she would n't marry him if he was President of the United States and plated with gold an inch thick. The very idea!"

"Well," said Mr. Clayton, "then we 've got to act quick. Alice must wrap up her throat—by the way, Alice, how *is* your throat?"

"It 's sore," sobbed Alice, who had been in tears almost from her father's return, "and I don't care if I do have diphtheria and die, no, I don't!" and she wept on.

"Wrap up your throat and go to bed, and I 'll go over to Doctor Pillsbury's and get a diphtheria card to nail up on the house. In the morning, first thing, we 'll have to write notes recalling the invitations for to-morrow evening, and have them delivered by messenger boys. We were fools for not finding out all about this man from some one who knew, before we invited him here. Sadler don't know more than half he thinks he does, anyway. And we 'll have to do this thing thoroughly, or our motives will be misconstrued, and people will say we are prejudiced and all that, when it is only a matter of principle with us."

The programme outlined above was carried out to the letter. The invitations were recalled, to the great disappointment of the invited guests. The family physician called several times during the day. Alice remained in bed, and the maid left without notice, in such a hurry that she forgot to take her best clothes.

Mr. Clayton himself remained at home. He had a telephone in the house, and was therefore in easy communication with his office, so that the business did not suffer materially by reason of his absence from the store. About ten o'clock in the morning a note came up from the hotel, expressing Mr. Brown's regrets and sympathy. Toward noon Mr. Clayton picked up the morning paper, which he had not theretofore had time to read, and was glancing over it casually, when his eye fell upon a column headed "A Colored Congressman." He read the article with astonishment that rapidly turned to chagrin and dismay. It was an interview describing the Congressman as a tall and shapely man, about thirty-five years old, with an olive complexion not noticeably darker than many a white man's, straight hair, and eyes as black as sloes.

"The bearing of this son of South Carolina reveals the polished manners of the Southern gentleman, and neither from his appearance nor his conversation would one suspect that the white blood which flows in his veins in such preponderating measure had ever been crossed by that of a darker race," wrote the reporter, who had received instructions at the office that for urgent business considerations the lake shipping interest wanted Representative Brown treated with marked consideration.

There was more of the article, but the introductory portion left Mr. Clayton in such a state of bewilderment that the paper fell from his hand. What was the meaning of it? Had he been mistaken? Obviously so, or else the reporter was wrong, which was manifestly improbable.

CHARLES W. CHESNUTT

When he had recovered himself somewhat, he picked up the newspaper and began reading where he had left off.

"Representative Brown traveled to Groveland in company with Bishop Jones of the African Methodist Jerusalem Church, who is *en route* to attend the general conference of his denomination at Detroit next week. The bishop, who came in while the writer was interviewing Mr. Brown, is a splendid type of the pure negro. He is said to be a man of great power among his people, which may easily be believed after one has looked upon his expressive countenance and heard him discuss the questions which affect the welfare of his church and his race."

Mr. Clayton stared at the paper. "'The bishop,'" he repeated, "'is a splendid type of the pure negro.' I must have mistaken the bishop for the Congressman! But how in the world did Jack get the thing balled up? I'll call up the store and demand an explanation of him.

"Jack," he asked, "what kind of a looking man was the fellow you gave the note to at the depot?"

"He was a very wicked-looking fellow, sir," came back the answer. "He had a bad eye, looked like a gambler, sir. I am not surprised that you did n't want to entertain him, even if he was a Congressman."

"What color was he—that's what I want to know—and what kind of hair did he have?"

"Why, he was about my complexion, sir, and had straight black hair."

The rules of the telephone company did not permit swearing over the line. Mr. Clayton broke the rules.

"Was there any one else with him?" he asked when he had relieved his mind.

"Yes, sir, Bishop Jones of the African Methodist Jerusalem Church was sitting there with him; they had traveled from Washington together. I drove the bishop to his stopping-place after I had left Mr. Brown at the hotel. I did n't suppose you'd mind."

Mr. Clayton fell into a chair, and indulged in thoughts unutterable.

He folded up the paper and slipped it under the family Bible, where it was least likely to be soon discovered.

"I'll hide the paper, anyway," he groaned. "I'll never hear the last of this till my dying day, so I may as well have a few hours' respite. It's too late to go back, and we've got to play the farce out. Alice is really sick with disappointment, and to let her know this now would only make her worse. Maybe he'll leave town in a day or two, and then she'll be in condition to stand it. Such luck is enough to disgust a man with trying to do right and live up to his principles."

Time hung a little heavy on Mr. Clayton's hands during the day. His wife was busy with the housework. He answered several telephone calls about Alice's health, and called up the store occasionally to ask how the business was getting on. After lunch he lay down on a sofa and took a nap, from which he was aroused by the sound of the door-bell. He went to the door. The evening paper was lying on the porch, and the newsboy, who had not observed the diphtheria sign until after he had rung, was hurrying away as fast as his legs would carry him.

Mr. Clayton opened the paper and looked it through to see if there was any reference to the visiting Congressman. He found what he sought and more. An article on the local page contained a resume of the information given in the morning paper, with the following additional paragraph:—

"A reporter, who called at the Forest Hill this morning to interview Representative Brown, was informed that the Congressman had been invited to spend the remainder of his time in Groveland as the guest of Mr. William Watkins, the proprietor of the popular livery establishment on Main Street. Mr. Brown will remain in the city several days, and a reception will be tendered him at Mr. Watkins's on Wednesday evening."

"That ends it," sighed Mr. Clayton. "The dove of peace will never again rest on my roof-tree."

But why dwell longer on the sufferings of Mr. Clayton, or attempt to describe the feelings or chronicle the remarks of his wife and daughter when they learned the facts in the case?

As to Representative Brown, he was made welcome in the hospitable home of Mr. William Watkins. There was a large and brilliant assemblage at the party on Wednesday evening, at which were displayed the costumes prepared for the Clayton reception. Mr. Brown took a fancy to Miss Lura Watkins, to whom, before the week was over, he became engaged to be married. Meantime poor Alice, the innocent victim of circumstances and principles, lay sick abed with a supposititious case of malignant diphtheria, and a real case of acute disappointment and chagrin.

"Oh, Jack!" exclaimed Alice, a few weeks later, on the way home from evening church in company with the young man, "what a dreadful thing it all was! And to think of that hateful Lura Watkins marrying the Congressman!"

The street was shaded by trees at the point where they were passing, and there was no one in sight. Jack put his arm around her waist, and, leaning over, kissed her.

"Never mind, dear," he said soothingly, "you still have your 'last chance' left, and I'll prove myself a better man than the Congressman."

Occasionally, at social meetings, when the vexed question of the future of the colored race comes up, as it often does, for discussion, Mr. Clayton may still be heard to remark sententiously:—

"What the white people of the United States need most, in dealing with this problem, is a higher conception of the brotherhood of man. For of one blood God made all the nations of the earth."

Cicely's Dream

I

THE OLD WOMAN STOOD AT the back door of the cabin, shading her eyes with her hand, and looking across the vegetable garden that ran up to the very door. Beyond the garden she saw, bathed in the sunlight, a field of corn, just in the ear, stretching for half a mile, its yellow, pollen-laden tassels overtopping the dark green mass of broad glistening blades; and in the distance, through the faint morning haze of evaporating dew, the line of the woods, of a still darker green, meeting the clear blue of the summer sky. Old Dinah saw, going down the path, a tall, brown girl, in a homespun frock, swinging a slat-bonnet in one hand and a splint basket in the other.

"Oh, Cicely!" she called.

The girl turned and answered in a resonant voice, vibrating with youth and life,—

"Yes, granny!"

"Be sho' and pick a good mess er peas, chile, fer yo' gran'daddy's gwine ter be home ter dinner ter-day."

The old woman stood a moment longer and then turned to go into the house. What she had not seen was that the girl was not only young, but lithe and shapely as a sculptor's model; that her bare feet seemed to spurn the earth as they struck it; that though brown, she was not so brown but that her cheek was darkly red with the blood of another race than that which gave her her name and station in life; and the old woman did not see that Cicely's face was as comely as her figure was superb, and that her eyes were dreamy with vague yearnings.

Cicely climbed the low fence between the garden and the cornfield, and started down one of the long rows leading directly away from the house. Old Needham was a good ploughman, and straight as an arrow ran the furrow between the rows of corn, until it vanished in the distant perspective. The peas were planted beside alternate hills of corn, the cornstalks serving as supports for the climbing pea-vines. The vines nearest the house had been picked more or less clear of the long green pods, and Cicely walked down the row for a quarter of a mile, to where the peas were more plentiful. And as she walked she thought of her dream of the night before.

CHARLES W. CHESNUTT

She had dreamed a beautiful dream. The fact that it was a beautiful dream, a delightful dream, her memory retained very vividly. She was troubled because she could not remember just what her dream had been about. Of one other fact she was certain, that in her dream she had found something, and that her happiness had been bound up with the thing she had found. As she walked down the corn-row she ran over in her mind the various things with which she had always associated happiness. Had she found a gold ring? No, it was not a gold ring—of that she felt sure. Was it a soft, curly plume for her hat? She had seen town people with them, and had indulged in day-dreams on the subject; but it was not a feather. Was it a bright-colored silk dress? No; as much as she had always wanted one, it was not a silk dress. For an instant, in a dream, she had tasted some great and novel happiness, and when she awoke it was dashed from her lips, and she could not even enjoy the memory of it, except in a vague, indefinite, and tantalizing way.

Cicely was troubled, too, because dreams were serious things. Dreams had certain meanings, most of them, and some dreams went by contraries. If her dream had been a prophecy of some good thing, she had by forgetting it lost the pleasure of anticipation. If her dream had been one of those that go by contraries, the warning would be in vain, because she would not know against what evil to provide. So, with a sigh, Cicely said to herself that it was a troubled world, more or less; and having come to a promising point, began to pick the tenderest pea-pods and throw them into her basket.

By the time she had reached the end of the line the basket was nearly full. Glancing toward the pine woods beyond the rail fence, she saw a brier bush loaded with large, luscious blackberries. Cicely was fond of blackberries, so she set her basket down, climbed the fence, and was soon busily engaged in gathering the fruit, delicious even in its wild state.

She had soon eaten all she cared for. But the berries were still numerous, and it occurred to her that her granddaddy would like a blackberry pudding for dinner. Catching up her apron, and using it as a receptacle for the berries, she had gathered scarcely more than a handful when she heard a groan.

Cicely was not timid, and her curiosity being aroused by the sound, she stood erect, and remained in a listening attitude. In a moment the sound was repeated, and, gauging the point from which it came, she plunged resolutely into the thick underbrush of the forest. She had gone but a few yards when she stopped short with an exclamation of surprise and concern.

Upon the ground, under the shadow of the towering pines, a man lay at full length,—a young man, several years under thirty, apparently, so far as his age could be guessed from a face that wore a short soft beard, and was so begrimed with dust and incrusted with blood that little could be seen of the underlying integument. What was visible showed a skin browned by nature or by exposure. His hands were of even a darker brown, almost as dark as Cicely's own. A tangled mass of very curly black hair, matted with burs, dank with dew, and clotted with blood, fell partly over his forehead, on the edge of which, extending back into the hair, an ugly scalp wound was gaping, and, though apparently not just inflicted, was still bleeding slowly, as though reluctant to stop, in spite of the coagulation that had almost closed it.

Cicely with a glance took in all this and more. But, first of all, she saw the man was wounded and bleeding, and the nurse latent in all womankind awoke in her to the requirements of the situation. She knew there was a spring a few rods away, and ran swiftly to it. There was usually a gourd at the spring, but now it was gone. Pouring out the blackberries in a little heap where they could be found again, she took off her apron, dipped one end of it into the spring, and ran back to the wounded man. The apron was clean, and she squeezed a little stream of water from it into the man's mouth. He swallowed it with avidity. Cicely then knelt by his side, and with the wet end of her apron washed the blood from the wound lightly, and the dust from the man's face. Then she looked at her apron a moment, debating whether she should tear it or not.

"I 'm feared granny 'll be mad," she said to herself. "I reckon I 'll jes' use de whole apron."

So she bound the apron around his head as well as she could, and then sat down a moment on a fallen tree trunk, to think what she should do next. The man already seemed more comfortable; he had ceased moaning, and lay quiet, though breathing heavily.

"What shall I do with that man?" she reflected. "I don' know whether he 's a w'ite man or a black man. Ef he 's a w'ite man, I oughter go an' tell de w'ite folks up at de big house, an' dey 'd take keer of 'im. If he 's a black man, I oughter go tell granny. He don' look lack a black man somehow er nuther, an' yet he don' look lack a w'ite man; he 's too dahk, an' his hair 's too curly. But I mus' do somethin'

CHARLES W. CHESNUTT

wid 'im. He can't be lef' here ter die in de woods all by hisse'f. Reckon I 'll go an' tell granny."

She scaled the fence, caught up the basket of peas from where she had left it, and ran, lightly and swiftly as a deer, toward the house. Her short skirt did not impede her progress, and in a few minutes she had covered the half mile and was at the cabin door, a slight heaving of her full and yet youthful breast being the only sign of any unusual exertion.

Her story was told in a moment. The old woman took down a black bottle from a high shelf, and set out with Cicely across the cornfield, toward the wounded man.

As they went through the corn Cicely recalled part of her dream. She had dreamed that under some strange circumstances—what they had been was still obscure—she had met a young man—a young man whiter than she and yet not all white—and that he had loved her and courted her and married her. Her dream had been all the sweeter because in it she had first tasted the sweetness of love, and she had not recalled it before because only in her dream had she known or thought of love as something supremely desirable.

With the memory of her dream, however, her fears revived. Dreams were solemn things. To Cicely the fabric of a vision was by no means baseless. Her trouble arose from her not being able to recall, though she was well versed in dream-lore, just what event was foreshadowed by a dream of finding a wounded man. If the wounded man were of her own race, her dream would thus far have been realized, and having met the young man, the other joys might be expected to follow. If he should turn out to be a white man, then her dream was clearly one of the kind that go by contraries, and she could expect only sorrow and trouble and pain as the proper sequences of this fateful discovery.

II

THE TWO WOMEN REACHED THE fence that separated the cornfield from the pine woods.

"How is I gwine ter git ovuh dat fence, chile?" asked the old woman.

"Wait a minute, granny," said Cicely; "I 'll take it down."

It was only an eight-rail fence, and it was a matter of but a few minutes for the girl to lift down and lay to either side the ends of the rails that formed one of the angles. This done, the old woman easily stepped across the remaining two or three rails. It was only a moment before they stood by the wounded man. He was lying still, breathing regularly, and seemingly asleep.

"What is he, granny," asked the girl anxiously, "a w'ite man, or not?"

Old Dinah pushed back the matted hair from the wounded man's brow, and looked at the skin beneath. It was fairer there, but yet of a decided brown. She raised his hand, pushed back the tattered sleeve from his wrist, and then she laid his hand down gently.

"Mos' lackly he's a mulatter man f'om up de country somewhar. He don' look lack dese yer niggers roun' yere, ner yet lack a w'ite man. But de po' boy's in a bad fix, w'ateber he is, an' I 'spec's we bettah do w'at we kin fer 'im, an' w'en he comes to he'll tell us w'at he is—er w'at he calls hisse'f. Hol' 'is head up, chile, an' I'll po' a drop er dis yer liquor down his th'oat; dat'll bring 'im to quicker'n anything e'se I knows."

Cicely lifted the sick man's head, and Dinah poured a few drops of the whiskey between his teeth. He swallowed it readily enough. In a few minutes he opened his eyes and stared blankly at the two women. Cicely saw that his eyes were large and black, and glistening with fever.

"How you feelin', suh?" asked the old woman.

There was no answer.

"Is you feelin' bettah now?"

The wounded man kept on staring blankly. Suddenly he essayed to put his hand to his head, gave a deep groan, and fell back again unconscious.

"He's gone ag'in," said Dinah. "I reckon we'll hafter tote 'im up ter de house and take keer er 'im dere. W'ite folks would n't want ter fool wid a nigger man, an' we doan know who his folks is. He's outer his head an' will be fer some time yet, an' we can't tell nuthin' 'bout 'im tel he comes ter his senses."

Cicely lifted the wounded man by the arms and shoulders. She was strong, with the strength of youth and a sturdy race. The man was pitifully emaciated; how much, the two women had not suspected until they raised him. They had no difficulty whatever, except for the awkwardness of such a burden, in lifting him over the fence and carrying him through the cornfield to the cabin.

They laid him on Cicely's bed in the little lean-to shed that formed a room separate from the main apartment of the cabin. The old woman sent Cicely to cook the dinner, while she gave her own attention exclusively to the still unconscious man. She brought water and washed him as though he were a child.

CHARLES W. CHESNUTT

"Po' boy," she said, "he doan feel lack he 's be'n eatin' nuff to feed a sparrer. He 'pears ter be mos' starved ter def."

She washed his wound more carefully, made some lint,—the art was well known in the sixties,—and dressed his wound with a fair degree of skill.

"Somebody must 'a' be'n tryin' ter put yo' light out, chile," she muttered to herself as she adjusted the bandage around his head. "A little higher er a little lower, an' you would n' 'a' be'n yere ter tell de tale. Dem clo's," she argued, lifting the tattered garments she had removed from her patient, "don' b'long 'roun' yere. Dat kinder weavin' come f'om down to'ds Souf Ca'lina. I wish Needham 'u'd come erlong. He kin tell who dis man is, an' all erbout 'im."

She made a bowl of gruel, and fed it, drop by drop, to the sick man. This roused him somewhat from his stupor, but when Dinah thought he had enough of the gruel, and stopped feeding him, he closed his eyes again and relapsed into a heavy sleep that was so closely akin to unconsciousness as to be scarcely distinguishable from it.

When old Needham came home at noon, his wife, who had been anxiously awaiting his return, told him in a few words the story of Cicely's discovery and of the subsequent events.

Needham inspected the stranger with a professional eye. He had been something of a plantation doctor in his day, and was known far and wide for his knowledge of simple remedies. The negroes all around, as well as many of the poorer white people, came to him for the treatment of common ailments.

"He 's got a fevuh," he said, after feeling the patient's pulse and laying his hand on his brow, "an' we 'll hafter gib 'im some yarb tea an' nuss 'im tel de fevuh w'ars off. I 'spec'," he added, "dat I knows whar dis boy come f'om. He 's mos' lackly one er dem bright mulatters, f'om Robeson County—some of 'em call deyse'ves Croatan Injins— w'at's been conscripted an' sent ter wu'k on de fo'tifications down at Wimbleton er some'er's er nuther, an' done 'scaped, and got mos' killed gittin' erway, an' wuz n' none too well fed befo', an' nigh 'bout starved ter def sence. We 'll hafter hide dis man, er e'se we is lackly ter git inter trouble ou'se'ves by harb'rin' 'im. Ef dey ketch 'im yere, dey 's liable ter take 'im out an' shoot 'im—an' des ez lackly us too."

Cicely was listening with bated breath.

"Oh, gran'daddy," she cried with trembling voice, "don' let 'em ketch 'im! Hide 'im somewhar."

"I reckon we 'll leave 'im yere fer a day er so. Ef he had come f'om roun' yere I 'd be skeered ter keep 'im, fer de w'ite folks 'u'd prob'ly be lookin' fer 'im. But I knows ev'ybody w'at's be'n conscripted fer ten miles 'roun', an' dis yere boy don' b'long in dis neighborhood. W'en 'e gits so 'e kin he'p 'isse'f we 'll put 'im up in de lof an' hide 'im till de Yankees come. Fer dey 're comin', sho'. I dremp' las' night dey wuz close ter han', and I hears de w'ite folks talkin' ter deyse'ves 'bout it. An' de time is comin' w'en de good Lawd gwine ter set his people free, an' it ain' gwine ter be long, nuther."

Needham's prophecy proved true. In less than a week the Confederate garrison evacuated the arsenal in the neighboring town of Patesville, blew up the buildings, destroyed the ordnance and stores, and retreated across the Cape Fear River, burning the river bridge behind them,—two acts of war afterwards unjustly attributed to General Sherman's army, which followed close upon the heels of the retreating Confederates.

When there was no longer any fear for the stranger's safety, no more pains were taken to conceal him. His wound had healed rapidly, and in a week he had been able with some help to climb up the ladder into the loft. In all this time, however, though apparently conscious, he had said no word to any one, nor had he seemed to comprehend a word that was spoken to him.

Cicely had been his constant attendant. After the first day, during which her granny had nursed him, she had sat by his bedside, had fanned his fevered brow, had held food and water and medicine to his lips. When it was safe for him to come down from the loft and sit in a chair under a spreading oak, Cicely supported him until he was strong enough to walk about the yard. When his strength had increased sufficiently to permit of greater exertion, she accompanied him on long rambles in the fields and woods.

In spite of his gain in physical strength, the newcomer changed very little in other respects. For a long time he neither spoke nor smiled. To questions put to him he simply gave no reply, but looked at his questioner with the blank unconsciousness of an infant. By and by he began to recognize Cicely, and to smile at her approach. The next step in returning consciousness was but another manifestation of the same sentiment. When Cicely would leave him he would look his regret, and be restless and uneasy until she returned.

The family were at a loss what to call him. To any inquiry as to his name he answered no more than to other questions.

CHARLES W. CHESNUTT

"He come jes' befo' Sherman," said Needham, after a few weeks, "lack John de Baptis' befo' de Lawd. I reckon we bettah call 'im John."

So they called him John. He soon learned the name. As time went on Cicely found that he was quick at learning things. She taught him to speak her own negro English, which he pronounced with absolute fidelity to her intonations; so that barring the quality of his voice, his speech was an echo of Cicely's own.

The summer wore away and the autumn came. John and Cicely wandered in the woods together and gathered walnuts, and chinquapins and wild grapes. When harvest time came, they worked in the fields side by side,—plucked the corn, pulled the fodder, and gathered the dried peas from the yellow pea-vines. Cicely was a phenomenal cotton-picker, and John accompanied her to the fields and stayed by her hours at a time, though occasionally he would complain of his head, and sit under a tree and rest part of the day while Cicely worked, the two keeping one another always in sight.

They did not have a great deal of intercourse with other people. Young men came to the cabin sometimes to see Cicely, but when they found her entirely absorbed in the stranger they ceased their visits. For a time Cicely kept him away, as much as possible, from others, because she did not wish them to see that there was anything wrong about him. This was her motive at first, but after a while she kept him to herself simply because she was happier so. He was hers—hers alone. She had found him, as Pharaoh's daughter had found Moses in the bulrushes; she had taught him to speak, to think, to love. She had not taught him to remember; she would not have wished him to; she would have been jealous of any past to which he might have proved bound by other ties. Her dream so far had come true. She had found him; he loved her. The rest of it would as surely follow, and that before long. For dreams were serious things, and time had proved hers to have been not a presage of misfortune, but one of the beneficent visions that are sent, that we may enjoy by anticipation the good things that are in store for us.

III

But a short interval of time elapsed after the passage of the warlike host that swept through North Carolina, until there appeared upon the scene the vanguard of a second army, which came to bring light and the fruits of liberty to a land which slavery and the havoc of war had brought to ruin. It is fashionable to assume that those who undertook the political rehabilitation of the Southern States merely rounded out the ruin that the war had wrought—merely ploughed up the desolate land and sowed it with salt. Perhaps the gentler judgments of the future may recognize that their task was a difficult one, and that wiser and honester men might have failed as egregiously. It may even, in time, be conceded that some good came out of the carpet-bag governments, as, for instance, the establishment of a system of popular education in the former slave States. Where it had been a crime to teach people to read or write, a schoolhouse dotted every hillside, and the State provided education for rich and poor, for white and black alike. Let us lay at least this token upon the grave of the carpet-baggers. The evil they did lives after them, and the statute of limitations does not seem to run against it. It is but just that we should not forget the good.

Long, however, before the work of political reconstruction had begun, a brigade of Yankee schoolmasters and schoolma'ams had invaded Dixie, and one of the latter had opened a Freedman's Bureau School in the town of Patesville, about four miles from Needham Green's cabin on the neighboring sandhills.

It had been quite a surprise to Miss Chandler's Boston friends when she had announced her intention of going South to teach the freedmen. Rich, accomplished, beautiful, and a social favorite, she was giving up the comforts and luxuries of Northern life to go among hostile strangers, where her associates would be mostly ignorant negroes. Perhaps she might meet occasionally an officer of some Federal garrison, or a traveler from the North; but to all intents and purposes her friends considered her as going into voluntary exile. But heroism was not rare in those days, and Martha Chandler was only one of the great multitude whose hearts went out toward an oppressed race, and who freely poured out their talents, their money, their lives,—whatever God had given them,—in the sublime and not unfruitful effort to transform three millions of slaves into intelligent freemen. Miss Chandler's friends knew, too, that she had met a great sorrow, and more than suspected that out of it had grown her determination to go South.

When Cicely Green heard that a school for colored people had been opened at Patesville she combed her hair, put on her Sunday frock and such bits of finery as she possessed, and set out for town early the next Monday morning.

There were many who came to learn the new gospel of education,

CHARLES W. CHESNUTT

which was to be the cure for all the freedmen's ills. The old and gray-haired, the full-grown man and woman, the toddling infant,—they came to acquire the new and wonderful learning that was to make them the equals of the white people. It was the teacher's task, by no means an easy one, to select from this incongruous mass the most promising material, and to distribute among them the second-hand books and clothing that were sent, largely by her Boston friends, to aid her in her work; to find out what they knew, to classify them by their intelligence rather than by their knowledge, for they were all lamentably ignorant. Some among them were the children of parents who had been free before the war, and of these some few could read and one or two could write. One paragon, who could repeat the multiplication table, was immediately promoted to the position of pupil teacher.

Miss Chandler took a liking to the tall girl who had come so far to sit under her instruction. There was a fine, free air in her bearing, a lightness in her step, a sparkle in her eye, that spoke of good blood,—whether fused by nature in its own alembic, out of material despised and spurned of men, or whether some obscure ancestral strain, the teacher could not tell. The girl proved intelligent and learned rapidly, indeed seemed almost feverishly anxious to learn. She was quiet, and was, though utterly untrained, instinctively polite, and profited from the first day by the example of her teacher's quiet elegance. The teacher dressed in simple black. When Cicely came back to school the second day, she had left off her glass beads and her red ribbon, and had arranged her hair as nearly like the teacher's as her skill and its quality would permit.

The teacher was touched by these efforts at imitation, and by the intense devotion Cicely soon manifested toward her. It was not a sycophantic, troublesome devotion, that made itself a burden to its object. It found expression in little things done rather than in any words the girl said. To the degree that the attraction was mutual, Martha recognized in it a sort of freemasonry of temperament that drew them together in spite of the differences between them. Martha felt sometimes, in the vague way that one speculates about the impossible, that if she were brown, and had been brought up in North Carolina, she would be like Cicely; and that if Cicely's ancestors had come over in the Mayflower, and Cicely had been reared on Beacon Street, in the shadow of the State House dome, Cicely would have been very much like herself.

Miss Chandler was lonely sometimes. Her duties kept her occupied all day. On Sundays she taught a Bible class in the schoolroom.

Correspondence with bureau officials and friends at home furnished her with additional occupation. At times, nevertheless, she felt a longing for the company of women of her own race; but the white ladies of the town did not call, even in the most formal way, upon the Yankee school-teacher. Miss Chandler was therefore fain to do the best she could with such companionship as was available. She took Cicely to her home occasionally, and asked her once to stay all night. Thinking, however, that she detected a reluctance on the girl's part to remain away from home, she did not repeat her invitation.

Cicely, indeed, was filling a double rôle. The learning acquired from Miss Chandler she imparted to John at home. Every evening, by the light of the pine-knots blazing on Needham's ample hearth, she taught John to read the simple words she had learned during the day. Why she did not take him to school she had never asked herself; there were several other pupils as old as he seemed to be. Perhaps she still thought it necessary to protect him from curious remark. He worked with Needham by day, and she could see him at night, and all of Saturdays and Sundays. Perhaps it was the jealous selfishness of love. She had found him; he was hers. In the spring, when school was over, her granny had said that she might marry him. Till then her dream would not yet have come true, and she must keep him to herself. And yet she did not wish him to lose this golden key to the avenues of opportunity. She would not take him to school, but she would teach him each day all that she herself had learned. He was not difficult to teach, but learned, indeed, with what seemed to Cicely marvelous ease,—always, however, by her lead, and never of his own initiative. For while he could do a man's work, he was in most things but a child, without a child's curiosity. His love for Cicely appeared the only thing for which he needed no suggestion; and even that possessed an element of childish dependence that would have seemed, to minds trained to thoughtful observation, infinitely pathetic.

The spring came and cotton-planting time. The children began to drop out of Miss Chandler's school one by one, as their services were required at home. Cicely was among those who intended to remain in school until the term closed with the "exhibition," in which she was assigned a leading part. She had selected her recitation, or "speech," from among half a dozen poems that her teacher had suggested, and to memorizing it she devoted considerable time and study. The exhibition, as the first of its kind, was sure to be a notable event. The parents and friends of the children were invited to attend, and a colored church, recently erected,—the largest available building,—was secured as the place where the exercises should take place.

On the morning of the eventful day, uncle Needham, assisted by John, harnessed the mule to the two-wheeled cart, on which a couple of splint-bottomed chairs were fastened to accommodate Dinah and Cicely. John put on his best clothes,—an ill-fitting suit of blue jeans,—a round wool hat, a pair of coarse brogans, a homespun shirt, and a bright blue necktie. Cicely wore her best frock, a red ribbon at her throat, another in her hair, and carried a bunch of flowers in her hand. Uncle Needham and aunt Dinah were also in holiday array. Needham and John took their seats on opposite sides of the cart-frame, with their feet dangling down, and thus the equipage set out leisurely for the town.

Cicely had long looked forward impatiently to this day. She was going to marry John the next week, and then her dream would have come entirely true. But even this anticipated happiness did not overshadow the importance of the present occasion, which would be an epoch in her life, a day of joy and triumph. She knew her speech perfectly, and timidity was not one of her weaknesses. She knew that the red ribbons set off her dark beauty effectively, and that her dress fitted neatly the curves of her shapely figure. She confidently expected to win the first prize, a large morocco-covered Bible, offered by Miss Chandler for the best exercise.

Cicely and her companions soon arrived at Patesville. Their entrance into the church made quite a sensation, for Cicely was not only an acknowledged belle, but a general favorite, and to John there attached a tinge of mystery which inspired a respect not bestowed upon those who had grown up in the neighborhood. Cicely secured a seat in the front part of the church, next to the aisle, in the place reserved for the pupils. As the house was already partly filled by townspeople when the party from the country arrived, Needham and his wife and John were forced to content themselves with places somewhat in the rear of the room, from which they could see and hear what took place on the platform, but where they were not at all conspicuously visible to those at the front of the church.

The schoolmistress had not yet arrived, and order was preserved in the audience by two of the elder pupils, adorned with large rosettes of red, white, and blue, who ushered the most important visitors to the seats reserved for them. A national flag was gracefully draped over the platform, and under it hung a lithograph of the Great Emancipator, for it was thus these people thought of him. He had saved the Union, but the Union had never meant anything good to them. He had proclaimed liberty to the captive, which meant all to them; and to them he was and would ever be the Great Emancipator.

The schoolmistress came in at a rear door and took her seat upon the platform. Martha was dressed in white; for once she had laid aside the sombre garb in which alone she had been seen since her arrival at Patesville. She wore a yellow rose at her throat, a bunch of jasmine in her belt. A sense of responsibility for the success of the exhibition had deepened the habitual seriousness of her face, yet she greeted the audience with a smile.

"Don' Miss Chan'ler look sweet," whispered the little girls to one another, devouring her beauty with sparkling eyes, their lips parted over a wealth of ivory.

"De Lawd will bress dat chile," said one old woman, in soliloquy. "I t'ank de good Marster I 's libbed ter see dis day."

Even envy could not hide its noisome head: a pretty quadroon whispered to her neighbor:—

"I don't b'liebe she 's natch'ly ez white ez dat. I 'spec' she 's be'n powd'rin'! An' I know all dat hair can't be her'n; she 's got on a switch, sho 's you bawn."

"You knows dat ain' so, Ma'y 'Liza Smif," rejoined the other, with a look of stern disapproval; "you *knows* dat ain' so. You 'd gib yo' everlastin' soul 'f you wuz ez white ez Miss Chan'ler, en yo' ha'r wuz ez long ez her'n."

"By Jove, Maxwell!" exclaimed a young officer, who belonged to the Federal garrison stationed in the town, "but that girl is a beauty." The speaker and a companion were in fatigue uniform, and had merely dropped in for an hour between garrison duty. The ushers had wished to give them seats on the platform, but they had declined, thinking that perhaps their presence there might embarrass the teacher. They sought rather to avoid observation by sitting behind a pillar in the rear of the room, around which they could see without attracting undue attention.

"To think," the lieutenant went on, "of that Junonian figure, those lustrous orbs, that golden coronal, that flower of Northern civilization, being wasted on these barbarians!" The speaker uttered an exaggerated but suppressed groan.

His companion, a young man of clean-shaven face and serious aspect, nodded assent, but whispered reprovingly,—

CHARLES W. CHESNUTT

"'Sh! some one will hear you. The exercises are going to begin."

When Miss Chandler stepped forward to announce the hymn to be sung by the school as the first exercise, every eye in the room was fixed upon her, except John's, which saw only Cicely. When the teacher had uttered a few words, he looked up to her, and from that moment did not take his eyes off Martha's face.

After the singing, a little girl, dressed in white, crossed by ribbons of red and blue, recited with much spirit a patriotic poem.

When Martha announced the third exercise, John's face took on a more than usually animated expression, and there was a perceptible deepening of the troubled look in his eyes, never entirely absent since Cicely had found him in the woods.

A little yellow boy, with long curls, and a frightened air, next ascended the platform.

"Now, Jimmie, be a man, and speak right out," whispered his teacher, tapping his arm reassuringly with her fan as he passed her.

Jimmie essayed to recite the lines so familiar to a past generation of schoolchildren:—

> *"I knew a widow very poor,*
> *Who four small children had;*
> *The eldest was but six years old,*
> *A gentle, modest lad."*

He ducked his head hurriedly in a futile attempt at a bow; then, following instructions previously given him, fixed his eyes upon a large cardboard motto hanging on the rear wall of the room, which admonished him in bright red letters to

"ALWAYS SPEAK THE TRUTH,"

and started off with assumed confidence

> *"I knew a widow very poor,*
> *Who"*—

At this point, drawn by an irresistible impulse, his eyes sought the level of the audience. Ah, fatal blunder! He stammered, but with an effort raised his eyes and began again:

> *"I knew a widow very poor,*
> *Who four"*—

Again his treacherous eyes fell, and his little remaining self-possession utterly forsook him. He made one more despairing effort:—

> *"I knew a widow very poor,*
> *Who four small"*—

and then, bursting into tears, turned and fled amid a murmur of sympathy.

Jimmie's inglorious retreat was covered by the singing in chorus of "The Star-spangled Banner," after which Cicely Green came forward to recite her poem.

"By Jove, Maxwell!" whispered the young officer, who was evidently a connoisseur of female beauty, "that is n't bad for a bronze Venus. I 'll tell you"—

"'Sh!" said the other. "Keep still."

When Cicely finished her recitation, the young officers began to applaud, but stopped suddenly in some confusion as they realized that they were the only ones in the audience so engaged. The colored people had either not learned how to express their approval in orthodox fashion, or else their respect for the sacred character of the edifice forbade any such demonstration. Their enthusiasm found vent, however, in a subdued murmur, emphasized by numerous nods and winks and suppressed exclamations. During the singing that followed Cicely's recitation the two officers quietly withdrew, their duties calling them away at this hour.

At the close of the exercises, a committee on prizes met in the vestibule, and unanimously decided that Cicely Green was entitled to the first prize. Proudly erect, with sparkling eyes and cheeks flushed with victory, Cicely advanced to the platform to receive the coveted reward. As she turned away, her eyes, shining with gratified vanity, sought those of her lover.

John sat bent slightly forward in an attitude of strained attention; and Cicely's triumph lost half its value when she saw that it was not at her, but at Miss Chandler, that his look was directed. Though she watched him thenceforward, not one glance did he vouchsafe to his jealous sweetheart, and never for an instant withdrew his eyes from

CHARLES W. CHESNUTT

Martha, or relaxed the unnatural intentness of his gaze. The imprisoned mind, stirred to unwonted effort, was struggling for liberty; and from Martha had come the first ray of outer light that had penetrated its dungeon.

Before the audience was dismissed, the teacher rose to bid her school farewell. Her intention was to take a vacation of three months; but what might happen in that time she did not know, and there were duties at home of such apparent urgency as to render her return to North Carolina at least doubtful; so that in her own heart her *au revoir* sounded very much like a farewell.

She spoke to them of the hopeful progress they had made, and praised them for their eager desire to learn. She told them of the serious duties of life, and of the use they should make of their acquirements. With prophetic finger she pointed them to the upward way which they must climb with patient feet to raise themselves out of the depths.

Then, an unusual thing with her, she spoke of herself. Her heart was full; it was with difficulty that she maintained her composure; for the faces that confronted her were kindly faces, and not critical, and some of them she had learned to love right well.

"I am going away from you, my children," she said; "but before I go I want to tell you how I came to be in North Carolina; so that if I have been able to do anything here among you for which you might feel inclined, in your good nature, to thank me, you may thank not me alone, but another who came before me, and whose work I have but taken up where *he* laid it down. I had a friend,—a dear friend,—why should I be ashamed to say it?—a lover, to whom I was to be married,—as I hope all you girls may some day be happily married. His country needed him, and I gave him up. He came to fight for the Union and for Freedom, for he believed that all men are brothers. He did not come back again—he gave up his life for you. Could I do less than he? I came to the land that he sanctified by his death, and I have tried in my weak way to tend the plant he watered with his blood, and which, in the fullness of time, will blossom forth into the perfect flower of liberty."

She could say no more, and as the whole audience thrilled in sympathy with her emotion, there was a hoarse cry from the men's side of the room, and John forced his way to the aisle and rushed forward to the platform.

"Martha! Martha!"

"Arthur! O Arthur!"

Pent-up love burst the flood-gates of despair and oblivion, and caught these two young hearts in its torrent. Captain Arthur Carey, of the 1st Massachusetts, long since reported missing, and mourned as dead, was restored to reason and to his world.

It seemed to him but yesterday that he had escaped from the Confederate prison at Salisbury; that in an encounter with a guard he had received a wound in the head; that he had wandered on in the woods, keeping himself alive by means of wild berries, with now and then a piece of bread or a potato from a friendly negro. It seemed but the night before that he had laid himself down, tortured with fever, weak from loss of blood, and with no hope that he would ever rise again. From that moment his memory of the past was a blank until he recognized Martha on the platform and took up again the thread of his former existence where it had been broken off.

AND CICELY? WELL, THERE IS often another woman, and Cicely, all unwittingly to Carey or to Martha, had been the other woman. For, after all, her beautiful dream had been one of the kind that go by contraries.

The Passing of Grandison

I

WHEN IT IS SAID THAT it was done to please a woman, there ought perhaps to be enough said to explain anything; for what a man will not do to please a woman is yet to be discovered. Nevertheless, it might be well to state a few preliminary facts to make it clear why young Dick Owens tried to run one of his father's negro men off to Canada.

In the early fifties, when the growth of anti-slavery sentiment and the constant drain of fugitive slaves into the North had so alarmed the slaveholders of the border States as to lead to the passage of the Fugitive Slave Law, a young white man from Ohio, moved by compassion for the sufferings of a certain bondman who happened to have a "hard master," essayed to help the slave to freedom. The attempt was discovered and frustrated; the abductor was tried and convicted for slave-stealing, and sentenced to a term of imprisonment in the penitentiary. His death, after the expiration of only a small part of the sentence, from cholera contracted while nursing stricken fellow prisoners, lent to the case a melancholy interest that made it famous in anti-slavery annals.

Dick Owens had attended the trial. He was a youth of about twenty-two, intelligent, handsome, and amiable, but extremely indolent, in a graceful and gentlemanly way; or, as old Judge Fenderson put it more than once, he was lazy as the Devil,—a mere figure of speech, of course, and not one that did justice to the Enemy of Mankind. When asked why he never did anything serious, Dick would good-naturedly reply, with a well-modulated drawl, that he didn't have to. His father was rich; there was but one other child, an unmarried daughter, who because of poor health would probably never marry, and Dick was therefore heir presumptive to a large estate. Wealth or social position he did not need to seek, for he was born to both. Charity Lomax had shamed him into studying law, but notwithstanding an hour or so a day spent at old Judge Fenderson's office, he did not make remarkable headway in his legal studies.

"What Dick needs," said the judge, who was fond of tropes, as became a scholar, and of horses, as was befitting a Kentuckian, "is the whip of necessity, or the spur of ambition. If he had either, he would soon need the snaffle to hold him back."

But all Dick required, in fact, to prompt him to the most remarkable thing he accomplished before he was twenty-five, was a mere suggestion from Charity Lomax. The story was never really known to but two persons until after the war, when it came out because it was a good story and there was no particular reason for its concealment.

Young Owens had attended the trial of this slave-stealer, or martyr,— either or both,—and, when it was over, had gone to call on Charity Lomax, and, while they sat on the veranda after sundown, had told her all about the trial. He was a good talker, as his career in later years disclosed, and described the proceedings very graphically.

"I confess," he admitted, "that while my principles were against the prisoner, my sympathies were on his side. It appeared that he was of good family, and that he had an old father and mother, respectable people, dependent upon him for support and comfort in their declining years. He had been led into the matter by pity for a negro whose master ought to have been run out of the county long ago for abusing his slaves. If it had been merely a question of old Sam Briggs's negro, nobody would have cared anything about it. But father and the rest of them stood on the principle of the thing, and told the judge so, and the fellow was sentenced to three years in the penitentiary."

Miss Lomax had listened with lively interest.

"I 've always hated old Sam Briggs," she said emphatically, "ever since the time he broke a negro's leg with a piece of cordwood. When I hear of a cruel deed it makes the Quaker blood that came from my grandmother assert itself. Personally I wish that all Sam Briggs's negroes would run away. As for the young man, I regard him as a hero. He dared something for humanity. I could love a man who would take such chances for the sake of others."

"Could you love me, Charity, if I did something heroic?"

"You never will, Dick. You 're too lazy for any use. You 'll never do anything harder than playing cards or fox-hunting."

"Oh, come now, sweetheart! I 've been courting you for a year, and it 's the hardest work imaginable. Are you never going to love me?" he pleaded.

His hand sought hers, but she drew it back beyond his reach.

"I 'll never love you, Dick Owens, until you have done something. When that time comes, I 'll think about it."

"But it takes so long to do anything worth mentioning, and I don't want to wait. One must read two years to become a lawyer, and work five more to make a reputation. We shall both be gray by then."

CHARLES W. CHESNUTT

"Oh, I don't know," she rejoined. "It does n't require a lifetime for a man to prove that he is a man. This one did something, or at least tried to."

"Well, I 'm willing to attempt as much as any other man. What do you want me to do, sweetheart? Give me a test."

"Oh, dear me!" said Charity, "I don't care what you *do*, so you do *something*. Really, come to think of it, why should I care whether you do anything or not?"

"I 'm sure I don't know why you should, Charity," rejoined Dick humbly, "for I 'm aware that I 'm not worthy of it."

"Except that I do hate," she added, relenting slightly, "to see a really clever man so utterly lazy and good for nothing."

"Thank you, my dear; a word of praise from you has sharpened my wits already. I have an idea! Will you love me if I run a negro off to Canada?"

"What nonsense!" said Charity scornfully. "You must be losing your wits. Steal another man's slave, indeed, while your father owns a hundred!"

"Oh, there 'll be no trouble about that," responded Dick lightly; "I 'll run off one of the old man's; we 've got too many anyway. It may not be quite as difficult as the other man found it, but it will be just as unlawful, and will demonstrate what I am capable of."

"Seeing 's believing," replied Charity. "Of course, what you are talking about now is merely absurd. I 'm going away for three weeks, to visit my aunt in Tennessee. If you 're able to tell me, when I return, that you've done something to prove your quality, I 'll—well, you may come and tell me about it."

II

Young Owens got up about nine o'clock next morning, and while making his toilet put some questions to his personal attendant, a rather bright looking young mulatto of about his own age.

"Tom," said Dick.

"Yas, Mars Dick," responded the servant.

"I 'm going on a trip North. Would you like to go with me?"

Now, if there was anything that Tom would have liked to make, it was a trip North. It was something he had long contemplated in the abstract, but had never been able to muster up sufficient courage to attempt in the concrete. He was prudent enough, however, to dissemble his feelings.

"I would n't min' it, Mars Dick, ez long ez you 'd take keer er me an' fetch me home all right."

Tom's eyes belied his words, however, and his young master felt well assured that Tom needed only a good opportunity to make him run away. Having a comfortable home, and a dismal prospect in case of failure, Tom was not likely to take any desperate chances; but young Owens was satisfied that in a free State but little persuasion would be required to lead Tom astray. With a very logical and characteristic desire to gain his end with the least necessary expenditure of effort, he decided to take Tom with him, if his father did not object.

Colonel Owens had left the house when Dick went to breakfast, so Dick did not see his father till luncheon.

"Father," he remarked casually to the colonel, over the fried chicken, "I 'm feeling a trifle run down. I imagine my health would be improved somewhat by a little travel and change of scene."

"Why don't you take a trip North?" suggested his father. The colonel added to paternal affection a considerable respect for his son as the heir of a large estate. He himself had been "raised" in comparative poverty, and had laid the foundations of his fortune by hard work; and while he despised the ladder by which he had climbed, he could not entirely forget it, and unconsciously manifested, in his intercourse with his son, some of the poor man's deference toward the wealthy and well-born.

"I think I 'll adopt your suggestion, sir," replied the son, "and run up to New York; and after I 've been there awhile I may go on to Boston for a week or so. I 've never been there, you know."

"There are some matters you can talk over with my factor in New York," rejoined the colonel, "and while you are up there among the Yankees, I hope you 'll keep your eyes and ears open to find out what the rascally abolitionists are saying and doing. They 're becoming altogether too active for our comfort, and entirely too many ungrateful niggers are running away. I hope the conviction of that fellow yesterday may discourage the rest of the breed. I 'd just like to catch any one trying to run off one of my darkeys. He 'd get short shrift; I don't think any Court would have a chance to try him."

"They are a pestiferous lot," assented Dick, "and dangerous to our institutions. But say, father, if I go North I shall want to take Tom with me."

Now, the colonel, while a very indulgent father, had pronounced views on the subject of negroes, having studied them, as he often said, for a great many years, and, as he asserted oftener still, understanding them perfectly. It is scarcely worth while to say, either, that he valued more highly than if he had inherited them the slaves he had toiled and schemed for.

"I don't think it safe to take Tom up North," he declared, with promptness and decision. "He's a good enough boy, but too smart to trust among those low-down abolitionists. I strongly suspect him of having learned to read, though I can't imagine how. I saw him with a newspaper the other day, and while he pretended to be looking at a woodcut, I'm almost sure he was reading the paper. I think it by no means safe to take him."

Dick did not insist, because he knew it was useless. The colonel would have obliged his son in any other matter, but his negroes were the outward and visible sign of his wealth and station, and therefore sacred to him.

"Whom do you think it safe to take?" asked Dick. "I suppose I'll have to have a body-servant."

"What's the matter with Grandison?" suggested the colonel. "He's handy enough, and I reckon we can trust him. He's too fond of good eating, to risk losing his regular meals; besides, he's sweet on your mother's maid, Betty, and I've promised to let 'em get married before long. I'll have Grandison up, and we'll talk to him. Here, you boy Jack," called the colonel to a yellow youth in the next room who was catching flies and pulling their wings off to pass the time, "go down to the barn and tell Grandison to come here."

"Grandison," said the colonel, when the negro stood before him, hat in hand.

"Yas, marster."

"Have n't I always treated you right?"

"Yas, marster."

"Have n't you always got all you wanted to eat?"

"Yas, marster."

"And as much whiskey and tobacco as was good for you, Grandison?"

"Y-a-s, marster."

"I should just like to know, Grandison, whether you don't think yourself a great deal better off than those poor free negroes down by the plank road, with no kind master to look after them and no mistress to give them medicine when they're sick and—and"—

"Well, I sh'd jes' reckon I is better off, suh, dan dem low-down free niggers, suh! Ef anybody ax 'em who dey b'long ter, dey has ter say nobody, er e'se lie erbout it. Anybody ax me who I b'longs ter, I ain' got no 'casion ter be shame' ter tell 'em, no, suh, 'deed I ain', suh!"

The colonel was beaming. This was true gratitude, and his feudal heart thrilled at such appreciative homage. What cold-blooded, heartless monsters they were who would break up this blissful relationship of kindly protection on the one hand, of wise subordination and loyal dependence on the other! The colonel always became indignant at the mere thought of such wickedness.

"Grandison," the colonel continued, "your young master Dick is going North for a few weeks, and I am thinking of letting him take you along. I shall send you on this trip, Grandison, in order that you may take care of your young master. He will need some one to wait on him, and no one can ever do it so well as one of the boys brought up with him on the old plantation. I am going to trust him in your hands, and I'm sure you'll do your duty faithfully, and bring him back home safe and sound—to old Kentucky."

Grandison grinned. "Oh yas, marster, I'll take keer er young Mars Dick."

"I want to warn you, though, Grandison," continued the colonel impressively, "against these cussed abolitionists, who try to entice servants from their comfortable homes and their indulgent masters, from the blue skies, the green fields, and the warm sunlight of their southern home, and send them away off yonder to Canada, a dreary country, where the woods are full of wildcats and wolves and bears, where the snow lies up to the eaves of the houses for six months of the year, and the cold is so severe that it freezes your breath and curdles your blood; and where, when runaway niggers get sick and can't work, they are turned out to starve and die, unloved and uncared for. I reckon, Grandison, that you have too much sense to permit yourself to be led astray by any such foolish and wicked people."

"'Deed, suh, I would n' low none er dem cussed, low-down abolitioners ter come nigh me, suh. I'd—I'd—would I be 'lowed ter hit 'em, suh?"

"Certainly, Grandison," replied the colonel, chuckling, "hit 'em as hard as you can. I reckon they'd rather like it. Begad, I believe they would! It would serve 'em right to be hit by a nigger!"

"Er ef I did n't hit 'em, suh," continued Grandison reflectively, "I'd tell Mars Dick, en *he'd* fix 'em. He'd smash de face off 'n 'em, suh, I jes' knows he would."

"Oh yes, Grandison, your young master will protect you. You need fear no harm while he is near."

"Dey won't try ter steal me, will dey, marster?" asked the negro, with sudden alarm.

"I don't know, Grandison," replied the colonel, lighting a fresh cigar. "They're a desperate set of lunatics, and there's no telling what they may resort to. But if you stick close to your young master, and remember always that he is your best friend, and understands your real needs, and has your true interests at heart, and if you will be careful to avoid strangers who try to talk to you, you'll stand a fair chance of getting back to your home and your friends. And if you please your master Dick, he'll buy you a present, and a string of beads for Betty to wear when you and she get married in the fall."

"Thanky, marster, thanky, suh," replied Grandison, oozing gratitude at every pore; "you is a good marster, to be sho', suh; yas, 'deed you is. You kin jes' bet me and Mars Dick gwine git 'long jes' lack I wuz own boy ter Mars Dick. En it won't be my fault ef he don' want me fer his boy all de time, w'en we come back home ag'in."

"All right, Grandison, you may go now. You need n't work any more to-day, and here's a piece of tobacco for you off my own plug."

"Thanky, marster, thanky, marster! You is de bes' marster any nigger ever had in dis worl'." And Grandison bowed and scraped and disappeared round the corner, his jaws closing around a large section of the colonel's best tobacco.

"You may take Grandison," said the colonel to his son. "I allow he's abolitionist-proof."

III

Richard Owens, Esq., and servant, from Kentucky, registered at the fashionable New York hostelry for Southerners in those days, a hotel where an atmosphere congenial to Southern institutions was sedulously maintained. But there were negro waiters in the dining-room, and mulatto bell-boys, and Dick had no doubt that Grandison, with the native gregariousness and garrulousness of his race, would foregather and palaver with them sooner or later, and Dick hoped that they would speedily inoculate him with the virus of freedom. For it was not Dick's intention to say anything to his servant about his plan to free him, for obvious reasons. To mention one of them, if Grandison should go away, and by legal process be recaptured, his young master's part in the matter would doubtless become known, which would be embarrassing to Dick, to say the least. If, on the other hand, he should merely give Grandison sufficient latitude, he had no doubt he would eventually lose him. For while not exactly skeptical about Grandison's perfervid loyalty, Dick had been a somewhat keen observer of human nature, in his own indolent way, and based his expectations upon the force of the example and argument that his servant could scarcely fail to encounter. Grandison should have a fair chance to become free by his own initiative; if it should become necessary to adopt other measures to get rid of him, it would be time enough to act when the necessity arose; and Dick Owens was not the youth to take needless trouble.

The young master renewed some acquaintances and made others, and spent a week or two very pleasantly in the best society of the metropolis, easily accessible to a wealthy, well-bred young Southerner, with proper introductions. Young women smiled on him, and young men of convivial habits pressed their hospitalities; but the memory of Charity's sweet, strong face and clear blue eyes made him proof against the blandishments of the one sex and the persuasions of the other. Meanwhile he kept Grandison supplied with pocket-money, and left him mainly to his own devices. Every night when Dick came in he hoped he might have to wait upon himself, and every morning he looked forward with pleasure to the prospect of making his toilet unaided. His hopes, however, were doomed to disappointment, for every night when he came in Grandison was on hand with a bootjack, and a nightcap mixed for his young master as the colonel had taught him to mix it, and every morning Grandison appeared with his master's boots blacked and his clothes brushed, and laid his linen out for the day.

"Grandison," said Dick one morning, after finishing his toilet, "this is the chance of your life to go around among your own people and see how they live. Have you met any of them?"

"Yas, suh, I 's seen some of 'em. But I don' keer nuffin fer 'em, suh. Dey 're diffe'nt f'm de niggers down ou' way. Dey 'lows dey 're free, but dey ain' got sense 'nuff ter know dey ain' half as well off as dey would be down Souf, whar dey 'd be 'predated."

When two weeks had passed without any apparent effect of evil example upon Grandison, Dick resolved to go on to Boston, where

CHARLES W. CHESNUTT

he thought the atmosphere might prove more favorable to his ends. After he had been at the Revere House for a day or two without losing Grandison, he decided upon slightly different tactics.

Having ascertained from a city directory the addresses of several well-known abolitionists, he wrote them each a letter something like this:—

Dear Friend and Brother:

A wicked slaveholder from Kentucky, stopping at the Revere House, has dared to insult the liberty-loving people of Boston by bringing his slave into their midst. Shall this be tolerated? Or shall steps be taken in the name of liberty to rescue a fellow-man from bondage? For obvious reasons I can only sign myself,

A Friend of Humanity

That his letter might have an opportunity to prove effective, Dick made it a point to send Grandison away from the hotel on various errands. On one of these occasions Dick watched him for quite a distance down the street. Grandison had scarcely left the hotel when a long-haired, sharp-featured man came out behind him, followed him, soon overtook him, and kept along beside him until they turned the next corner. Dick's hopes were roused by this spectacle, but sank correspondingly when Grandison returned to the hotel. As Grandison said nothing about the encounter, Dick hoped there might be some self-consciousness behind this unexpected reticence, the results of which might develop later on.

But Grandison was on hand again when his master came back to the hotel at night, and was in attendance again in the morning, with hot water, to assist at his master's toilet. Dick sent him on further errands from day to day, and upon one occasion came squarely up to him—inadvertently of course—while Grandison was engaged in conversation with a young white man in clerical garb. When Grandison saw Dick approaching, he edged away from the preacher and hastened toward his master, with a very evident expression of relief upon his countenance.

"Mars Dick," he said, "dese yer abolitioners is jes' pesterin' de life out er me tryin' ter git me ter run away. I don' pay no 'tention ter 'em, but dey riles me so sometimes dat I 'm feared I 'll hit some of 'em some er dese days, an' dat mought git me inter trouble. I ain' said nuffin' ter you 'bout it, Mars Dick, fer I did n' wanter 'sturb yo' min'; but I don' like it, suh; no, suh, I don'! Is we gwine back home 'fo' long, Mars Dick?"

"We 'll be going back soon enough," replied Dick somewhat shortly, while he inwardly cursed the stupidity of a slave who could be free and would not, and registered a secret vow that if he were unable to get rid of Grandison without assassinating him, and were therefore compelled to take him back to Kentucky, he would see that Grandison got a taste of an article of slavery that would make him regret his wasted opportunities. Meanwhile he determined to tempt his servant yet more strongly.

"Grandison," he said next morning, "I 'm going away for a day or two, but I shall leave you here. I shall lock up a hundred dollars in this drawer and give you the key. If you need any of it, use it and enjoy yourself,—spend it all if you like,—for this is probably the last chance you 'll have for some time to be in a free State, and you 'd better enjoy your liberty while you may."

When he came back a couple of days later and found the faithful Grandison at his post, and the hundred dollars intact, Dick felt seriously annoyed. His vexation was increased by the fact that he could not express his feelings adequately. He did not even scold Grandison; how could he, indeed, find fault with one who so sensibly recognized his true place in the economy of civilization, and kept it with such touching fidelity?

"I can't say a thing to him," groaned Dick. "He deserves a leather medal, made out of his own hide tanned. I reckon I 'll write to father and let him know what a model servant he has given me."

He wrote his father a letter which made the colonel swell with pride and pleasure. "I really think," the colonel observed to one of his friends, "that Dick ought to have the nigger interviewed by the Boston papers, so that they may see how contented and happy our darkeys really are."

Dick also wrote a long letter to Charity Lomax, in which he said, among many other things, that if she knew how hard he was working, and under what difficulties, to accomplish something serious for her sake, she would no longer keep him in suspense, but overwhelm him with love and admiration.

Having thus exhausted without result the more obvious methods of getting rid of Grandison, and diplomacy having also proved a failure, Dick was forced to consider more radical measures. Of course he might

CHARLES W. CHESNUTT

run away himself, and abandon Grandison, but this would be merely to leave him in the United States, where he was still a slave, and where, with his notions of loyalty, he would speedily be reclaimed. It was necessary, in order to accomplish the purpose of his trip to the North, to leave Grandison permanently in Canada, where he would be legally free.

"I might extend my trip to Canada," he reflected, "but that would be too palpable. I have it! I 'll visit Niagara Falls on the way home, and lose him on the Canada side. When he once realizes that he is actually free, I 'll warrant that he 'll stay."

So the next day saw them westward bound, and in due course of time, by the somewhat slow conveyances of the period, they found themselves at Niagara. Dick walked and drove about the Falls for several days, taking Grandison along with him on most occasions. One morning they stood on the Canadian side, watching the wild whirl of the waters below them.

"Grandison," said Dick, raising his voice above the roar of the cataract, "do you know where you are now?"

"I 's wid you, Mars Dick; dat 's all I keers."

"You are now in Canada, Grandison, where your people go when they run away from their masters. If you wished, Grandison, you might walk away from me this very minute, and I could not lay my hand upon you to take you back."

Grandison looked around uneasily.

"Let 's go back ober de ribber, Mars Dick. I 's feared I 'll lose you ovuh heah, an' den I won' hab no marster, an' won't nebber be able to git back home no mo'."

Discouraged, but not yet hopeless, Dick said, a few minutes later,—

"Grandison, I 'm going up the road a bit, to the inn over yonder. You stay here until I return. I 'll not be gone a great while."

Grandison's eyes opened wide and he looked somewhat fearful.

"Is dey any er dem dadblasted abolitioners roun' heah, Mars Dick?"

"I don't imagine that there are," replied his master, hoping there might be. "But I 'm not afraid of *your* running away, Grandison. I only wish I were," he added to himself.

Dick walked leisurely down the road to where the whitewashed inn, built of stone, with true British solidity, loomed up through the trees by the roadside. Arrived there he ordered a glass of ale and a sandwich, and took a seat at a table by a window, from which he could see Grandison in the distance. For a while he hoped that the seed he had sown might have fallen on fertile ground, and that Grandison, relieved from the restraining power of a master's eye, and finding himself in a free country, might get up and walk away; but the hope was vain, for Grandison remained faithfully at his post, awaiting his master's return. He had seated himself on a broad flat stone, and, turning his eyes away from the grand and awe-inspiring spectacle that lay close at hand, was looking anxiously toward the inn where his master sat cursing his ill-timed fidelity.

By and by a girl came into the room to serve his order, and Dick very naturally glanced at her; and as she was young and pretty and remained in attendance, it was some minutes before he looked for Grandison. When he did so his faithful servant had disappeared.

To pay his reckoning and go away without the change was a matter quickly accomplished. Retracing his footsteps toward the Falls, he saw, to his great disgust, as he approached the spot where he had left Grandison, the familiar form of his servant stretched out on the ground, his face to the sun, his mouth open, sleeping the time away, oblivious alike to the grandeur of the scenery, the thunderous roar of the cataract, or the insidious voice of sentiment.

"Grandison," soliloquized his master, as he stood gazing down at his ebony encumbrance, "I do not deserve to be an American citizen; I ought not to have the advantages I possess over you; and I certainly am not worthy of Charity Lomax, if I am not smart enough to get rid of you. I have an idea! You shall yet be free, and I will be the instrument of your deliverance. Sleep on, faithful and affectionate servitor, and dream of the blue grass and the bright skies of old Kentucky, for it is only in your dreams that you will ever see them again!"

Dick retraced his footsteps towards the inn. The young woman chanced to look out of the window and saw the handsome young gentleman she had waited on a few minutes before, standing in the road a short distance away, apparently engaged in earnest conversation with a colored man employed as hostler for the inn. She thought she saw something pass from the white man to the other, but at that moment her duties called her away from the window, and when she looked out again the young gentleman had disappeared, and the hostler, with two other young men of the neighborhood, one white and one colored, were walking rapidly towards the Falls.

CHARLES W. CHESNUTT

IV

DICK MADE THE JOURNEY HOMEWARD alone, and as rapidly as the conveyances of the day would permit. As he drew near home his conduct in going back without Grandison took on a more serious aspect than it had borne at any previous time, and although he had prepared the colonel by a letter sent several days ahead, there was still the prospect of a bad quarter of an hour with him; not, indeed, that his father would upbraid him, but he was likely to make searching inquiries. And notwithstanding the vein of quiet recklessness that had carried Dick through his preposterous scheme, he was a very poor liar, having rarely had occasion or inclination to tell anything but the truth. Any reluctance to meet his father was more than offset, however, by a stronger force drawing him homeward, for Charity Lomax must long since have returned from her visit to her aunt in Tennessee.

Dick got off easier than he had expected. He told a straight story, and a truthful one, so far as it went.

The colonel raged at first, but rage soon subsided into anger, and anger moderated into annoyance, and annoyance into a sort of garrulous sense of injury. The colonel thought he had been hardly used; he had trusted this negro, and he had broken faith. Yet, after all, he did not blame Grandison so much as he did the abolitionists, who were undoubtedly at the bottom of it.

As for Charity Lomax, Dick told her, privately of course, that he had run his father's man, Grandison, off to Canada, and left him there.

"Oh, Dick," she had said with shuddering alarm, "what have you done? If they knew it they'd send you to the penitentiary, like they did that Yankee."

"But they don't know it," he had replied seriously; adding, with an injured tone, "you don't seem to appreciate my heroism like you did that of the Yankee; perhaps it's because I wasn't caught and sent to the penitentiary. I thought you wanted me to do it."

"Why, Dick Owens!" she exclaimed. "You know I never dreamed of any such outrageous proceeding.

"But I presume I'll have to marry you," she concluded, after some insistence on Dick's part, "if only to take care of you. You are too reckless for anything; and a man who goes chasing all over the North, being entertained by New York and Boston society and having negroes to throw away, needs some one to look after him."

"It 's a most remarkable thing," replied Dick fervently, "that your views correspond exactly with my profoundest convictions. It proves beyond question that we were made for one another."

THEY WERE MARRIED THREE WEEKS later. As each of them had just returned from a journey, they spent their honeymoon at home.

A week after the wedding they were seated, one afternoon, on the piazza of the colonel's house, where Dick had taken his bride, when a negro from the yard ran down the lane and threw open the big gate for the colonel's buggy to enter. The colonel was not alone. Beside him, ragged and travel-stained, bowed with weariness, and upon his face a haggard look that told of hardship and privation, sat the lost Grandison.

The colonel alighted at the steps.

"Take the lines, Tom," he said to the man who had opened the gate, "and drive round to the barn. Help Grandison down,—poor devil, he 's so stiff he can hardly move!—and get a tub of water and wash him and rub him down, and feed him, and give him a big drink of whiskey, and then let him come round and see his young master and his new mistress."

The colonel's face wore an expression compounded of joy and indignation,—joy at the restoration of a valuable piece of property; indignation for reasons he proceeded to state.

"It 's astounding, the depths of depravity the human heart is capable of! I was coming along the road three miles away, when I heard some one call me from the roadside. I pulled up the mare, and who should come out of the woods but Grandison. The poor nigger could hardly crawl along, with the help of a broken limb. I was never more astonished in my life. You could have knocked me down with a feather. He seemed pretty far gone,—he could hardly talk above a whisper,— and I had to give him a mouthful of whiskey to brace him up so he could tell his story. It 's just as I thought from the beginning, Dick; Grandison had no notion of running away; he knew when he was well off, and where his friends were. All the persuasions of abolition liars and runaway niggers did not move him. But the desperation of those fanatics knew no bounds; their guilty consciences gave them no rest. They got the notion somehow that Grandison belonged to a nigger-catcher, and had been brought North as a spy to help capture ungrateful runaway servants. They actually kidnaped him—just think of it!—and gagged him and bound him and threw him rudely into a wagon, and carried him into the gloomy depths of a Canadian forest, and locked him in a lonely hut, and fed him on bread and water for three weeks. One of the scoundrels wanted to kill him, and persuaded the others that it ought to be done; but they got to quarreling about how they should do it, and before they had their minds made up Grandison escaped, and, keeping his back steadily to the North Star, made his way, after suffering incredible hardships, back to the old plantation, back to his master, his friends, and his home. Why, it 's as good as one of Scott's novels! Mr. Simms or some other one of our Southern authors ought to write it up."

"Don't you think, sir," suggested Dick, who had calmly smoked his cigar throughout the colonel's animated recital, "that that kidnaping yarn sounds a little improbable? Is n't there some more likely explanation?"

"Nonsense, Dick; it 's the gospel truth! Those infernal abolitionists are capable of anything—everything! Just think of their locking the poor, faithful nigger up, beating him, kicking him, depriving him of his liberty, keeping him on bread and water for three long, lonesome weeks, and he all the time pining for the old plantation!"

There were almost tears in the colonel's eyes at the picture of Grandison's sufferings that he conjured up. Dick still professed to be slightly skeptical, and met Charity's severely questioning eye with bland unconsciousness.

The colonel killed the fatted calf for Grandison, and for two or three weeks the returned wanderer's life was a slave's dream of pleasure. His fame spread throughout the county, and the colonel gave him a permanent place among the house servants, where he could always have him conveniently at hand to relate his adventures to admiring visitors.

About three weeks after Grandison's return the colonel's faith in sable humanity was rudely shaken, and its foundations almost broken up. He came near losing his belief in the fidelity of the negro to his master,—the servile virtue most highly prized and most sedulously cultivated by the colonel and his kind. One Monday morning Grandison was missing. And not only Grandison, but his wife, Betty the maid; his mother, aunt Eunice; his father, uncle Ike; his brothers, Tom and John, and his little sister Elsie, were likewise absent from the plantation; and a hurried search and inquiry in the neighborhood resulted in no information as to their whereabouts. So much valuable property could not be lost without an effort to recover it, and the wholesale nature of the transaction carried consternation to the hearts of those whose ledgers were chiefly bound in black. Extremely energetic measures were taken by the colonel and his friends. The fugitives were traced, and followed from point to point, on their northward run through Ohio. Several times the hunters were close upon their heels, but the magnitude of the escaping party begot unusual vigilance on the part of those who sympathized with the fugitives, and strangely enough, the underground railroad seemed to have had its tracks cleared and signals set for this particular train. Once, twice, the colonel thought he had them, but they slipped through his fingers.

One last glimpse he caught of his vanishing property, as he stood, accompanied by a United States marshal, on a wharf at a port on the south shore of Lake Erie. On the stern of a small steamboat which was receding rapidly from the wharf, with her nose pointing toward Canada, there stood a group of familiar dark faces, and the look they cast backward was not one of longing for the fleshpots of Egypt. The colonel saw Grandison point him out to one of the crew of the vessel, who waved his hand derisively toward the colonel. The latter shook his fist impotently—and the incident was closed.

Uncle Wellington's Wives

I

Uncle Wellington Braboy was so deeply absorbed in thought as he walked slowly homeward from the weekly meeting of the Union League, that he let his pipe go out, a fact of which he remained oblivious until he had reached the little frame house in the suburbs of Patesville, where he lived with aunt Milly, his wife. On this particular occasion the club had been addressed by a visiting brother from the North, Professor Patterson, a tall, well-formed mulatto, who wore a perfectly fitting suit of broadcloth, a shiny silk hat, and linen of dazzling whiteness,—in short, a gentleman of such distinguished appearance that the doors and windows of the offices and stores on Front Street were filled with curious observers as he passed through that thoroughfare in the early part of the day. This polished stranger was a traveling organizer of Masonic lodges, but he also claimed to be a high officer in the Union League, and had been invited to lecture before the local chapter of that organization at Patesville.

The lecture had been largely attended, and uncle* Wellington Braboy had occupied a seat just in front of the platform. The subject of the lecture was "The Mental, Moral, Physical, Political, Social, and Financial Improvement of the Negro Race in America," a theme much dwelt upon, with slight variations, by colored orators. For to this struggling people, then as now, the problem of their uncertain present and their doubtful future was the chief concern of life. The period was the hopeful one. The Federal Government retained some vestige of authority in the South, and the newly emancipated race cherished the delusion that under the Constitution, that enduring rock on which our liberties are founded, and under the equal laws it purported to guarantee, they would enter upon the era of freedom and opportunity which their Northern friends had inaugurated with such solemn sanctions. The speaker pictured in eloquent language the state of ideal equality and happiness enjoyed by colored people at the North: how they sent their children to school with the white children; how they sat by white people in the churches and theatres, ate with them in the public restaurants, and buried their dead in the same cemeteries. The professor waxed eloquent with the development of his theme, and, as a finishing touch to an alluring picture, assured the excited audience that the intermarriage of the races was common, and that he himself had espoused a white woman.

Uncle Wellington Braboy was a deeply interested listener. He had heard something of these facts before, but his information had always come in such vague and questionable shape that he had paid little attention to it. He knew that the Yankees had freed the slaves, and that runaway negroes had always gone to the North to seek liberty; any such equality, however, as the visiting brother had depicted, was more than uncle Wellington had ever conceived as actually existing anywhere in the world. At first he felt inclined to doubt the truth of the speaker's statements; but the cut of his clothes, the eloquence of his language, and the flowing length of his whiskers, were so far superior to anything uncle Wellington had ever met among the colored people of his native State, that he felt irresistibly impelled to the conviction that nothing less than the advantages claimed for the North by the visiting brother could have produced such an exquisite flower of civilization. Any lingering doubts uncle Wellington may have felt were entirely dispelled by the courtly bow and cordial grasp of the hand with which the visiting brother acknowledged the congratulations showered upon him by the audience at the close of his address.

The more uncle Wellington's mind dwelt upon the professor's speech, the more attractive seemed the picture of Northern life presented. Uncle Wellington possessed in large measure the imaginative faculty so freely bestowed by nature upon the race from which the darker half of his blood was drawn. He had indulged in occasional day-dreams of an ideal state of social equality, but his wildest flights of fancy had never located it nearer than heaven, and he had felt some misgivings about its practical working even there. Its desirability he had never doubted, and the speech of the evening before had given a local habitation and a name to the forms his imagination had bodied forth. Giving full rein to his fancy, he saw in the North a land flowing with milk and honey,—a land peopled by noble men and beautiful women, among whom colored men and women moved with the ease and grace of acknowledged right. Then he placed himself in the foreground of the picture. What a fine figure he would have made in the world if he had been born at the free North! He imagined himself dressed like the professor, and passing the contribution-box in a white church; and most pleasant of his dreams, and the hardest to realize as possible, was that of the gracious white lady he might have called wife. Uncle Wellington was a mulatto, and his features were those of his white father, though tinged with the hue of his mother's race; and as he lifted the kerosene lamp at evening, and took a long look at his image in the little mirror over the mantelpiece, he said to himself that he was a very good-looking man, and could have adorned a much higher sphere in life than that in which the accident of birth had placed him. He fell asleep and dreamed that he lived in a two-story brick house, with a spacious flower garden in front, the whole inclosed by a high iron fence; that he kept a carriage and servants, and never did a stroke of work. This was the highest style of living in Patesville, and he could conceive of nothing finer.

Uncle Wellington slept later than usual the next morning, and the sunlight was pouring in at the open window of the bedroom, when his dreams were interrupted by the voice of his wife, in tones meant to be harsh, but which no ordinary degree of passion could rob of their native unctuousness.

"Git up f'm dere, you lazy, good-fuh-nuffin' nigger! Is you gwine ter sleep all de mawnin'? I 's ti'ed er dis yer runnin' 'roun' all night an' den sleepin' all day. You won't git dat tater patch hoed ovuh ter-day 'less'n you git up f'm dere an' git at it."

Uncle Wellington rolled over, yawned cavernously, stretched himself, and with a muttered protest got out of bed and put on his clothes. Aunt Milly had prepared a smoking breakfast of hominy and fried bacon, the odor of which was very grateful to his nostrils.

"Is breakfus' done ready?" he inquired, tentatively, as he came into the kitchen and glanced at the table.

"No, it ain't ready, an' 't ain't gwine ter be ready 'tel you tote dat wood an' water in," replied aunt Milly severely, as she poured two teacups of boiling water on two tablespoonfuls of ground coffee.

Uncle Wellington went down to the spring and got a pail of water, after which he brought in some oak logs for the fire place and some lightwood for kindling. Then he drew a chair towards the table and started to sit down.

"Wonduh what 's de matter wid you dis mawnin' anyhow," remarked aunt Milly. "You must 'a' be'n up ter some devilment las' night, fer yo' recommemb'ance is so po' dat you fus' fergit ter git up, an' den fergit ter wash yo' face an' hands fo' you set down ter de table. I don' 'low nobody ter eat at my table dat a-way."

"I don' see no use 'n washin' 'em so much," replied Wellington wearily. "Dey gits dirty ag'in right off, an' den you got ter wash 'em ovuh ag'in; it 's jes' pilin' up wuk what don' fetch in nuffin'. De dirt don' show nohow, 'n' I don' see no advantage in bein' black, ef you got to keep on washin' yo' face 'n' han's jes' lack w'ite folks." He nevertheless performed his ablutions in a perfunctory way, and resumed his seat at the breakfast-table.

"Ole 'oman," he asked, after the edge of his appetite had been taken off, "how would you lack ter live at de Norf?"

"I dunno nuffin' 'bout de Norf," replied aunt Milly. "It 's hard 'nuff ter git erlong heah, whar we knows all erbout it."

"De brother what 'dressed de meetin' las' night say dat de wages at de Norf is twicet ez big ez dey is heah."

"You could make a sight mo' wages heah ef you 'd 'ten' ter yo' wuk better," replied aunt Milly.

Uncle Wellington ignored this personality, and continued, "An' he say de cullud folks got all de privileges er de w'ite folks,—dat dey chillen goes ter school tergedder, dat dey sets on same seats in chu'ch, an' sarves on jury, 'n' rides on de kyars an' steamboats wid de w'ite folks, an' eats at de fus' table."

"Dat 'u'd suit you," chuckled aunt Milly, "an' you 'd stay dere fer de secon' table, too. How dis man know 'bout all dis yer foolis'ness?" she asked incredulously.

"He come f'm de Norf," said uncle Wellington, "an' he 'speunced it all hisse'f."

"Well, he can't make me b'lieve it," she rejoined, with a shake of her head.

"An' you would n' lack ter go up dere an' 'joy all dese privileges?" asked uncle Wellington, with some degree of earnestness.

The old woman laughed until her sides shook. "Who gwine ter take me up dere?" she inquired.

"You got de money yo'se'f."

"I ain' got no money fer ter was'e," she replied shortly, becoming serious at once; and with that the subject was dropped.

Uncle Wellington pulled a hoe from under the house, and took his way wearily to the potato patch. He did not feel like working, but aunt Milly was the undisputed head of the establishment, and he did not dare to openly neglect his work.

In fact, he regarded work at any time as a disagreeable necessity to be avoided as much as possible.

His wife was cast in a different mould. Externally she would have impressed the casual observer as a neat, well-preserved, and good-looking black woman, of middle age, every curve of whose ample figure—and her figure was all curves—was suggestive of repose. So far from being indolent, or even deliberate in her movements, she was the most active and energetic woman in the town. She went through the physical exercises of a prayer-meeting with astonishing vigor. It was exhilarating to see her wash a shirt, and a study to watch her do it up. A quick jerk shook out the dampened garment; one pass of her ample palm spread it over the ironing-board, and a few well-directed strokes with the iron accomplished what would have occupied the ordinary laundress for half an hour.

To this uncommon, and in uncle Wellington's opinion unnecessary and unnatural activity, his own habits were a steady protest. If aunt Milly had been willing to support him in idleness, he would have acquiesced without a murmur in her habits of industry. This she would not do, and, moreover, insisted on his working at least half the time. If she had invested the proceeds of her labor in rich food and fine clothing, he might have endured it better; but to her passion for work was added a most detestable thrift. She absolutely refused to pay for Wellington's clothes, and required him to furnish a certain proportion of the family supplies. Her savings were carefully put by, and with them she had bought and paid for the modest cottage which she and her husband occupied. Under her careful hand it was always neat and clean; in summer the little yard was gay with bright-colored flowers, and woe to the heedless pickaninny who should stray into her yard and pluck a rose or a verbena! In a stout oaken chest under her bed she kept a capacious stocking, into which flowed a steady stream of fractional currency. She carried the key to this chest in her pocket, a proceeding regarded by uncle Wellington with no little disfavor. He was of the opinion— an opinion he would not have dared to assert in her presence—that his wife's earnings were his own property; and he looked upon this stocking as a drunkard's wife might regard the saloon which absorbed her husband's wages.

Uncle Wellington hurried over the potato patch on the morning of the conversation above recorded, and as soon as he saw aunt Milly go away with a basket of clothes on her head, returned to the house, put on his coat, and went uptown.

He directed his steps to a small frame building fronting on the main street of the village, at a point where the street was intersected by one of the several creeks meandering through the town, cooling the air, providing numerous swimming-holes for the amphibious small boy, and furnishing water-power for grist-mills and saw-mills. The rear of the building rested on long brick pillars, built up from the bottom of the steep bank of the creek, while the front was level with the street. This was the office of Mr. Matthew Wright, the sole representative of the colored race at the bar of Chinquapin County. Mr. Wright came of an "old issue" free colored family, in which, though the negro blood was present in an attenuated strain, a line of free ancestry could be traced beyond the Revolutionary War. He had enjoyed exceptional opportunities, and enjoyed the distinction of being the first, and for a long time the only colored lawyer in North Carolina. His services were frequently called into requisition by impecunious people of his own race; when they had money they went to white lawyers, who, they shrewdly conjectured, would have more influence with judge or jury than a colored lawyer, however able.

Uncle Wellington found Mr. Wright in his office. Having inquired after the health of the lawyer's family and all his relations in detail, uncle Wellington asked for a professional opinion.

"Mistah Wright, ef a man's wife got money, whose money is dat befo' de law—his'n er her'n?"

The lawyer put on his professional air, and replied:—

"Under the common law, which in default of special legislative enactment is the law of North Carolina, the personal property of the wife belongs to her husband."

"But dat don' jes' tech de p'int, suh. I wuz axin' 'bout money."

"You see, uncle Wellington, your education has not rendered you familiar with legal phraseology. The term 'personal property' or 'estate' embraces, according to Blackstone, all property other than land, and therefore includes money. Any money a man's wife has is his, constructively, and will be recognized as his actually, as soon as he can secure possession of it."

"Dat is ter say, suh—my eddication don' quite 'low me ter understan' dat—dat is ter say"—

"That is to say, it's yours when you get it. It is n't yours so that the law will help you get it; but on the other hand, when you once lay your hands on it, it is yours so that the law won't take it away from you."

Uncle Wellington nodded to express his full comprehension of the law as expounded by Mr. Wright, but scratched his head in a way that

CHARLES W. CHESNUTT

expressed some disappointment. The law seemed to wobble. Instead of enabling him to stand up fearlessly and demand his own, it threw him back upon his own efforts; and the prospect of his being able to overpower or outwit aunt Milly by any ordinary means was very poor.

He did not leave the office, but hung around awhile as though there were something further he wished to speak about. Finally, after some discursive remarks about the crops and politics, he asked, in an offhand, disinterested manner, as though the thought had just occurred to him:—

"Mistah Wright, w'ile's we 're talkin' 'bout law matters, what do it cos' ter git a defoce?"

"That depends upon circumstances. It is n't altogether a matter of expense. Have you and aunt Milly been having trouble?"

"Oh no, suh; I was jes' a-wond'rin'."

"You see," continued the lawyer, who was fond of talking, and had nothing else to do for the moment, "a divorce is not an easy thing to get in this State under any circumstances. It used to be the law that divorce could be granted only by special act of the legislature; and it is but recently that the subject has been relegated to the jurisdiction of the courts."

Uncle Wellington understood a part of this, but the answer had not been exactly to the point in his mind.

"S'pos'n', den, jes' fer de argyment, me an' my ole 'oman sh'd fall out en wanter separate, how could I git a defoce?"

"That would depend on what you quarreled about. It 's pretty hard work to answer general questions in a particular way. If you merely wished to separate, it would n't be necessary to get a divorce; but if you should want to marry again, you would have to be divorced, or else you would be guilty of bigamy, and could be sent to the penitentiary. But, by the way, uncle Wellington, when were you married?"

"I got married 'fo' de wah, when I was livin' down on Rockfish Creek."

"When you were in slavery?"

"Yas, suh."

"Did you have your marriage registered after the surrender?"

"No, suh; never knowed nuffin' 'bout dat."

After the war, in North Carolina and other States, the freed people who had sustained to each other the relation of husband and wife as it existed among slaves, were required by law to register their consent to continue in the marriage relation. By this simple expedient their former marriages of convenience received the sanction of law, and their children the seal of legitimacy. In many cases, however, where the parties lived in districts remote from the larger towns, the ceremony was neglected, or never heard of by the freedmen.

"Well," said the lawyer, "if that is the case, and you and aunt Milly should disagree, it would n't be necessary for you to get a divorce, even if you should want to marry again. You were never legally married."

"So Milly ain't my lawful wife, den?"

"She may be your wife in one sense of the word, but not in such a sense as to render you liable to punishment for bigamy if you should marry another woman. But I hope you will never want to do anything of the kind, for you have a very good wife now."

Uncle Wellington went away thoughtfully, but with a feeling of unaccustomed lightness and freedom. He had not felt so free since the memorable day when he had first heard of the Emancipation Proclamation. On leaving the lawyer's office, he called at the workshop of one of his friends, Peter Williams, a shoemaker by trade, who had a brother living in Ohio.

"Is you hearn f'm Sam lately?" uncle Wellington inquired, after the conversation had drifted through the usual generalities.

"His mammy got er letter f'm 'im las' week; he 's livin' in de town er Groveland now."

"How 's he gittin' on?"

"He says he gittin' on monst'us well. He 'low ez how he make five dollars a day w'ite-washin', an' have all he kin do."

The shoemaker related various details of his brother's prosperity, and uncle Wellington returned home in a very thoughtful mood, revolving in his mind a plan of future action. This plan had been vaguely assuming form ever since the professor's lecture, and the events of the morning had brought out the detail in bold relief.

Two days after the conversation with the shoemaker, aunt Milly went, in the afternoon, to visit a sister of hers who lived several miles out in the country. During her absence, which lasted until nightfall, uncle Wellington went uptown and purchased a cheap oilcloth valise from a shrewd son of Israel, who had penetrated to this locality with a stock of notions and cheap clothing. Uncle Wellington had his purchase done up in brown paper, and took the parcel under his arm. Arrived at home he unwrapped the valise, and thrust into its capacious jaws his best suit of clothes, some underwear, and a few other small articles for

CHARLES W. CHESNUTT

personal use and adornment. Then he carried the valise out into the yard, and, first looking cautiously around to see if there was any one in sight, concealed it in a clump of bushes in a corner of the yard.

It may be inferred from this proceeding that uncle Wellington was preparing for a step of some consequence. In fact, he had fully made up his mind to go to the North; but he still lacked the most important requisite for traveling with comfort, namely, the money to pay his expenses. The idea of tramping the distance which separated him from the promised land of liberty and equality had never occurred to him. When a slave, he had several times been importuned by fellow servants to join them in the attempt to escape from bondage, but he had never wanted his freedom badly enough to walk a thousand miles for it; if he could have gone to Canada by stage-coach, or by rail, or on horseback, with stops for regular meals, he would probably have undertaken the trip. The funds he now needed for his journey were in aunt Milly's chest. He had thought a great deal about his right to this money. It was his wife's savings, and he had never dared to dispute, openly, her right to exercise exclusive control over what she earned; but the lawyer had assured him of his right to the money, of which he was already constructively in possession, and he had therefore determined to possess himself actually of the coveted stocking. It was impracticable for him to get the key of the chest. Aunt Milly kept it in her pocket by day and under her pillow at night. She was a light sleeper, and, if not awakened by the abstraction of the key, would certainly have been disturbed by the unlocking of the chest. But one alternative remained, and that was to break open the chest in her absence.

There was a revival in progress at the colored Methodist church. Aunt Milly was as energetic in her religion as in other respects, and had not missed a single one of the meetings. She returned at nightfall from her visit to the country and prepared a frugal supper. Uncle Wellington did not eat as heartily as usual. Aunt Milly perceived his want of appetite, and spoke of it. He explained it by saying that he did not feel very well.

"Is you gwine ter chu'ch ter-night?" inquired his wife.

"I reckon I 'll stay home an' go ter bed," he replied. "I ain't be'n feelin' well dis evenin', an' I 'spec' I better git a good night's res'."

"Well, you kin stay ef you mineter. Good preachin' 'u'd make you feel better, but ef you ain't gwine, don' fergit ter tote in some wood an' lighterd 'fo' you go ter bed. De moon is shinin' bright, an' you can't have no 'scuse 'bout not bein' able ter see."

Uncle Wellington followed her out to the gate, and watched her receding form until it disappeared in the distance. Then he re-entered the house with a quick step, and taking a hatchet from a corner of the room, drew the chest from under the bed. As he applied the hatchet to the fastenings, a thought struck him, and by the flickering light of the pine-knot blazing on the hearth, a look of hesitation might have been seen to take the place of the determined expression his face had worn up to that time. He had argued himself into the belief that his present action was lawful and justifiable. Though this conviction had not prevented him from trembling in every limb, as though he were committing a mere vulgar theft, it had still nerved him to the deed. Now even his moral courage began to weaken. The lawyer had told him that his wife's property was his own; in taking it he was therefore only exercising his lawful right. But at the point of breaking open the chest, it occurred to him that he was taking this money in order to get away from aunt Milly, and that he justified his desertion of her by the lawyer's opinion that she was not his lawful wife. If she was not his wife, then he had no right to take the money; if she was his wife, he had no right to desert her, and would certainly have no right to marry another woman. His scheme was about to go to shipwreck on this rock, when another idea occurred to him.

"De lawyer say dat in one sense er de word de ole 'oman is my wife, an' in anudder sense er de word she ain't my wife. Ef I goes ter de Norf an' marry a w'ite 'oman, I ain't commit no brigamy, 'caze in dat sense er de word she ain't my wife; but ef I takes dis money, I ain't stealin' it, 'caze in dat sense er de word she is my wife. Dat 'splains all de trouble away."

Having reached this ingenious conclusion, uncle Wellington applied the hatchet vigorously, soon loosened the fastenings of the chest, and with trembling hands extracted from its depths a capacious blue cotton stocking. He emptied the stocking on the table. His first impulse was to take the whole, but again there arose in his mind a doubt—a very obtrusive, unreasonable doubt, but a doubt, nevertheless—of the absolute rectitude of his conduct; and after a moment's hesitation he hurriedly counted the money—it was in bills of small denominations— and found it to be about two hundred and fifty dollars. He then divided it into two piles of one hundred and twenty-five dollars each. He put one pile into his pocket, returned the remainder to the stocking, and replaced it where he had found it. He then closed the chest and shoved it under the bed. After having arranged the fire so that it could safely

CHARLES W. CHESNUTT

be left burning, he took a last look around the room, and went out into the moonlight, locking the door behind him, and hanging the key on a nail in the wall, where his wife would be likely to look for it. He then secured his valise from behind the bushes, and left the yard. As he passed by the wood-pile, he said to himself:—

"Well, I declar' ef I ain't done fergot ter tote in dat lighterd; I reckon de ole 'oman 'll ha' ter fetch it in herse'f dis time."

He hastened through the quiet streets, avoiding the few people who were abroad at that hour, and soon reached the railroad station, from which a North-bound train left at nine o'clock. He went around to the dark side of the train, and climbed into a second-class car, where he shrank into the darkest corner and turned his face away from the dim light of the single dirty lamp. There were no passengers in the car except one or two sleepy negroes, who had got on at some other station, and a white man who had gone into the car to smoke, accompanied by a gigantic bloodhound.

Finally the train crept out of the station. From the window uncle Wellington looked out upon the familiar cabins and turpentine stills, the new barrel factory, the brickyard where he had once worked for some time; and as the train rattled through the outskirts of the town, he saw gleaming in the moonlight the white headstones of the colored cemetery where his only daughter had been buried several years before.

Presently the conductor came around. Uncle Wellington had not bought a ticket, and the conductor collected a cash fare. He was not acquainted with uncle Wellington, but had just had a drink at the saloon near the depot, and felt at peace with all mankind.

"Where are you going, uncle?" he inquired carelessly.

Uncle Wellington's face assumed the ashen hue which does duty for pallor in dusky countenances, and his knees began to tremble. Controlling his voice as well as he could, he replied that he was going up to Jonesboro, the terminus of the railroad, to work for a gentleman at that place. He felt immensely relieved when the conductor pocketed the fare, picked up his lantern, and moved away. It was very unphilosophical and very absurd that a man who was only doing right should feel like a thief, shrink from the sight of other people, and lie instinctively. Fine distinctions were not in uncle Wellington's line, but he was struck by the unreasonableness of his feelings, and still more by the discomfort they caused him. By and by, however, the motion of the train made him drowsy; his thoughts all ran together in confusion; and he fell asleep with his head on his valise, and one hand in his pocket, clasped tightly around the roll of money.

II

THE TRAIN FROM PITTSBURG DREW into the Union Depot at Groveland, Ohio, one morning in the spring of 187-, with bell ringing and engine puffing; and from a smoking-car emerged the form of uncle Wellington Braboy, a little dusty and travel-stained, and with a sleepy look about his eyes. He mingled in the crowd, and, valise in hand, moved toward the main exit from the depot. There were several tracks to be crossed, and more than once a watchman snatched him out of the way of a baggage-truck, or a train backing into the depot. He at length reached the door, beyond which, and as near as the regulations would permit, stood a number of hackmen, vociferously soliciting patronage. One of them, a colored man, soon secured several passengers. As he closed the door after the last one he turned to uncle Wellington, who stood near him on the sidewalk, looking about irresolutely.

"Is you goin' uptown?" asked the hackman, as he prepared to mount the box.

"Yas, suh."

"I 'll take you up fo' a quahtah, ef you want ter git up here an' ride on de box wid me."

Uncle Wellington accepted the offer and mounted the box. The hackman whipped up his horses, the carriage climbed the steep hill leading up to the town, and the passengers inside were soon deposited at their hotels.

"Whereabouts do you want to go?" asked the hackman of uncle Wellington, when the carriage was emptied of its last passengers.

"I want ter go ter Brer Sam Williams's," said Wellington.

"What 's his street an' number?"

Uncle Wellington did not know the street and number, and the hackman had to explain to him the mystery of numbered houses, to which he was a total stranger.

"Where is he from?" asked the hackman, "and what is his business?"

"He is f'm Norf Ca'lina," replied uncle Wellington, "an' makes his livin' w'itewashin'."

"I reckon I knows de man," said the hackman. "I 'spec' he 's changed his name. De man I knows is name' Johnson. He b'longs ter my chu'ch.

I 'm gwine out dat way ter git a passenger fer de ten o'clock train, an I 'll take you by dere."

They followed one of the least handsome streets of the city for more than a mile, turned into a cross street, and drew up before a small frame house, from the front of which a sign, painted in white upon a black background, announced to the reading public, in letters inclined to each other at various angles, that whitewashing and kalsomining were "dun" there. A knock at the door brought out a slatternly looking colored woman. She had evidently been disturbed at her toilet, for she held a comb in one hand, and the hair on one side of her head stood out loosely, while on the other side it was braided close to her head. She called her husband, who proved to be the Patesville shoemaker's brother. The hackman introduced the traveler, whose name he had learned on the way out, collected his quarter, and drove away.

Mr. Johnson, the shoemaker's brother, welcomed uncle Wellington to Groveland, and listened with eager delight to the news of the old town, from which he himself had run away many years before, and followed the North Star to Groveland. He had changed his name from "Williams" to "Johnson," on account of the Fugitive Slave Law, which, at the time of his escape from bondage, had rendered it advisable for runaway slaves to court obscurity. After the war he had retained the adopted name. Mrs. Johnson prepared breakfast for her guest, who ate it with an appetite sharpened by his journey. After breakfast he went to bed, and slept until late in the afternoon.

After supper Mr. Johnson took uncle Wellington to visit some of the neighbors who had come from North Carolina before the war. They all expressed much pleasure at meeting "Mr. Braboy," a title which at first sounded a little odd to uncle Wellington. At home he had been "Wellin'ton," "Brer Wellin'ton," or "uncle Wellin'ton;" it was a novel experience to be called "Mister," and he set it down, with secret satisfaction, as one of the first fruits of Northern liberty.

"Would you lack ter look 'roun' de town a little?" asked Mr. Johnson at breakfast next morning. "I ain' got no job dis mawnin', an' I kin show you some er de sights."

Uncle Wellington acquiesced in this arrangement, and they walked up to the corner to the street-car line. In a few moments a car passed. Mr. Johnson jumped on the moving car, and uncle Wellington followed his example, at the risk of life or limb, as it was his first experience of street cars.

There was only one vacant seat in the car and that was between two white women in the forward end. Mr. Johnson motioned to the seat, but Wellington shrank from walking between those two rows of white people, to say nothing of sitting between the two women, so he remained standing in the rear part of the car. A moment later, as the car rounded a short curve, he was pitched sidewise into the lap of a stout woman magnificently attired in a ruffled blue calico gown. The lady colored up, and uncle Wellington, as he struggled to his feet amid the laughter of the passengers, was absolutely helpless with embarrassment, until the conductor came up behind him and pushed him toward the vacant place.

"Sit down, will you," he said; and before uncle Wellington could collect himself, he was seated between the two white women. Everybody in the car seemed to be looking at him. But he came to the conclusion, after he had pulled himself together and reflected a few moments, that he would find this method of locomotion pleasanter when he got used to it, and then he could score one more glorious privilege gained by his change of residence.

They got off at the public square, in the heart of the city, where there were flowers and statues, and fountains playing. Mr. Johnson pointed out the court-house, the post-office, the jail, and other public buildings fronting on the square. They visited the market near by, and from an elevated point, looked down upon the extensive lumber yards and factories that were the chief sources of the city's prosperity. Beyond these they could see the fleet of ships that lined the coal and iron ore docks of the harbor. Mr. Johnson, who was quite a fluent talker, enlarged upon the wealth and prosperity of the city; and Wellington, who had never before been in a town of more than three thousand inhabitants, manifested sufficient interest and wonder to satisfy the most exacting *cicerone*. They called at the office of a colored lawyer and member of the legislature, formerly from North Carolina, who, scenting a new constituent and a possible client, greeted the stranger warmly, and in flowing speech pointed out the superior advantages of life at the North, citing himself as an illustration of the possibilities of life in a country really free. As they wended their way homeward to dinner uncle Wellington, with quickened pulse and rising hopes, felt that this was indeed the promised land, and that it must be flowing with milk and honey.

Uncle Wellington remained at the residence of Mr. Johnson for several weeks before making any effort to find employment. He spent

CHARLES W. CHESNUTT

this period in looking about the city. The most commonplace things possessed for him the charm of novelty, and he had come prepared to admire. Shortly after his arrival, he had offered to pay for his board, intimating at the same time that he had plenty of money. Mr. Johnson declined to accept anything from him for board, and expressed himself as being only too proud to have Mr. Braboy remain in the house on the footing of an honored guest, until he had settled himself. He lightened in some degree, however, the burden of obligation under which a prolonged stay on these terms would have placed his guest, by soliciting from the latter occasional small loans, until uncle Wellington's roll of money began to lose its plumpness, and with an empty pocket staring him in the face, he felt the necessity of finding something to do.

During his residence in the city he had met several times his first acquaintance, Mr. Peterson, the hackman, who from time to time inquired how he was getting along. On one of these occasions Wellington mentioned his willingness to accept employment. As good luck would have it, Mr. Peterson knew of a vacant situation. He had formerly been coachman for a wealthy gentleman residing on Oakwood Avenue, but had resigned the situation to go into business for himself. His place had been filled by an Irishman, who had just been discharged for drunkenness, and the gentleman that very day had sent word to Mr. Peterson, asking him if he could recommend a competent and trustworthy coachman.

"Does you know anything erbout hosses?" asked Mr. Peterson.

"Yas, indeed, I does," said Wellington. "I wuz raise' 'mongs' hosses."

"I tol' my ole boss I'd look out fer a man, an' ef you reckon you kin fill de 'quirements er de situation, I'll take yo' roun' dere ter-morrer mornin'. You wants ter put on yo' bes' clothes an' slick up, fer dey 're partic'lar people. Ef you git de place I'll expec' you ter pay me fer de time I lose in 'tendin' ter yo' business, fer time is money in dis country, an' folks don't do much fer nuthin'."

Next morning Wellington blacked his shoes carefully, put on a clean collar, and with the aid of Mrs. Johnson tied his cravat in a jaunty bow which gave him quite a sprightly air and a much younger look than his years warranted. Mr. Peterson called for him at eight o'clock. After traversing several cross streets they turned into Oakwood Avenue and walked along the finest part of it for about half a mile. The handsome houses of this famous avenue, the stately trees, the wide-spreading lawns, dotted with flower beds, fountains and statuary, made up a picture so far surpassing anything in Wellington's experience as to fill him with an almost oppressive sense of its beauty.

"Hit looks lack hebben," he said softly.

"It 's a pootty fine street," rejoined his companion, with a judicial air, "but I don't like dem big lawns. It 's too much trouble ter keep de grass down. One er dem lawns is big enough to pasture a couple er cows."

They went down a street running at right angles to the avenue, and turned into the rear of the corner lot. A large building of pressed brick, trimmed with stone, loomed up before them.

"Do de gemman lib in dis house?" asked Wellington, gazing with awe at the front of the building.

"No, dat 's de barn," said Mr. Peterson with good-natured contempt; and leading the way past a clump of shrubbery to the dwelling-house, he went up the back steps and rang the door-bell.

The ring was answered by a buxom Irishwoman, of a natural freshness of complexion deepened to a fiery red by the heat of a kitchen range. Wellington thought he had seen her before, but his mind had received so many new impressions lately that it was a minute or two before he recognized in her the lady whose lap he had involuntarily occupied for a moment on his first day in Groveland.

"Faith," she exclaimed as she admitted them, "an' it 's mighty glad I am to see ye ag'in, Misther Payterson! An' how hev ye be'n, Misther Payterson, sence I see ye lahst?"

"Middlin' well, Mis' Flannigan, middlin' well, 'ceptin' a tech er de rheumatiz. S'pose you be'n doin' well as usual?"

"Oh yis, as well as a dacent woman could do wid a drunken baste about the place like the lahst coachman. O Misther Payterson, it would make yer heart bleed to see the way the spalpeen cut up a-Saturday! But Misther Todd discharged 'im the same avenin', widout a characther, bad 'cess to 'im, an' we 've had no coachman sence at all, at all. An' it 's sorry I am"—

The lady's flow of eloquence was interrupted at this point by the appearance of Mr. Todd himself, who had been informed of the men's arrival. He asked some questions in regard to Wellington's qualifications and former experience, and in view of his recent arrival in the city was willing to accept Mr. Peterson's recommendation instead of a reference. He said a few words about the nature of the work, and stated his willingness to pay Wellington the wages formerly allowed Mr. Peterson, thirty dollars a month and board and lodging.

CHARLES W. CHESNUTT

This handsome offer was eagerly accepted, and it was agreed that Wellington's term of service should begin immediately. Mr. Peterson, being familiar with the work, and financially interested, conducted the new coachman through the stables and showed him what he would have to do. The silver-mounted harness, the variety of carriages, the names of which he learned for the first time, the arrangements for feeding and watering the horses,—these appointments of a rich man's stable impressed Wellington very much, and he wondered that so much luxury should be wasted on mere horses. The room assigned to him, in the second story of the barn, was a finer apartment than he had ever slept in; and the salary attached to the situation was greater than the combined monthly earnings of himself and aunt Milly in their Southern home. Surely, he thought, his lines had fallen in pleasant places.

Under the stimulus of new surroundings Wellington applied himself diligently to work, and, with the occasional advice of Mr. Peterson, soon mastered the details of his employment. He found the female servants, with whom he took his meals, very amiable ladies. The cook, Mrs. Katie Flannigan, was a widow. Her husband, a sailor, had been lost at sea. She was a woman of many words, and when she was not lamenting the late Flannigan's loss,—according to her story he had been a model of all the virtues,—she would turn the batteries of her tongue against the former coachman. This gentleman, as Wellington gathered from frequent remarks dropped by Mrs. Flannigan, had paid her attentions clearly susceptible of a serious construction. These attentions had not borne their legitimate fruit, and she was still a widow unconsoled,—hence Mrs. Flannigan's tears. The housemaid was a plump, good-natured German girl, with a pronounced German accent. The presence on washdays of a Bohemian laundress, of recent importation, added another to the variety of ways in which the English tongue was mutilated in Mr. Todd's kitchen. Association with the white women drew out all the native gallantry of the mulatto, and Wellington developed quite a helpful turn. His politeness, his willingness to lend a hand in kitchen or laundry, and the fact that he was the only male servant on the place, combined to make him a prime favorite in the servants' quarters.

It was the general opinion among Wellington's acquaintances that he was a single man. He had come to the city alone, had never been heard to speak of a wife, and to personal questions bearing upon the subject of matrimony had always returned evasive answers. Though he had never questioned the correctness of the lawyer's opinion in regard to his slave marriage, his conscience had never been entirely at ease since his departure from the South, and any positive denial of his married condition would have stuck in his throat. The inference naturally drawn from his reticence in regard to the past, coupled with his expressed intention of settling permanently in Groveland, was that he belonged in the ranks of the unmarried, and was therefore legitimate game for any widow or old maid who could bring him down. As such game is bagged easiest at short range, he received numerous invitations to tea-parties, where he feasted on unlimited chicken and pound cake. He used to compare these viands with the plain fare often served by aunt Milly, and the result of the comparison was another item to the credit of the North upon his mental ledger. Several of the colored ladies who smiled upon him were blessed with good looks, and uncle Wellington, naturally of a susceptible temperament, as people of lively imagination are apt to be, would probably have fallen a victim to the charms of some woman of his own race, had it not been for a strong counter-attraction in the person of Mrs. Flannigan. The attentions of the lately discharged coachman had lighted anew the smouldering fires of her widowed heart, and awakened longings which still remained unsatisfied. She was thirty-five years old, and felt the need of some one else to love. She was not a woman of lofty ideals; with her a man was a man—

"For a' that an' a' that;"

and, aside from the accident of color, uncle Wellington was as personable a man as any of her acquaintance. Some people might have objected to his complexion; but then, Mrs. Flannigan argued, he was at least half white; and, this being the case, there was no good reason why he should be regarded as black.

Uncle Wellington was not slow to perceive Mrs. Flannigan's charms of person, and appreciated to the full the skill that prepared the choice tidbits reserved for his plate at dinner. The prospect of securing a white wife had been one of the principal inducements offered by a life at the North; but the awe of white people in which he had been reared was still too strong to permit his taking any active steps toward the object of his secret desire, had not the lady herself come to his assistance with a little of the native coquetry of her race.

CHARLES W. CHESNUTT

"Ah, Misther Braboy," she said one evening when they sat at the supper table alone,—it was the second girl's afternoon off, and she had not come home to supper,—"it must be an awful lonesome life ye've been afther l'adin', as a single man, wid no one to cook fer ye, or look afther ye."

"It are a kind er lonesome life, Mis' Flannigan, an' dat's a fac'. But sence I had de privilege er eatin' yo' cookin' an' 'joyin' yo' society, I ain' felt a bit lonesome."

"Yer flatthrin' me, Misther Braboy. An' even if ye mane it"—

"I means eve'y word of it, Mis' Flannigan."

"An' even if ye mane it, Misther Braboy, the time is liable to come when things'll be different; for service is uncertain, Misther Braboy. An' then you'll wish you had some nice, clean woman, 'at knowed ter cook an' wash an' iron, ter look afther ye, an' make yer life comfortable."

Uncle Wellington sighed, and looked at her languishingly.

"It'u'd all be well ernuff, Mis' Flannigan, ef I had n' met you; but I don' know whar I's ter fin' a colored lady w'at'll begin ter suit me after habbin' libbed in de same house wid you."

"Colored lady, indade! Why, Misther Braboy, ye don't nade ter demane yerself by marryin' a colored lady—not but they're as good as anybody else, so long as they behave themselves. There's many a white woman 'u'd be glad ter git as fine a lookin' man as ye are."

"Now *you're* flattrin' *me*, Mis' Flannigan," said Wellington. But he felt a sudden and substantial increase in courage when she had spoken, and it was with astonishing ease that he found himself saying:—

"Dey ain' but one lady, Mis' Flannigan, dat could injuce me ter want ter change de lonesomeness er my singleness fer de 'sponsibilities er matermony, an' I'm feared she'd say no ef I'd ax her."

"Ye'd better ax her, Misther Braboy, an' not be wastin' time a-wond'rin'. Do I know the lady?"

"You knows 'er better 'n anybody else, Mis' Flannigan. *You* is de only lady I'd be satisfied ter marry after knowin' you. Ef you casts me off I'll spen' de rest er my days in lonesomeness an' mis'ry."

Mrs. Flannigan affected much surprise and embarrassment at this bold declaration.

"Oh, Misther Braboy," she said, covering him with a coy glance, "an' it's rale 'shamed I am to hev b'en talkin' ter ye ez I hev. It looks as though I'd b'en doin' the coortin'. I did n't drame that I'd b'en able ter draw yer affections to mesilf."

"I 's loved you ever sence I fell in yo' lap on de street car de fus' day I wuz in Groveland," he said, as he moved his chair up closer to hers.

One evening in the following week they went out after supper to the residence of Rev. Cæsar Williams, pastor of the colored Baptist church, and, after the usual preliminaries, were pronounced man and wife.

III

ACCORDING TO ALL HIS PRECONCEIVED notions, this marriage ought to have been the acme of uncle Wellington's felicity. But he soon found that it was not without its drawbacks. On the following morning Mr. Todd was informed of the marriage. He had no special objection to it, or interest in it, except that he was opposed on principle to having husband and wife in his employment at the same time. As a consequence, Mrs. Braboy, whose place could be more easily filled than that of her husband, received notice that her services would not be required after the end of the month. Her husband was retained in his place as coachman.

Upon the loss of her situation Mrs. Braboy decided to exercise the married woman's prerogative of letting her husband support her. She rented the upper floor of a small house in an Irish neighborhood. The newly wedded pair furnished their rooms on the installment plan and began housekeeping.

There was one little circumstance, however, that interfered slightly with their enjoyment of that perfect freedom from care which ought to characterize a honeymoon. The people who owned the house and occupied the lower floor had rented the upper part to Mrs. Braboy in person, it never occurring to them that her husband could be other than a white man. When it became known that he was colored, the landlord, Mr. Dennis O'Flaherty, felt that he had been imposed upon, and, at the end of the first month, served notice upon his tenants to leave the premises. When Mrs. Braboy, with characteristic impetuosity, inquired the meaning of this proceeding, she was informed by Mr. O'Flaherty that he did not care to live in the same house "wid naygurs." Mrs. Braboy resented the epithet with more warmth than dignity, and for a brief space of time the air was green with choice specimens of brogue, the altercation barely ceasing before it had reached the point of blows.

It was quite clear that the Braboys could not longer live comfortably in Mr. O'Flaherty's house, and they soon vacated the premises, first

CHARLES W. CHESNUTT

letting the rent get a couple of weeks in arrears as a punishment to the too fastidious landlord. They moved to a small house on Hackman Street, a favorite locality with colored people.

For a while, affairs ran smoothly in the new home. The colored people seemed, at first, well enough disposed toward Mrs. Braboy, and she made quite a large acquaintance among them. It was difficult, however, for Mrs. Braboy to divest herself of the consciousness that she was white, and therefore superior to her neighbors. Occasional words and acts by which she manifested this feeling were noticed and resented by her keen-eyed and sensitive colored neighbors. The result was a slight coolness between them. That her few white neighbors did not visit her, she naturally and no doubt correctly imputed to disapproval of her matrimonial relations.

Under these circumstances, Mrs. Braboy was left a good deal to her own company. Owing to lack of opportunity in early life, she was not a woman of many resources, either mental or moral. It is therefore not strange that, in order to relieve her loneliness, she should occasionally have recourse to a glass of beer, and, as the habit grew upon her, to still stronger stimulants. Uncle Wellington himself was no tee-totaler, and did not interpose any objection so long as she kept her potations within reasonable limits, and was apparently none the worse for them; indeed, he sometimes joined her in a glass. On one of these occasions he drank a little too much, and, while driving the ladies of Mr. Todd's family to the opera, ran against a lamp-post and overturned the carriage, to the serious discomposure of the ladies' nerves, and at the cost of his situation.

A coachman discharged under such circumstances is not in the best position for procuring employment at his calling, and uncle Wellington, under the pressure of need, was obliged to seek some other means of livelihood. At the suggestion of his friend Mr. Johnson, he bought a whitewash brush, a peck of lime, a couple of pails, and a hand-cart, and began work as a whitewasher. His first efforts were very crude, and for a while he lost a customer in every person he worked for. He nevertheless managed to pick up a living during the spring and summer months, and to support his wife and himself in comparative comfort.

The approach of winter put an end to the whitewashing season, and left uncle Wellington dependent for support upon occasional jobs of unskilled labor. The income derived from these was very uncertain, and Mrs. Braboy was at length driven, by stress of circumstances, to the washtub, that last refuge of honest, able-bodied poverty, in all countries where the use of clothing is conventional.

The last state of uncle Wellington was now worse than the first. Under the soft firmness of aunt Milly's rule, he had not been required to do a great deal of work, prompt and cheerful obedience being chiefly what was expected of him. But matters were very different here. He had not only to bring in the coal and water, but to rub the clothes and turn the wringer, and to humiliate himself before the public by emptying the tubs and hanging out the wash in full view of the neighbors; and he had to deliver the clothes when laundered.

At times Wellington found himself wondering if his second marriage had been a wise one. Other circumstances combined to change in some degree his once rose-colored conception of life at the North. He had believed that all men were equal in this favored locality, but he discovered more degrees of inequality than he had ever perceived at the South. A colored man might be as good as a white man in theory, but neither of them was of any special consequence without money, or talent, or position. Uncle Wellington found a great many privileges open to him at the North, but he had not been educated to the point where he could appreciate them or take advantage of them; and the enjoyment of many of them was expensive, and, for that reason alone, as far beyond his reach as they had ever been. When he once began to admit even the possibility of a mistake on his part, these considerations presented themselves to his mind with increasing force. On occasions when Mrs. Braboy would require of him some unusual physical exertion, or when too frequent applications to the bottle had loosened her tongue, uncle Wellington's mind would revert, with a remorseful twinge of conscience, to the *dolce far niente* of his Southern home; a film would come over his eyes and brain, and, instead of the red-faced Irishwoman opposite him, he could see the black but comely disk of aunt Milly's countenance bending over the washtub; the elegant brogue of Mrs. Braboy would deliquesce into the soft dialect of North Carolina; and he would only be aroused from this blissful reverie by a wet shirt or a handful of suds thrown into his face, with which gentle reminder his wife would recall his attention to the duties of the moment.

There came a time, one day in spring, when there was no longer any question about it: uncle Wellington was desperately homesick.

Liberty, equality, privileges,—all were but as dust in the balance when weighed against his longing for old scenes and faces. It was the

CHARLES W. CHESNUTT

natural reaction in the mind of a middle-aged man who had tried to force the current of a sluggish existence into a new and radically different channel. An active, industrious man, making the change in early life, while there was time to spare for the waste of adaptation, might have found in the new place more favorable conditions than in the old. In Wellington age and temperament combined to prevent the success of the experiment; the spirit of enterprise and ambition into which he had been temporarily galvanized could no longer prevail against the inertia of old habits of life and thought.

One day when he had been sent to deliver clothes he performed his errand quickly, and boarding a passing street car, paid one of his very few five-cent pieces to ride down to the office of the Hon. Mr. Brown, the colored lawyer whom he had visited when he first came to the city, and who was well known to him by sight and reputation.

"Mr. Brown," he said, "I ain' gitt'n' 'long very well wid my ole 'oman."

"What 's the trouble?" asked the lawyer, with business-like curtness, for he did not scent much of a fee.

"Well, de main trouble is she doan treat me right. An' den she gits drunk, an' wuss'n dat, she lays vi'lent han's on me. I kyars de marks er dat 'oman on my face now."

He showed the lawyer a long scratch on the neck.

"Why don't you defend yourself?"

"You don' know Mis' Braboy, suh; you don' know dat 'oman," he replied, with a shake of the head. "Some er dese yer w'ite women is monst'us strong in de wris'."

"Well, Mr. Braboy, it 's what you might have expected when you turned your back on your own people and married a white woman. You were n't content with being a slave to the white folks once, but you must try it again. Some people never know when they 've got enough. I don't see that there 's any help for you; unless," he added suggestively, "you had a good deal of money."

"'Pears ter me I heared somebody say sence I be'n up heah, dat it wuz 'gin de law fer w'ite folks an' colored folks ter marry."

"That was once the law, though it has always been a dead letter in Groveland. In fact, it was the law when you got married, and until I introduced a bill in the legislature last fall to repeal it. But even that law did n't hit cases like yours. It was unlawful to make such a marriage, but it was a good marriage when once made."

"I don' jes' git dat th'oo my head," said Wellington, scratching that member as though to make a hole for the idea to enter.

"It's quite plain, Mr. Braboy. It's unlawful to kill a man, but when he's killed he's just as dead as though the law permitted it. I'm afraid you have n't much of a case, but if you'll go to work and get twenty-five dollars together, I'll see what I can do for you. We may be able to pull a case through on the ground of extreme cruelty. I might even start the case if you brought in ten dollars."

Wellington went away sorrowfully. The laws of Ohio were very little more satisfactory than those of North Carolina. And as for the ten dollars,—the lawyer might as well have told him to bring in the moon, or a deed for the Public Square. He felt very, very low as he hurried back home to supper, which he would have to go without if he were not on hand at the usual supper-time.

But just when his spirits were lowest, and his outlook for the future most hopeless, a measure of relief was at hand. He noticed, when he reached home, that Mrs. Braboy was a little preoccupied, and did not abuse him as vigorously as he expected after so long an absence. He also perceived the smell of strange tobacco in the house, of a better grade than he could afford to use. He thought perhaps some one had come in to see about the washing; but he was too glad of a respite from Mrs. Braboy's rhetoric to imperil it by indiscreet questions.

Next morning she gave him fifty cents.

"Braboy," she said, "ye 've be'n helpin' me nicely wid the washin', an' I 'm going ter give ye a holiday. Ye can take yer hook an' line an' go fishin' on the breakwater. I 'll fix ye a lunch, an' ye need n't come back till night. An' there 's half a dollar; ye can buy yerself a pipe er terbacky. But be careful an' don't waste it," she added, for fear she was overdoing the thing.

Uncle Wellington was overjoyed at this change of front on the part of Mrs. Braboy; if she would make it permanent he did not see why they might not live together very comfortably.

The day passed pleasantly down on the breakwater. The weather was agreeable, and the fish bit freely. Towards evening Wellington started home with a bunch of fish that no angler need have been ashamed of. He looked forward to a good warm supper; for even if something should have happened during the day to alter his wife's mood for the worse, any ordinary variation would be more than balanced by the substantial

CHARLES W. CHESNUTT

addition of food to their larder. His mouth watered at the thought of the finny beauties sputtering in the frying-pan.

He noted, as he approached the house, that there was no smoke coming from the chimney. This only disturbed him in connection with the matter of supper. When he entered the gate he observed further that the window-shades had been taken down.

"'Spec' de ole 'oman's been house-cleanin'," he said to himself. "I wonder she did n' make me stay an' he'p 'er."

He went round to the rear of the house and tried the kitchen door. It was locked. This was somewhat of a surprise, and disturbed still further his expectations in regard to supper. When he had found the key and opened the door, the gravity of his next discovery drove away for the time being all thoughts of eating.

The kitchen was empty. Stove, table, chairs, wash-tubs, pots and pans, had vanished as if into thin air.

"Fo' de Lawd's sake!" he murmured in open-mouthed astonishment.

He passed into the other room,—they had only two,—which had served as bedroom and sitting-room. It was as bare as the first, except that in the middle of the floor were piled uncle Wellington's clothes. It was not a large pile, and on the top of it lay a folded piece of yellow wrapping-paper.

Wellington stood for a moment as if petrified. Then he rubbed his eyes and looked around him.

"W'at do dis mean?" he said. "Is I er-dreamin', er does I see w'at I 'pears ter see?" He glanced down at the bunch of fish which he still held. "Heah 's de fish; heah 's de house; heah I is; but whar 's de ole 'oman, an' whar 's de fu'niture? *I* can't figure out w'at dis yer all means."

He picked up the piece of paper and unfolded it. It was written on one side. Here was the obvious solution of the mystery,—that is, it would have been obvious if he could have read it; but he could not, and so his fancy continued to play upon the subject. Perhaps the house had been robbed, or the furniture taken back by the seller, for it had not been entirely paid for.

Finally he went across the street and called to a boy in a neighbor's yard.

"Does you read writin', Johnnie?"

"Yes, sir, I 'm in the seventh grade."

"Read dis yer paper fuh me."

The youngster took the note, and with much labor read the following:—

Mr. Braboy:

"In lavin' ye so suddint I have ter say that my first husban'
has turned up unixpected, having been saved onbeknownst
ter me from a wathry grave an' all the money wasted I spint
fer masses fer ter rist his sole an' I wish I had it back I feel it
my dooty ter go an' live wid 'im again. I take the furnacher
because I bought it yer close is yors I leave them and wishin'
yer the best of luck I remane oncet yer wife but now agin

Mrs. Katie Flannigan

"N.B. I'm lavin town terday so it won't be no use lookin'
fer me."

On inquiry uncle Wellington learned from the boy that shortly after
his departure in the morning a white man had appeared on the scene,
followed a little later by a moving-van, into which the furniture had
been loaded and carried away. Mrs. Braboy, clad in her best clothes, had
locked the door, and gone away with the strange white man.

The news was soon noised about the street. Wellington swapped
his fish for supper and a bed at a neighbor's, and during the evening
learned from several sources that the strange white man had been at
his house the afternoon of the day before. His neighbors intimated that
they thought Mrs. Braboy's departure a good riddance of bad rubbish,
and Wellington did not dispute the proposition.

Thus ended the second chapter of Wellington's matrimonial
experiences. His wife's departure had been the one thing needful to
convince him, beyond a doubt, that he had been a great fool. Remorse
and homesickness forced him to the further conclusion that he had
been knave as well as fool, and had treated aunt Milly shamefully. He
was not altogether a bad old man, though very weak and erring, and his
better nature now gained the ascendency. Of course his disappointment
had a great deal to do with his remorse; most people do not perceive
the hideousness of sin until they begin to reap its consequences. Instead
of the beautiful Northern life he had dreamed of, he found himself
stranded, penniless, in a strange land, among people whose sympathy
he had forfeited, with no one to lean upon, and no refuge from the
storms of life. His outlook was very dark, and there sprang up within
him a wild longing to get back to North Carolina,—back to the little
whitewashed cabin, shaded with china and mulberry trees; back to the

wood-pile and the garden; back to the old cronies with whom he had swapped lies and tobacco for so many years. He longed to kiss the rod of aunt Milly's domination. He had purchased his liberty at too great a price.

The next day he disappeared from Groveland. He had announced his departure only to Mr. Johnson, who sent his love to his relations in Patesville.

It would be painful to record in detail the return journey of uncle Wellington—Mr. Braboy no longer—to his native town; how many weary miles he walked; how many times he risked his life on railroad tracks and between freight cars; how he depended for sustenance on the grudging hand of back-door charity. Nor would it be profitable or delicate to mention any slight deviations from the path of rectitude, as judged by conventional standards, to which he may occasionally have been driven by a too insistent hunger; or to refer in the remotest degree to a compulsory sojourn of thirty days in a city where he had no references, and could show no visible means of support. True charity will let these purely personal matters remain locked in the bosom of him who suffered them.

IV

JUST FIFTEEN MONTHS AFTER THE date when uncle Wellington had left North Carolina, a weather-beaten figure entered the town of Patesville after nightfall, following the railroad track from the north. Few would have recognized in the hungry-looking old brown tramp, clad in dusty rags and limping along with bare feet, the trim-looking middle-aged mulatto who so few months before had taken the train from Patesville for the distant North; so, if he had but known it, there was no necessity for him to avoid the main streets and sneak around by unfrequented paths to reach the old place on the other side of the town. He encountered nobody that he knew, and soon the familiar shape of the little cabin rose before him. It stood distinctly outlined against the sky, and the light streaming from the half-opened shutters showed it to be occupied. As he drew nearer, every familiar detail of the place appealed to his memory and to his affections, and his heart went out to the old home and the old wife. As he came nearer still, the odor of fried chicken floated out upon the air and set his mouth to watering, and awakened unspeakable longings in his half-starved stomach.

At this moment, however, a fearful thought struck him; suppose the old woman had taken legal advice and married again during his absence? Turn about would have been only fair play. He opened the gate softly, and with his heart in his mouth approached the window on tiptoe and looked in.

A cheerful fire was blazing on the hearth, in front of which sat the familiar form of aunt Milly—and another, at the sight of whom uncle Wellington's heart sank within him. He knew the other person very well; he had sat there more than once before uncle Wellington went away. It was the minister of the church to which his wife belonged. The preacher's former visits, however, had signified nothing more than pastoral courtesy, or appreciation of good eating. His presence now was of serious portent; for Wellington recalled, with acute alarm, that the elder's wife had died only a few weeks before his own departure for the North. What was the occasion of his presence this evening? Was it merely a pastoral call? or was he courting? or had aunt Milly taken legal advice and married the elder?

Wellington remembered a crack in the wall, at the back of the house, through which he could see and hear, and quietly stationed himself there.

"Dat chicken smells mighty good, Sis' Milly," the elder was saying; "I can't fer de life er me see why dat low-down husban' er yo'n could ever run away f'm a cook like you. It 's one er de beatenis' things I ever heared. How he could lib wid you an' not 'preciate you I can't understan', no indeed I can't."

Aunt Milly sighed. "De trouble wid Wellin'ton wuz," she replied, "dat he did n' know when he wuz well off. He wuz alluz wishin' fer change, er studyin' 'bout somethin' new."

"Ez fer me," responded the elder earnestly, "I likes things what has be'n prove' an' tried an' has stood de tes', an' I can't 'magine how anybody could spec' ter fin' a better housekeeper er cook dan you is, Sis' Milly. I 'm a gittin' mighty lonesome sence my wife died. De Good Book say it is not good fer man ter lib alone, en it 'pears ter me dat you an' me mought git erlong tergether monst'us well."

Wellington's heart stood still, while he listened with strained attention. Aunt Milly sighed.

"I ain't denyin', elder, but what I 've be'n kinder lonesome myse'f fer quite a w'ile, an' I doan doubt dat w'at de Good Book say 'plies ter women as well as ter men."

CHARLES W. CHESNUTT

"You kin be sho' it do," averred the elder, with professional authoritativeness; "yas 'm, you kin be cert'n sho'."

"But, of co'se," aunt Milly went on, "havin' los' my ole man de way I did, it has tuk me some time fer ter git my feelin's straighten' out like dey oughter be."

"I kin 'magine yo' feelin's, Sis' Milly," chimed in the elder sympathetically, "w'en you come home dat night an' foun' yo' chist broke open, an' yo' money gone dat you had wukked an' slaved full f'm mawnin' 'tel night, year in an' year out, an' w'en you foun' dat no-'count nigger gone wid his clo's an' you lef' all alone in de worl' ter scuffle 'long by yo'self."

"Yas, elder," responded aunt Milly, "I wa'n't used right. An' den w'en I heared 'bout his goin' ter de lawyer ter fin' out 'bout a defoce, an' w'en I heared w'at de lawyer said 'bout my not bein' his wife 'less he wanted me, it made me so mad, I made up my min' dat ef he ever put his foot on my do'sill ag'in, I'd shet de do' in his face an' tell 'im ter go back whar he come f'm."

To Wellington, on the outside, the cabin had never seemed so comfortable, aunt Milly never so desirable, chicken never so appetizing, as at this moment when they seemed slipping away from his grasp forever.

"Yo' feelin's does you credit, Sis' Milly," said the elder, taking her hand, which for a moment she did not withdraw. "An' de way fer you ter close yo' do' tightes' ag'inst 'im is ter take me in his place. He ain' got no claim on you no mo'. He tuk his ch'ice 'cordin' ter w'at de lawyer tol' 'im, an' 'termine' dat he wa'n't yo' husban'. Ef he wa'n't yo' husban', he had no right ter take yo' money, an' ef he comes back here ag'in you kin hab 'im tuck up an' sent ter de penitenchy fer stealin' it."

Uncle Wellington's knees, already weak from fasting, trembled violently beneath him. The worst that he had feared was now likely to happen. His only hope of safety lay in flight, and yet the scene within so fascinated him that he could not move a step.

"It 'u'd serve him right," exclaimed aunt Milly indignantly, "ef he wuz sent ter de penitenchy fer life! Dey ain't nuthin' too mean ter be done ter 'im. What did I ever do dat he should use me like he did?"

The recital of her wrongs had wrought upon aunt Milly's feelings so that her voice broke, and she wiped her eyes with her apron.

The elder looked serenely confident, and moved his chair nearer hers in order the better to play the role of comforter. Wellington, on the outside, felt so mean that the darkness of the night was scarcely sufficient to hide him; it would be no more than right if the earth were to open and swallow him up.

"An' yet aftuh all, elder," said Milly with a sob, "though I knows you is a better man, an' would treat me right, I wuz so use' ter dat ole nigger, an' libbed wid 'im so long, dat ef he 'd open dat do' dis minute an' walk in, I 'm feared I 'd be foolish ernuff an' weak ernuff to forgive 'im an' take 'im back ag'in."

With a bound, uncle Wellington was away from the crack in the wall. As he ran round the house he passed the wood-pile and snatched up an armful of pieces. A moment later he threw open the door.

"Ole 'oman," he exclaimed, "here 's dat wood you tol' me ter fetch in! Why, elder," he said to the preacher, who had started from his seat with surprise, "w'at's yo' hurry? Won't you stay an' hab some supper wid us?"

CHARLES W. CHESNUTT

The Bouquet

M ary Myrover's friends were somewhat surprised when she began to teach a colored school. Miss Myrover's friends are mentioned here, because nowhere more than in a Southern town is public opinion a force which cannot be lightly contravened. Public opinion, however, did not oppose Miss Myrover's teaching colored children; in fact, all the colored public schools in town—and there were several—were taught by white teachers, and had been so taught since the State had undertaken to provide free public instruction for all children within its boundaries. Previous to that time, there had been a Freedman's Bureau school and a Presbyterian missionary school, but these had been withdrawn when the need for them became less pressing. The colored people of the town had been for some time agitating their right to teach their own schools, but as yet the claim had not been conceded.

The reason Miss Myrover's course created some surprise was not, therefore, the fact that a Southern white woman should teach a colored school; it lay in the fact that up to this time no woman of just her quality had taken up such work. Most of the teachers of colored schools were not of those who had constituted the aristocracy of the old régime; they might be said rather to represent the new order of things, in which labor was in time to become honorable, and men were, after a somewhat longer time, to depend, for their place in society, upon themselves rather than upon their ancestors. Mary Myrover belonged to one of the proudest of the old families. Her ancestors had been people of distinction in Virginia before a collateral branch of the main stock had settled in North Carolina. Before the war, they had been able to live up to their pedigree; but the war brought sad changes. Miss Myrover's father—the Colonel Myrover who led a gallant but desperate charge at Vicksburg—had fallen on the battlefield, and his tomb in the white cemetery was a shrine for the family. On the Confederate Memorial Day, no other grave was so profusely decorated with flowers, and, in the oration pronounced, the name of Colonel Myrover was always used to illustrate the highest type of patriotic devotion and self-sacrifice. Miss Myrover's brother, too, had fallen in the conflict; but his bones lay in some unknown trench, with those of a thousand others who had fallen on the same field. Ay, more, her lover, who had hoped to come home in the full tide of victory and claim his bride as a reward for gallantry, had shared the fate of her father and brother. When the war was over, the remnant of the family found itself involved in the common ruin,—more deeply involved, indeed, than some others; for Colonel Myrover had believed in the ultimate triumph of his cause, and had invested most of his wealth in Confederate bonds, which were now only so much waste paper.

There had been a little left. Mrs. Myrover was thrifty, and had laid by a few hundred dollars, which she kept in the house to meet unforeseen contingencies. There remained, too, their home, with an ample garden and a well-stocked orchard, besides a considerable tract of country land, partly cleared, but productive of very little revenue.

With their shrunken resources, Miss Myrover and her mother were able to hold up their heads without embarrassment for some years after the close of the war. But when things were adjusted to the changed conditions, and the stream of life began to flow more vigorously in the new channels, they saw themselves in danger of dropping behind, unless in some way they could add to their meagre income. Miss Myrover looked over the field of employment, never very wide for women in the South, and found it occupied. The only available position she could be supposed prepared to fill, and which she could take without distinct loss of caste, was that of a teacher, and there was no vacancy except in one of the colored schools. Even teaching was a doubtful experiment; it was not what she would have preferred, but it was the best that could be done. "I don't like it, Mary," said her mother. "It's a long step from owning such people to teaching them. What do they need with education? It will only make them unfit for work."

"They're free now, mother, and perhaps they'll work better if they're taught something. Besides, it's only a business arrangement, and does n't involve any closer contact than we have with our servants."

"Well, I should say not!" sniffed the old lady. "Not one of them will ever dare to presume on your position to take any liberties with us. I'll see to that."

Miss Myrover began her work as a teacher in the autumn, at the opening of the school year. It was a novel experience at first. Though there had always been negro servants in the house, and though on the streets colored people were more numerous than those of her own race, and though she was so familiar with their dialect that she might almost be said to speak it, barring certain characteristic grammatical inaccuracies, she had never been brought in personal contact with so

CHARLES W. CHESNUTT

many of them at once as when she confronted the fifty or sixty faces—of colors ranging from a white almost as clear as her own to the darkest livery of the sun—which were gathered in the schoolroom on the morning when she began her duties. Some of the inherited prejudice of her caste, too, made itself felt, though she tried to repress any outward sign of it; and she could perceive that the children were not altogether responsive; they, likewise, were not entirely free from antagonism. The work was unfamiliar to her. She was not physically very strong, and at the close of the first day went home with a splitting headache. If she could have resigned then and there without causing comment or annoyance to others, she would have felt it a privilege to do so. But a night's rest banished her headache and improved her spirits, and the next morning she went to her work with renewed vigor, fortified by the experience of the first day.

Miss Myrover's second day was more satisfactory. She had some natural talent for organization, though hitherto unaware of it, and in the course of the day she got her classes formed and lessons under way. In a week or two she began to classify her pupils in her own mind, as bright or stupid, mischievous or well behaved, lazy or industrious, as the case might be, and to regulate her discipline accordingly. That she had come of a long line of ancestors who had exercised authority and mastership was perhaps not without its effect upon her character, and enabled her more readily to maintain good order in the school. When she was fairly broken in, she found the work rather to her liking, and derived much pleasure from such success as she achieved as a teacher.

It was natural that she should be more attracted to some of her pupils than to others. Perhaps her favorite—or, rather, the one she liked best, for she was too fair and just for conscious favoritism—was Sophy Tucker. Just the ground for the teacher's liking for Sophy might not at first be apparent. The girl was far from the whitest of Miss Myrover's pupils; in fact, she was one of the darker ones. She was not the brightest in intellect, though she always tried to learn her lessons. She was not the best dressed, for her mother was a poor widow, who went out washing and scrubbing for a living. Perhaps the real tie between them was Sophy's intense devotion to the teacher. It had manifested itself almost from the first day of the school, in the rapt look of admiration Miss Myrover always saw on the little black face turned toward her. In it there was nothing of envy, nothing of regret; nothing but worship for the beautiful white lady—she was not especially handsome, but to

Sophy her beauty was almost divine—who had come to teach her. If Miss Myrover dropped a book, Sophy was the first to spring and pick it up; if she wished a chair moved, Sophy seemed to anticipate her wish; and so of all the numberless little services that can be rendered in a schoolroom.

Miss Myrover was fond of flowers, and liked to have them about her. The children soon learned of this taste of hers, and kept the vases on her desk filled with blossoms during their season. Sophy was perhaps the most active in providing them. If she could not get garden flowers, she would make excursions to the woods in the early morning, and bring in great dew-laden bunches of bay, or jasmine, or some other fragrant forest flower which she knew the teacher loved.

"When I die, Sophy," Miss Myrover said to the child one day, "I want to be covered with roses. And when they bury me, I'm sure I shall rest better if my grave is banked with flowers, and roses are planted at my head and at my feet."

Miss Myrover was at first amused at Sophy's devotion; but when she grew more accustomed to it, she found it rather to her liking. It had a sort of flavor of the old régime, and she felt, when she bestowed her kindly notice upon her little black attendant, some of the feudal condescension of the mistress toward the slave. She was kind to Sophy, and permitted her to play the rôle she had assumed, which caused sometimes a little jealousy among the other girls. Once she gave Sophy a yellow ribbon which she took from her own hair. The child carried it home, and cherished it as a priceless treasure, to be worn only on the greatest occasions.

Sophy had a rival in her attachment to the teacher, but the rivalry was altogether friendly. Miss Myrover had a little dog, a white spaniel, answering to the name of Prince. Prince was a dog of high degree, and would have very little to do with the children of the school; he made an exception, however, in the case of Sophy, whose devotion for his mistress he seemed to comprehend. He was a clever dog, and could fetch and carry, sit up on his haunches, extend his paw to shake hands, and possessed several other canine accomplishments. He was very fond of his mistress, and always, unless shut up at home, accompanied her to school, where he spent most of his time lying under the teacher's desk, or, in cold weather, by the stove, except when he would go out now and then and chase an imaginary rabbit round the yard, presumably for exercise.

CHARLES W. CHESNUTT

At school Sophy and Prince vied with each other in their attentions to Miss Myrover. But when school was over, Prince went away with her, and Sophy stayed behind; for Miss Myrover was white and Sophy was black, which they both understood perfectly well. Miss Myrover taught the colored children, but she could not be seen with them in public. If they occasionally met her on the street, they did not expect her to speak to them, unless she happened to be alone and no other white person was in sight. If any of the children felt slighted, she was not aware of it, for she intended no slight; she had not been brought up to speak to negroes on the street, and she could not act differently from other people. And though she was a woman of sentiment and capable of deep feeling, her training had been such that she hardly expected to find in those of darker hue than herself the same susceptibility— varying in degree, perhaps, but yet the same in kind—that gave to her own life the alternations of feeling that made it most worth living.

Once Miss Myrover wished to carry home a parcel of books. She had the bundle in her hand when Sophy came up.

"Lemme tote yo' bundle fer yer, Miss Ma'y?" she asked eagerly. "I'm gwine yo' way."

"Thank you, Sophy," was the reply. "I'll be glad if you will."

Sophy followed the teacher at a respectful distance. When they reached Miss Myrover's home, Sophy carried the bundle to the doorstep, where Miss Myrover took it and thanked her.

Mrs. Myrover came out on the piazza as Sophy was moving away. She said, in the child's hearing, and perhaps with the intention that she should hear: "Mary, I wish you would n't let those little darkeys follow you to the house. I don't want them in the yard. I should think you'd have enough of them all day."

"Very well, mother," replied her daughter. "I won't bring any more of them. The child was only doing me a favor."

Mrs. Myrover was an invalid, and opposition or irritation of any kind brought on nervous paroxysms that made her miserable, and made life a burden to the rest of the household, so that Mary seldom crossed her whims. She did not bring Sophy to the house again, nor did Sophy again offer her services as porter.

One day in spring Sophy brought her teacher a bouquet of yellow roses.

"Dey come off'n my own bush, Miss Ma'y," she said proudly, "an' I didn' let nobody e'se pull 'em, but saved 'em all fer you, 'cause I know you likes roses so much. I'm gwine bring 'em all ter you as long as dey las'."

"Thank you, Sophy," said the teacher; "you are a very good girl."

For another year Mary Myrover taught the colored school, and did excellent service. The children made rapid progress under her tuition, and learned to love her well; for they saw and appreciated, as well as children could, her fidelity to a trust that she might have slighted, as some others did, without much fear of criticism. Toward the end of her second year she sickened, and after a brief illness died.

Old Mrs. Myrover was inconsolable. She ascribed her daughter's death to her labors as teacher of negro children. Just how the color of the pupils had produced the fatal effects she did not stop to explain. But she was too old, and had suffered too deeply from the war, in body and mind and estate, ever to reconcile herself to the changed order of things following the return of peace; and, with an unsound yet perfectly explainable logic, she visited some of her displeasure upon those who had profited most, though passively, by her losses.

"I always feared something would happen to Mary," she said. "It seemed unnatural for her to be wearing herself out teaching little negroes who ought to have been working for her. But the world has hardly been a fit place to live in since the war, and when I follow her, as I must before long, I shall not be sorry to go."

She gave strict orders that no colored people should be admitted to the house. Some of her friends heard of this, and remonstrated. They knew the teacher was loved by the pupils, and felt that sincere respect from the humble would be a worthy tribute to the proudest. But Mrs. Myrover was obdurate.

"They had my daughter when she was alive," she said, "and they've killed her. But she's mine now, and I won't have them come near her. I don't want one of them at the funeral or anywhere around."

For a month before Miss Myrover's death Sophy had been watching her rosebush—the one that bore the yellow roses—for the first buds of spring, and, when these appeared, had awaited impatiently their gradual unfolding. But not until her teacher's death had they become full-blown roses. When Miss Myrover died, Sophy determined to pluck the roses and lay them on her coffin. Perhaps, she thought, they might even put them in her hand or on her breast. For Sophy remembered Miss Myrover's thanks and praise when she had brought her the yellow roses the spring before.

On the morning of the day set for the funeral, Sophy washed her face until it shone, combed and brushed her hair with painful

CHARLES W. CHESNUTT

conscientiousness, put on her best frock, plucked her yellow roses, and, tying them with the treasured ribbon her teacher had given her, set out for Miss Myrover's home.

She went round to the side gate—the house stood on a corner—and stole up the path to the kitchen. A colored woman, whom she did not know, came to the door.

"Wat yer want, chile?" she inquired.

"Kin I see Miss Ma'y?" asked Sophy timidly.

"I don't know, honey. Ole Miss Myrover say she don't want no cullud folks roun' de house endyoin' dis fun'al. I'll look an' see if she's roun' de front room, whar de co'pse is. You sed down heah an' keep still, an' ef she's upstairs maybe I kin git yer in dere a minute. Ef I can't, I kin put yo' bokay 'mongs' de res', whar she won't know nuthin' erbout it."

A moment after she had gone, there was a step in the hall, and old Mrs. Myrover came into the kitchen.

"Dinah!" she said in a peevish tone; "Dinah!"

Receiving no answer, Mrs. Myrover peered around the kitchen, and caught sight of Sophy.

"What are you doing here?" she demanded.

"I-I'm-m waitin' ter see de cook, ma'am," stammered Sophy.

"The cook is n't here now. I don't know where she is. Besides, my daughter is to be buried to-day, and I won't have any one visiting the servants until the funeral is over. Come back some other day, or see the cook at her own home in the evening."

She stood waiting for the child to go, and under the keen glance of her eyes Sophy, feeling as though she had been caught in some disgraceful act, hurried down the walk and out of the gate, with her bouquet in her hand.

"Dinah," said Mrs. Myrover, when the cook came back, "I don't want any strange people admitted here to-day. The house will be full of our friends, and we have no room for others."

"Yas 'm," said the cook. She understood perfectly what her mistress meant; and what the cook thought about her mistress was a matter of no consequence.

The funeral services were held at St. Paul's Episcopal Church, where the Myrovers had always worshiped. Quite a number of Miss Myrover's pupils went to the church to attend the services. The building was not a large one. There was a small gallery at the rear, to which colored people were admitted, if they chose to come, at ordinary services; and those who wished to be present at the funeral supposed that the usual custom would prevail. They were therefore surprised, when they went to the side entrance, by which colored people gained access to the gallery stairs, to be met by an usher who barred their passage.

"I 'm sorry," he said, "but I have had orders to admit no one until the friends of the family have all been seated. If you wish to wait until the white people have all gone in, and there 's any room left, you may be able to get into the back part of the gallery. Of course I can't tell yet whether there 'll be any room or not."

Now the statement of the usher was a very reasonable one; but, strange to say, none of the colored people chose to remain except Sophy. She still hoped to use her floral offering for its destined end, in some way, though she did not know just how. She waited in the yard until the church was filled with white people, and a number who could not gain admittance were standing about the doors. Then she went round to the side of the church, and, depositing her bouquet carefully on an old mossy gravestone, climbed up on the projecting sill of a window near the chancel. The window was of stained glass, of somewhat ancient make. The church was old, had indeed been built in colonial times, and the stained glass had been brought from England. The design of the window showed Jesus blessing little children. Time had dealt gently with the window, but just at the feet of the figure of Jesus a small triangular piece of glass had been broken out. To this aperture Sophy applied her eyes, and through it saw and heard what she could of the services within.

Before the chancel, on trestles draped in black, stood the sombre casket in which lay all that was mortal of her dear teacher. The top of the casket was covered with flowers; and lying stretched out underneath it she saw Miss Myrover's little white dog, Prince. He had followed the body to the church, and, slipping in unnoticed among the mourners, had taken his place, from which no one had the heart to remove him.

The white-robed rector read the solemn service for the dead, and then delivered a brief address, in which he dwelt upon the uncertainty of life, and, to the believer, the certain blessedness of eternity. He spoke of Miss Myrover's kindly spirit, and, as an illustration of her love and self-sacrifice for others, referred to her labors as a teacher of the poor ignorant negroes who had been placed in their midst by an all-wise Providence, and whom it was their duty to guide and direct in the station in which God had put them. Then the organ pealed, a prayer was said, and the long cortege moved from the church to the cemetery, about half a mile away, where the body was to be interred.

When the services were over, Sophy sprang down from her perch, and, taking her flowers, followed the procession. She did not walk with the rest, but at a proper and respectful distance from the last mourner. No one noticed the little black girl with the bunch of yellow flowers, or thought of her as interested in the funeral.

The cortege reached the cemetery and filed slowly through the gate; but Sophy stood outside, looking at a small sign in white letters on a black background:—

"*Notice*. This cemetery is for white people only. Others please keep out."

Sophy, thanks to Miss Myrover's painstaking instruction, could read this sign very distinctly. In fact, she had often read it before. For Sophy was a child who loved beauty, in a blind, groping sort of way, and had sometimes stood by the fence of the cemetery and looked through at the green mounds and shaded walks and blooming flowers within, and wished that she might walk among them. She knew, too, that the little sign on the gate, though so courteously worded, was no mere formality; for she had heard how a colored man, who had wandered into the cemetery on a hot night and fallen asleep on the flat top of a tomb, had been arrested as a vagrant and fined five dollars, which he had worked out on the streets, with a ball-and-chain attachment, at twenty-five cents a day. Since that time the cemetery gate had been locked at night.

So Sophy stayed outside, and looked through the fence. Her poor bouquet had begun to droop by this time, and the yellow ribbon had lost some of its freshness. Sophy could see the rector standing by the grave, the mourners gathered round; she could faintly distinguish the solemn words with which ashes were committed to ashes, and dust to dust. She heard the hollow thud of the earth falling on the coffin; and she leaned against the iron fence, sobbing softly, until the grave was filled and rounded off, and the wreaths and other floral pieces were disposed upon it. When the mourners began to move toward the gate, Sophy walked slowly down the street, in a direction opposite to that taken by most of the people who came out.

When they had all gone away, and the sexton had come out and locked the gate behind him, Sophy crept back. Her roses were faded now, and from some of them the petals had fallen. She stood there irresolute, loath to leave with her heart's desire unsatisfied, when, as her eyes sought again the teacher's last resting-place, she saw lying beside the new-made grave what looked like a small bundle of white wool. Sophy's eyes lighted up with a sudden glow.

"Prince! Here, Prince!" she called.

The little dog rose, and trotted down to the gate. Sophy pushed the poor bouquet between the iron bars. "Take that ter Miss Ma'y, Prince," she said, "that's a good doggie."

The dog wagged his tail intelligently, took the bouquet carefully in his mouth, carried it to his mistress's grave, and laid it among the other flowers. The bunch of roses was so small that from where she stood Sophy could see only a dash of yellow against the white background of the mass of flowers.

When Prince had performed his mission he turned his eyes toward Sophy inquiringly, and when she gave him a nod of approval lay down and resumed his watch by the graveside. Sophy looked at him a moment with a feeling very much like envy, and then turned and moved slowly away.

The Web of Circumstance

I

Within a low clapboarded hut, with an open front, a forge was glowing. In front a blacksmith was shoeing a horse, a sleek, well-kept animal with the signs of good blood and breeding. A young mulatto stood by and handed the blacksmith such tools as he needed from time to time. A group of negroes were sitting around, some in the shadow of the shop, one in the full glare of the sunlight. A gentleman was seated in a buggy a few yards away, in the shade of a spreading elm. The horse had loosened a shoe, and Colonel Thornton, who was a lover of fine horseflesh, and careful of it, had stopped at Ben Davis's blacksmith shop, as soon as he discovered the loose shoe, to have it fastened on.

"All right, Kunnel," the blacksmith called out. "Tom," he said, addressing the young man, "he'p me hitch up."

Colonel Thornton alighted from the buggy, looked at the shoe, signified his approval of the job, and stood looking on while the blacksmith and his assistant harnessed the horse to the buggy.

"Dat's a mighty fine whip yer got dere, Kunnel," said Ben, while the young man was tightening the straps of the harness on the opposite side of the horse. "I wush I had one like it. Where kin yer git dem whips?"

"My brother brought me this from New York," said the Colonel. "You can't buy them down here."

The whip in question was a handsome one. The handle was wrapped with interlacing threads of variegated colors, forming an elaborate pattern, the lash being dark green. An octagonal ornament of glass was set in the end of the handle.

"It cert'n'y is fine," said Ben; "I wish I had one like it." He looked at the whip longingly as Colonel Thornton drove away.

"'Pears ter me Ben gittin' mighty blooded," said one of the bystanders, "drivin' a hoss an' buggy, an' wantin' a whip like Colonel Thornton's."

"What's de reason I can't hab a hoss an' buggy an' a whip like Kunnel Tho'nton's, ef I pay fer 'em?" asked Ben. "We colored folks never had no chance ter git nothin' befo' de wah, but ef eve'y nigger in dis town had a tuck keer er his money sence de wah, like I has, an' bought as much lan' as I has, de niggers might 'a' got half de lan' by dis time," he went on, giving a finishing blow to a horseshoe, and throwing it on the ground to cool.

Carried away by his own eloquence, he did not notice the approach of two white men who came up the street from behind him.

"An' ef you niggers," he continued, raking the coals together over a fresh bar of iron, "would stop wastin' yo' money on 'scursions to put money in w'ite folks' pockets, an' stop buildin' fine chu'ches, an' buil' houses fer yo'se'ves, you'd git along much faster."

"You're talkin' sense, Ben," said one of the white men. "Yo'r people will never be respected till they've got property."

The conversation took another turn. The white men transacted their business and went away. The whistle of a neighboring steam sawmill blew a raucous blast for the hour of noon, and the loafers shuffled away in different directions.

"You kin go ter dinner, Tom," said the blacksmith. "An' stop at de gate w'en yer go by my house, and tell Nancy I'll be dere in'bout twenty minutes. I got ter finish dis yer plough p'int fus'."

The young man walked away. One would have supposed, from the rapidity with which he walked, that he was very hungry. A quarter of an hour later the blacksmith dropped his hammer, pulled off his leather apron, shut the front door of the shop, and went home to dinner. He came into the house out of the fervent heat, and, throwing off his straw hat, wiped his brow vigorously with a red cotton handkerchief.

"Dem collards smells good," he said, sniffing the odor that came in through the kitchen door, as his good-looking yellow wife opened it to enter the room where he was. "I've got a monst'us good appetite ter-day. I feels good, too. I paid Majah Ransom de intrus' on de mortgage dis mawnin' an' a hund'ed dollahs besides, an' I spec's ter hab de balance ready by de fust of nex' Jiniwary; an' den we won't owe nobody a cent. I tell yer dere ain' nothin' like propputy ter make a pusson feel like a man. But w'at's de matter wid yer, Nancy? Is sump'n' skeered yer?"

The woman did seem excited and ill at ease. There was a heaving of the full bust, a quickened breathing, that betokened suppressed excitement.

"I-I-jes' seen a rattlesnake out in de gyahden," she stammered.

The blacksmith ran to the door. "Which way? Whar wuz he?" he cried.

He heard a rustling in the bushes at one side of the garden, and the sound of a breaking twig, and, seizing a hoe which stood by the door, he sprang toward the point from which the sound came.

CHARLES W. CHESNUTT

"No, no," said the woman hurriedly, "it wuz over here," and she directed her husband's attention to the other side of the garden.

The blacksmith, with the uplifted hoe, its sharp blade gleaming in the sunlight, peered cautiously among the collards and tomato plants, listening all the while for the ominous rattle, but found nothing.

"I reckon he's got away," he said, as he set the hoe up again by the door. "Whar's de chillen?" he asked with some anxiety. "Is dey playin' in de woods?"

"No," answered his wife, "dey've gone ter de spring."

The spring was on the opposite side of the garden from that on which the snake was said to have been seen, so the blacksmith sat down and fanned himself with a palm-leaf fan until the dinner was served.

"Yer ain't quite on time ter-day, Nancy," he said, glancing up at the clock on the mantel, after the edge of his appetite had been taken off. "Got ter make time ef yer wanter make money. Did n't Tom tell yer I'd be heah in twenty minutes?"

"No," she said; "I seen him goin' pas'; he did n' say nothin'."

"I dunno w'at's de matter wid dat boy," mused the blacksmith over his apple dumpling. "He's gittin' mighty keerless heah lately; mus' hab sump'n' on 'is min',—some gal, I reckon."

The children had come in while he was speaking,—a slender, shapely boy, yellow like his mother, a girl several years younger, dark like her father: both bright-looking children and neatly dressed.

"I seen cousin Tom down by de spring," said the little girl, as she lifted off the pail of water that had been balanced on her head. "He come out er de woods jest ez we wuz fillin' our buckets."

"Yas," insisted the blacksmith, "he's got some gal on his min'."

II

THE CASE OF THE STATE of North Carolina *vs.* Ben Davis was called. The accused was led into court, and took his seat in the prisoner's dock.

"Prisoner at the bar, stand up."

The prisoner, pale and anxious, stood up. The clerk read the indictment, in which it was charged that the defendant by force and arms had entered the barn of one G.W. Thornton, and feloniously taken therefrom one whip, of the value of fifteen dollars.

"Are you guilty or not guilty?" asked the judge.

"Not guilty, yo' Honah; not guilty, Jedge. I never tuck de whip."

The State's attorney opened the case. He was young and zealous. Recently elected to the office, this was his first batch of cases, and he was anxious to make as good a record as possible. He had no doubt of the prisoner's guilt. There had been a great deal of petty thieving in the county, and several gentlemen had suggested to him the necessity for greater severity in punishing it. The jury were all white men. The prosecuting attorney stated the case.

"We expect to show, gentlemen of the jury, the facts set out in the indictment,—not altogether by direct proof, but by a chain of circumstantial evidence which is stronger even than the testimony of eyewitnesses. Men might lie, but circumstances cannot. We expect to show that the defendant is a man of dangerous character, a surly, impudent fellow; a man whose views of property are prejudicial to the welfare of society, and who has been heard to assert that half the property which is owned in this county has been stolen, and that, if justice were done, the white people ought to divide up the land with the negroes; in other words, a negro nihilist, a communist, a secret devotee of Tom Paine and Voltaire, a pupil of the anarchist propaganda, which, if not checked by the stern hand of the law, will fasten its insidious fangs on our social system, and drag it down to ruin."

"We object, may it please your Honor," said the defendant's attorney. "The prosecutor should defer his argument until the testimony is in."

"Confine yourself to the facts, Major," said the court mildly.

The prisoner sat with half-open mouth, overwhelmed by this flood of eloquence. He had never heard of Tom Paine or Voltaire. He had no conception of what a nihilist or an anarchist might be, and could not have told the difference between a propaganda and a potato.

"We expect to show, may it please the court, that the prisoner had been employed by Colonel Thornton to shoe a horse; that the horse was taken to the prisoner's blacksmith shop by a servant of Colonel Thornton's; that, this servant expressing a desire to go somewhere on an errand before the horse had been shod, the prisoner volunteered to return the horse to Colonel Thornton's stable; that he did so, and the following morning the whip in question was missing; that, from circumstances, suspicion naturally fell upon the prisoner, and a search was made of his shop, where the whip was found secreted; that the prisoner denied that the whip was there, but when confronted with the evidence of his crime, showed by his confusion that he was guilty beyond a peradventure."

The prisoner looked more anxious; so much eloquence could not but be effective with the jury.

The attorney for the defendant answered briefly, denying the defendant's guilt, dwelling upon his previous good character for honesty, and begging the jury not to pre-judge the case, but to remember that the law is merciful, and that the benefit of the doubt should be given to the prisoner.

The prisoner glanced nervously at the jury. There was nothing in their faces to indicate the effect upon them of the opening statements. It seemed to the disinterested listeners as if the defendant's attorney had little confidence in his client's cause.

Colonel Thornton took the stand and testified to his ownership of the whip, the place where it was kept, its value, and the fact that it had disappeared. The whip was produced in court and identified by the witness. He also testified to the conversation at the blacksmith shop in the course of which the prisoner had expressed a desire to possess a similar whip. The cross-examination was brief, and no attempt was made to shake the Colonel's testimony.

The next witness was the constable who had gone with a warrant to search Ben's shop. He testified to the circumstances under which the whip was found.

"He wuz brazen as a mule at fust, an' wanted ter git mad about it. But when we begun ter turn over that pile er truck in the cawner, he kinder begun ter trimble; when the whip-handle stuck out, his eyes commenced ter grow big, an' when we hauled the whip out he turned pale ez ashes, an' begun to swear he did n' take the whip an' did n' know how it got thar."

"You may cross-examine," said the prosecuting attorney triumphantly.

The prisoner felt the weight of the testimony, and glanced furtively at the jury, and then appealingly at his lawyer.

"You say that Ben denied that he had stolen the whip," said the prisoner's attorney, on cross-examination. "Did it not occur to you that what you took for brazen impudence might have been but the evidence of conscious innocence?"

The witness grinned incredulously, revealing thereby a few blackened fragments of teeth.

"I 've tuck up more 'n a hundred niggers fer stealin', Kurnel, an' I never seed one yit that did n' 'ny it ter the las'."

"Answer my question. Might not the witness's indignation have been a manifestation of conscious innocence? Yes or no?"

"Yes, it mought, an' the moon mought fall—but it don't."

Further cross-examination did not weaken the witness's testimony, which was very damaging, and every one in the court room felt instinctively that a strong defense would be required to break down the State's case.

"The State rests," said the prosecuting attorney, with a ring in his voice which spoke of certain victory.

There was a temporary lull in the proceedings, during which a bailiff passed a pitcher of water and a glass along the line of jury-men. The defense was then begun.

The law in its wisdom did not permit the defendant to testify in his own behalf. There were no witnesses to the facts, but several were called to testify to Ben's good character. The colored witnesses made him out possessed of all the virtues. One or two white men testified that they had never known anything against his reputation for honesty.

The defendant rested his case, and the State called its witnesses in rebuttal. They were entirely on the point of character. One testified that he had heard the prisoner say that, if the negroes had their rights, they would own at least half the property. Another testified that he had heard the defendant say that the negroes spent too much money on churches, and that they cared a good deal more for God than God had ever seemed to care for them.

Ben Davis listened to this testimony with half-open mouth and staring eyes. Now and then he would lean forward and speak perhaps a word, when his attorney would shake a warning finger at him, and he would fall back helplessly, as if abandoning himself to fate; but for a moment only, when he would resume his puzzled look.

The arguments followed. The prosecuting attorney briefly summed up the evidence, and characterized it as almost a mathematical proof of the prisoner's guilt. He reserved his eloquence for the closing argument.

The defendant's attorney had a headache, and secretly believed his client guilty. His address sounded more like an appeal for mercy than a demand for justice. Then the State's attorney delivered the maiden argument of his office, the speech that made his reputation as an orator, and opened up to him a successful political career.

The judge's charge to the jury was a plain, simple statement of the law as applied to circumstantial evidence, and the mere statement of the law foreshadowed the verdict.

The eyes of the prisoner were glued to the jury-box, and he looked more and more like a hunted animal. In the rear of the crowd of blacks who filled the back part of the room, partly concealed by the projecting angle of the fireplace, stood Tom, the blacksmith's assistant. If the face is the mirror of the soul, then this man's soul, taken off its guard in this moment of excitement, was full of lust and envy and all evil passions.

The jury filed out of their box, and into the jury room behind the judge's stand. There was a moment of relaxation in the court room. The lawyers fell into conversation across the table. The judge beckoned to Colonel Thornton, who stepped forward, and they conversed together a few moments. The prisoner was all eyes and ears in this moment of waiting, and from an involuntary gesture on the part of the judge he divined that they were speaking of him. It is a pity he could not hear what was said.

"How do you feel about the case, Colonel?" asked the judge.

"Let him off easy," replied Colonel Thornton. "He 's the best blacksmith in the county."

The business of the court seemed to have halted by tacit consent, in anticipation of a quick verdict. The suspense did not last long. Scarcely ten minutes had elapsed when there was a rap on the door, the officer opened it, and the jury came out.

The prisoner, his soul in his eyes, sought their faces, but met no reassuring glance; they were all looking away from him.

"Gentlemen of the jury, have you agreed upon a verdict?"

"We have," responded the foreman. The clerk of the court stepped forward and took the fateful slip from the foreman's hand.

The clerk read the verdict: "We, the jury impaneled and sworn to try the issues in this cause, do find the prisoner guilty as charged in the indictment."

There was a moment of breathless silence. Then a wild burst of grief from the prisoner's wife, to which his two children, not understanding it all, but vaguely conscious of some calamity, added their voices in two long, discordant wails, which would have been ludicrous had they not been heartrending.

The face of the young man in the back of the room expressed relief and badly concealed satisfaction. The prisoner fell back upon the seat from which he had half risen in his anxiety, and his dark face assumed an ashen hue. What he thought could only be surmised. Perhaps, knowing his innocence, he had not believed conviction possible; perhaps, conscious of guilt, he dreaded the punishment, the extent of which was optional with the judge, within very wide limits. Only one other person present knew whether or not he was guilty, and that other had slunk furtively from the court room.

Some of the spectators wondered why there should be so much ado about convicting a negro of stealing a buggy-whip. They had forgotten their own interest of the moment before. They did not realize out of what trifles grow the tragedies of life.

It was four o'clock in the afternoon, the hour for adjournment, when the verdict was returned. The judge nodded to the bailiff.

"Oyez, oyez! this court is now adjourned until ten o'clock to-morrow morning," cried the bailiff in a singsong voice. The judge left the bench, the jury filed out of the box, and a buzz of conversation filled the court room.

"Brace up, Ben, brace up, my boy," said the defendant's lawyer, half apologetically. "I did what I could for you, but you can never tell what a jury will do. You won't be sentenced till to-morrow morning. In the meantime I'll speak to the judge and try to get him to be easy with you. He may let you off with a light fine."

The negro pulled himself together, and by an effort listened.

"Thanky, Majah," was all he said. He seemed to be thinking of something far away.

He barely spoke to his wife when she frantically threw herself on him, and clung to his neck, as he passed through the side room on his way to jail. He kissed his children mechanically, and did not reply to the soothing remarks made by the jailer.

III

THERE WAS A GOOD DEAL of excitement in town the next morning. Two white men stood by the post office talking.

"Did yer hear the news?"

"No, what wuz it?"

"Ben Davis tried ter break jail las' night."

"You don't say so! What a fool! He ain't be'n sentenced yit."

"Well, now," said the other, "I've knowed Ben a long time, an' he wuz a right good nigger. I kinder found it hard ter b'lieve he did steal that whip. But what's a man's feelin's ag'in' the proof?"

They spoke on awhile, using the past tense as if they were speaking of a dead man.

CHARLES W. CHESNUTT

"Ef I know Jedge Hart, Ben 'll wish he had slep' las' night, 'stidder tryin' ter break out'n jail."

At ten o'clock the prisoner was brought into court. He walked with shambling gait, bent at the shoulders, hopelessly, with downcast eyes, and took his seat with several other prisoners who had been brought in for sentence. His wife, accompanied by the children, waited behind him, and a number of his friends were gathered in the court room.

The first prisoner sentenced was a young white man, convicted several days before of manslaughter. The deed was done in the heat of passion, under circumstances of great provocation, during a quarrel about a woman. The prisoner was admonished of the sanctity of human life, and sentenced to one year in the penitentiary.

The next case was that of a young clerk, eighteen or nineteen years of age, who had committed a forgery in order to procure the means to buy lottery tickets. He was well connected, and the case would not have been prosecuted if the judge had not refused to allow it to be nolled, and, once brought to trial, a conviction could not have been avoided.

"You are a young man," said the judge gravely, yet not unkindly, "and your life is yet before you. I regret that you should have been led into evil courses by the lust for speculation, so dangerous in its tendencies, so fruitful of crime and misery. I am led to believe that you are sincerely penitent, and that, after such punishment as the law cannot remit without bringing itself into contempt, you will see the error of your ways and follow the strict path of rectitude. Your fault has entailed distress not only upon yourself, but upon your relatives, people of good name and good family, who suffer as keenly from your disgrace as you yourself. Partly out of consideration for their feelings, and partly because I feel that, under the circumstances, the law will be satisfied by the penalty I shall inflict, I sentence you to imprisonment in the county jail for six months, and a fine of one hundred dollars and the costs of this action."

"The jedge talks well, don't he?" whispered one spectator to another.

"Yes, and kinder likes ter hear hisse'f talk," answered the other.

"Ben Davis, stand up," ordered the judge.

He might have said "Ben Davis, wake up," for the jailer had to touch the prisoner on the shoulder to rouse him from his stupor. He stood up, and something of the hunted look came again into his eyes, which shifted under the stern glance of the judge.

"Ben Davis, you have been convicted of larceny, after a fair trial before twelve good men of this county. Under the testimony, there can be no doubt of your guilt. The case is an aggravated one. You are not an ignorant, shiftless fellow, but a man of more than ordinary intelligence among your people, and one who ought to know better. You have not even the poor excuse of having stolen to satisfy hunger or a physical appetite. Your conduct is wholly without excuse, and I can only regard your crime as the result of a tendency to offenses of this nature, a tendency which is only too common among your people; a tendency which is a menace to civilization, a menace to society itself, for society rests upon the sacred right of property. Your opinions, too, have been given a wrong turn; you have been heard to utter sentiments which, if disseminated among an ignorant people, would breed discontent, and give rise to strained relations between them and their best friends, their old masters, who understand their real nature and their real needs, and to whose justice and enlightened guidance they can safely trust. Have you anything to say why sentence should not be passed upon you?"

"Nothin', suh, cep'n dat I did n' take de whip."

"The law, largely, I think, in view of the peculiar circumstances of your unfortunate race, has vested a large discretion in courts as to the extent of the punishment for offenses of this kind. Taking your case as a whole, I am convinced that it is one which, for the sake of the example, deserves a severe punishment. Nevertheless, I do not feel disposed to give you the full extent of the law, which would be twenty years in the penitentiary,* but, considering the fact that you have a family, and have heretofore borne a good reputation in the community, I will impose upon you the light sentence of imprisonment for five years in the penitentiary at hard labor. And I hope that this will be a warning to you and others who may be similarly disposed, and that after your sentence has expired you may lead the life of a law-abiding citizen."

"O Ben! O my husband! O God!" moaned the poor wife, and tried to press forward to her husband's side.

"Keep back, Nancy, keep back," said the jailer. "You can see him in jail."

Several people were looking at Ben's face. There was one flash of despair, and then nothing but a stony blank, behind which he masked his real feelings, whatever they were.

Human character is a compound of tendencies inherited and habits

---

* There are no degrees of larceny in North Carolina, and the penalty for any offense lies in the discretion of the judge, to the limit of twenty years.

acquired. In the anxiety, the fear of disgrace, spoke the nineteenth century civilization with which Ben Davis had been more or less closely in touch during twenty years of slavery and fifteen years of freedom. In the stolidity with which he received this sentence for a crime which he had not committed, spoke who knows what trait of inherited savagery? For stoicism is a savage virtue.

IV

ONE MORNING IN JUNE, FIVE years later, a black man limped slowly along the old Lumberton plank road; a tall man, whose bowed shoulders made him seem shorter than he was, and a face from which it was difficult to guess his years, for in it the wrinkles and flabbiness of age were found side by side with firm white teeth, and eyes not sunken,—eyes bloodshot, and burning with something, either fever or passion. Though he limped painfully with one foot, the other hit the ground impatiently, like the good horse in a poorly matched team. As he walked along, he was talking to himself:—

"I wonder what dey 'll do w'en I git back? I wonder how Nancy 's s'ported the fambly all dese years? Tuck in washin', I s'ppose,—she was a monst'us good washer an' ironer. I wonder ef de chillun 'll be too proud ter reco'nize deir daddy come back f'um de penetenchy? I 'spec' Billy must be a big boy by dis time. He won' b'lieve his daddy ever stole anything. I 'm gwine ter slip roun' an' s'prise 'em."

Five minutes later a face peered cautiously into the window of what had once been Ben Davis's cabin,—at first an eager face, its coarseness lit up with the fire of hope; a moment later a puzzled face; then an anxious, fearful face as the man stepped away from the window and rapped at the door.

"Is Mis' Davis home?" he asked of the woman who opened the door.

"Mis' Davis don' live here. You er mistook in de house."

"Whose house is dis?"

"It b'longs ter my husban', Mr. Smith,—Primus Smith."

"'Scuse me, but I knowed de house some years ago w'en I wuz here oncet on a visit, an' it b'longed ter a man name' Ben Davis."

"Ben Davis—Ben Davis?—oh yes, I 'member now. Dat wuz de gen'man w'at wuz sent ter de penetenchy fer sump'n er nuther,—sheep-stealin', I b'lieve. Primus," she called, "w'at wuz Ben Davis, w'at useter own dis yer house, sent ter de penetenchy fer?"

"Hoss-stealin'," came back the reply in sleepy accents, from the man seated by the fireplace.

The traveler went on to the next house. A neat-looking yellow woman came to the door when he rattled the gate, and stood looking suspiciously at him.

"W'at you want?" she asked.

"Please, ma'am, will you tell me whether a man name' Ben Davis useter live in dis neighborhood?"

"Useter live in de nex' house; wuz sent ter de penitenchy fer killin' a man."

"Kin yer tell me w'at went wid Mis' Davis?"

"Umph! I 's a 'spectable 'oman, I is, en don' mix wid dem kind er people. She wuz 'n' no better 'n her husban'. She tuk up wid a man dat useter wuk fer Ben, an' dey 're livin' down by de ole wagon-ya'd, where no 'spectable 'oman ever puts her foot."

"An' de chillen?"

"De gal 's dead. Wuz 'n' no better 'n she oughter be'n. She fell in de crick an' got drown'; some folks say she wuz 'n' sober w'en it happen'. De boy tuck atter his pappy. He wuz 'rested las' week fer shootin' a w'ite man, an' wuz lynch' de same night. Dey wa'n't none of 'em no 'count after deir pappy went ter de penitenchy."

"What went wid de proputty?"

"Hit wuz sol' fer de mortgage, er de taxes, er de lawyer, er sump'n,—I don' know w'at. A w'ite man got it."

The man with the bundle went on until he came to a creek that crossed the road. He descended the sloping bank, and, sitting on a stone in the shade of a water-oak, took off his coarse brogans, unwound the rags that served him in lieu of stockings, and laved in the cool water the feet that were chafed with many a weary mile of travel.

After five years of unrequited toil, and unspeakable hardship in convict camps,—five years of slaving by the side of human brutes, and of nightly herding with them in vermin-haunted huts,—Ben Davis had become like them. For a while he had received occasional letters from home, but in the shifting life of the convict camp they had long since ceased to reach him, if indeed they had been written. For a year or two, the consciousness of his innocence had helped to make him resist the debasing influences that surrounded him. The hope of shortening his sentence by good behavior, too, had worked a similar end. But the transfer from one contractor to another, each interested in keeping as long as possible a good worker, had speedily dissipated any such hope. When hope took flight, its place was not long vacant. Despair followed, and black hatred of all mankind, hatred especially of the man to whom he attributed all his misfortunes. One who is suffering unjustly is not apt to indulge in fine abstractions, nor to balance probabilities. By long brooding over his wrongs, his mind became, if not unsettled, at least warped, and he imagined that Colonel Thornton had deliberately set a trap into which he had fallen. The Colonel, he convinced himself, had disapproved of his prosperity, and had schemed to destroy it. He reasoned himself into the belief that he represented in his person the accumulated wrongs of a whole race, and Colonel Thornton the race who had oppressed them. A burning desire for revenge sprang up in him, and he nursed it until his sentence expired and he was set at liberty. What he had learned since reaching home had changed his desire into a deadly purpose.

When he had again bandaged his feet and slipped them into his shoes, he looked around him, and selected a stout sapling from among the undergrowth that covered the bank of the stream. Taking from his pocket a huge clasp-knife, he cut off the length of an ordinary walking stick and trimmed it. The result was an ugly-looking bludgeon, a dangerous weapon when in the grasp of a strong man.

With the stick in his hand, he went on down the road until he approached a large white house standing some distance back from the street. The grounds were filled with a profusion of shrubbery. The negro entered the gate and secreted himself in the bushes, at a point where he could hear any one that might approach.

It was near midday, and he had not eaten. He had walked all night, and had not slept. The hope of meeting his loved ones had been meat and drink and rest for him. But as he sat waiting, outraged nature asserted itself, and he fell asleep, with his head on the rising root of a tree, and his face upturned.

And as he slept, he dreamed of his childhood; of an old black mammy taking care of him in the daytime, and of a younger face, with soft eyes, which bent over him sometimes at night, and a pair of arms which clasped him closely. He dreamed of his past,—of his young wife, of his bright children. Somehow his dreams all ran to pleasant themes for a while.

Then they changed again. He dreamed that he was in the convict camp, and, by an easy transition, that he was in hell, consumed with hunger, burning with thirst. Suddenly the grinning devil who stood over him with a barbed whip faded away, and a little white angel came and handed him a drink of water. As he raised it to his lips the glass slipped, and he struggled back to consciousness.

"Poo' man! Poo' man sick, an' sleepy. Dolly b'ing Powers to cover poo' man up. Poo' man mus' be hungry. Wen Dolly get him covered up, she go b'ing poo' man some cake."

A sweet little child, as beautiful as a cherub escaped from Paradise, was standing over him. At first he scarcely comprehended the words the baby babbled out. But as they became clear to him, a novel feeling crept slowly over his heart. It had been so long since he had heard anything but curses and stern words of command, or the ribald songs of obscene merriment, that the clear tones of this voice from heaven cooled his calloused heart as the water of the brook had soothed his blistered feet. It was so strange, so unwonted a thing, that he lay there with half-closed eyes while the child brought leaves and flowers and laid them on his face and on his breast, and arranged them with little caressing taps.

She moved away, and plucked a flower. And then she spied another farther on, and then another, and, as she gathered them, kept increasing the distance between herself and the man lying there, until she was several rods away.

Ben Davis watched her through eyes over which had come an unfamiliar softness. Under the lingering spell of his dream, her golden hair, which fell in rippling curls, seemed like a halo of purity and innocence and peace, irradiating the atmosphere around her. It is true the thought occurred to Ben, vaguely, that through harm to her he might inflict the greatest punishment upon her father; but the idea came like a dark shape that faded away and vanished into nothingness as soon as it came within the nimbus that surrounded the child's person.

The child was moving on to pluck still another flower, when there came a sound of hoof-beats, and Ben was aware that a horseman, visible through the shrubbery, was coming along the curved path that led from the gate to the house. It must be the man he was waiting for, and now was the time to wreak his vengeance. He sprang to his feet, grasped his club, and stood for a moment irresolute. But either the instinct of the convict, beaten, driven, and debased, or the influence of the child, which was still strong upon him, impelled him, after the first momentary pause, to flee as though seeking safety.

His flight led him toward the little girl, whom he must pass in order to make his escape, and as Colonel Thornton turned the corner of the path he saw a desperate-looking negro, clad in filthy rags, and carrying in his hand a murderous bludgeon, running toward the child, who, startled by the sound of footsteps, had turned and was looking toward the approaching man with wondering eyes. A sickening fear came over the father's heart, and drawing the ever-ready revolver, which according to the Southern custom he carried always upon his person, he fired with unerring aim. Ben Davis ran a few yards farther, faltered, threw out his hands, and fell dead at the child's feet.

Some time, we are told, when the cycle of years has rolled around, there is to be another golden age, when all men will dwell together in love and harmony, and when peace and righteousness shall prevail for a thousand years. God speed the day, and let not the shining thread of hope become so enmeshed in the web of circumstance that we lose sight of it; but give us here and there, and now and then, some little foretaste of this golden age, that we may the more patiently and hopefully await its coming!

Appendix

Three essays on the Color Line:
  What is a White Man? (1889)
  The Future American (1900)
  The Disfranchisement of the Negro (1903)

What is a White Man?

THE FIAT HAVING GONE FORTH from the wise men of the South that the "all-pervading, all-conquering Anglo-Saxon race" must continue forever to exercise exclusive control and direction of the government of this so-called Republic, it becomes important to every citizen who values his birthright to know who are included in this grandiloquent term. It is of course perfectly obvious that the writer or speaker who used this expression—perhaps Mr. Grady of Georgia—did not say what he meant. It is not probable that he meant to exclude from full citizenship the Celts and Teutons and Gauls and Slavs who make up so large a proportion of our population; he hardly meant to exclude the Jews, for even the most ardent fire-eater would hardly venture to advocate the disfranchisement of the thrifty race whose mortgages cover so large a portion of Southern soil. What the eloquent gentleman really meant by this high-sounding phrase was simply the white race; and the substance of the argument of that school of Southern writers to which he belongs, is simply that for the good of the country the Negro should have no voice in directing the government or public policy of the Southern States or of the nation.

But it is evident that where the intermingling of the races has made such progress as it has in this country, the line which separates the races must in many instances have been practically obliterated. And there has arisen in the United States a very large class of the population who are certainly not Negroes in an ethnological sense, and whose children will be no nearer Negroes than themselves. In view, therefore, of the very positive ground taken by the white leaders of the South, where most of these people reside, it becomes in the highest degree important to them to know what race they belong to. It ought to be also a matter of serious concern to the Southern white people; for if their zeal for good government is so great that they contemplate the practical overthrow of the Constitution and laws of the United States to secure it, they ought at least to be sure that no man entitled to it by their own argument, is robbed of a right so precious as that of free citizenship; the "all-pervading, all conquering Anglo-Saxon" ought to set as high a value on American citizenship as the all-conquering Roman placed upon the franchise of his State two thousand years ago. This discussion would of course be of little interest to the genuine Negro, who is entirely outside of the charmed circle, and must content himself with the acquisition of wealth, the pursuit of learning and such other privileges as his "best friends" may find it consistent with the welfare of the nation to allow him; but to every other good citizen the inquiry ought to be a momentous one. What is a white man?

In spite of the virulence and universality of race prejudice in the United States, the human intellect long ago revolted at the manifest absurdity of classifying men fifteen-sixteenths white as black men; and hence there grew up a number of laws in different states of the Union defining the limit which separated the white and colored races, which was, when these laws took their rise and is now to a large extent, the line which separated freedom and opportunity from slavery or hopeless degradation. Some of these laws are of legislative origin; others are judge-made laws, brought out by the exigencies of special cases which came before the courts for determination. Some day they will, perhaps, become mere curiosities of jurisprudence; the "black laws" will be bracketed with the "blue laws," and will be at best but landmarks by which to measure the progress of the nation. But to-day these laws are in active operation, and they are, therefore, worthy of attention; for every good citizen ought to know the law, and, if possible, to respect it; and if not worthy of respect, it should be changed by the authority which enacted it. Whether any of the laws referred to here have been in any manner changed by very recent legislation the writer cannot say, but they are certainly embodied in the latest editions of the revised statutes of the states referred to.

The colored people were divided, in most of the Southern States, into two classes, designated by law as Negroes and mulattoes respectively. The term Negro was used in its ethnological sense, and needed no definition; but the term "mulatto" was held by legislative enactment to embrace all persons of color not Negroes. The words "quadroon" and "mestizo" are employed in some of the law books, tho not defined; but the term "octoroon," as indicating a person having

CHARLES W. CHESNUTT

one-eighth of Negro blood, is not used at all, so far as the writer has been able to observe.

The states vary slightly in regard to what constitutes a mulatto or person of color, and as to what proportion of white blood should be sufficient to remove the disability of color. As a general rule, less than one-fourth of Negro blood left the individual white—in theory; race questions being, however, regulated very differently in practice. In Missouri, by the code of 1855, still in operation, so far as not inconsistent with the Federal Constitution and laws, "any person other than a Negro, any one of whose grandmothers or grandfathers is or shall have been a Negro, tho all of his or her progenitors except those descended from the Negro may have been white persons, shall be deemed a mulatto." Thus the color-line is drawn at one-fourth of Negro blood, and persons with only one-eighth are white.

By the Mississippi code of 1880, the color-line is drawn at one-fourth of Negro blood, all persons having less being theoretically white.

Under the *code noir* of Louisiana, the descendant of a white and a quadroon is white, thus drawing the line at one-eighth of Negro blood. The code of 1876 abolished all distinctions of color; as to whether they have been re-enacted since the Republican Party went out of power in that state the writer is not informed.

Jumping to the extreme North, persons are white within the meaning of the Constitution of Michigan who have less than one-fourth of Negro blood.

In Ohio the rule, as established by numerous decisions of the Supreme Court, was that a preponderance of white blood constituted a person a white man in the eye of the law, and entitled him to the exercise of all the civil rights of a white man. By a retrogressive step the color-line was extended in 1861 in the case of marriage, which by statute was forbidden between a person of pure white blood and one having a visible admixture of African blood. But by act of legislature, passed in the spring of 1887, all laws establishing or permitting distinctions of color were repealed. In many parts of the state these laws were always ignored, and they would doubtless have been repealed long ago but for the sentiment of the southern counties, separated only by the width of the Ohio River from a former slave-holding state. There was a bill introduced in the legislature during the last session to re-enact the "black laws," but it was hopelessly defeated; the member who introduced it evidently mistook his latitude; he ought to be a member of the Georgia legislature.

But the state which, for several reasons, one might expect to have the strictest laws in regard to the relations of the races, has really the loosest. Two extracts from decisions of the Supreme Court of South Carolina will make clear the law of that state in regard to the color line.

The definition of the term mulatto, as understood in this state, seems to be vague, signifying generally a person of mixed white or European and Negro parentage, in whatever proportions the blood of the two races may be mingled in the individual. But it is not invariably applicable to every admixture of African blood with the European, nor is one having all the features of a white to be ranked with the degraded class designated by the laws of this state as persons of color, because of some remote taint of the Negro race. The line of distinction, however, is not ascertained by any rule of law. . . Juries would probably be justified in holding a person to be white in whom the admixture of African blood did not exceed the proportion of one-eighth. But it is in all cases a question for the jury, to be determined by them upon the evidence of features and complexion afforded by inspection, the evidence of reputation as to parentage, and the evidence of the rank and station in society occupied by the party. The only rule which can be laid down by the courts is that where there is a distinct and visible admixture of Negro blood, the individual is to be denominated a mulatto or person of color.

In a later case the court held: "The question whether persons are colored or white, where color or feature are doubtful, is for the jury to decide by reputation, by reception into society, and by their exercise of the privileges of the white man, as well as by admixture of blood."

It is an interesting question why such should have been, and should still be, for that matter, the law of South Carolina, and why there should exist in that state a condition of public opinion which would accept such a law. Perhaps it may be attributed to the fact that the colored population of South Carolina always outnumbered the white population, and the eagerness of the latter to recruit their ranks was sufficient to overcome in some measure their prejudice against the Negro blood. It is certainly true that the color-line is, in practice as in law, more loosely drawn in South Carolina than in any other Southern State, and that no inconsiderable element of the population of that state consists of these legal white persons, who were either born in the state, or, attracted thither by this feature of the laws, have come in from surrounding states, and, forsaking home and kindred, have taken their social position as white people. A reasonable degree of reticence in regard to one's antecedents is, however, usual in such cases.

Before the War the color-line, as fixed by law, regulated in theory the civil and political status of persons of color. What that status was, was expressed in the Dred Scott decision. But since the War, or rather since the enfranchisement of the colored people, these laws have been mainly confined—in theory, be it always remembered—to the regulation of the intercourse of the races in schools and in the marriage relation. The extension of the color-line to places of public entertainment and resort, to inns and public highways, is in most states entirely a matter of custom. A colored man can sue in the courts of any Southern State for the violation of his common-law rights, and recover damages of say fifty cents without costs. A colored minister who sued a Baltimore steamboat company a few weeks ago for refusing him first-class accommodation, he having paid first-class fare, did not even meet with that measure of success; the learned judge, a Federal judge by the way, held that the plaintiff's rights had been invaded, and that he had suffered humiliation at the hands of the defendant company, but that "the humiliation was not sufficient to entitle him to damages." And the learned judge dismissed the action without costs to either party.

Having thus ascertained what constitutes a white man, the good citizen may be curious to know what steps have been taken to preserve the purity of the white race. Nature, by some unaccountable oversight having to some extent neglected a matter so important to the future prosperity and progress of mankind. The marriage laws referred to here are in active operation, and cases under them are by no means infrequent. Indeed, instead of being behind the age, the marriage laws in the Southern States are in advance of public opinion; for very rarely will a Southern community stop to figure on the pedigree of the contracting parties to a marriage where one is white and the other is known to have any strain of Negro blood.

In Virginia, under the title "Offenses against Morality," the law provides that "any white person who shall intermarry with a Negro shall be confined in jail not more than one year and fined not exceeding one hundred dollars." In a marginal note on the statute-book, attention is called to the fact that "a similar penalty is not imposed on the Negro"—a stretch of magnanimity to which the laws of other states are strangers. A person who performs the ceremony of marriage in such a case is fined two hundred dollars, one-half of which goes to the informer.

In Maryland, a minister who performs the ceremony of marriage between a Negro and a white person is liable to a fine of one hundred dollars.

In Mississippi, code of 1880, it is provided that "the marriage of a white person to a Negro or mulatto or person who shall have one-fourth or more of Negro blood, shall be unlawful"; and as this prohibition does not seem sufficiently emphatic, it is further declared to be "incestuous and void," and is punished by the same penalty prescribed for marriage within the forbidden degrees of consanguinity.

But it is Georgia, the *alma genetrix* of the chain-gang, which merits the questionable distinction of having the harshest set of color laws. By the law of Georgia the term "person of color" is defined to mean "all such as have an admixture of Negro blood, and the term 'Negro,' includes mulattoes."

This definition is perhaps restricted somewhat by another provision, by which "all Negroes, mestizoes, and their descendants, having one-eighth of Negro or mulatto blood in their veins, shall be known in this State as persons of color." A colored minister is permitted to perform the ceremony of marriage between colored persons only, tho white ministers are not forbidden to join persons of color in wedlock. It is further provided that "the marriage relation between white persons and persons of African descent is forever prohibited, and such marriages shall be null and void." This is a very sweeping provision; it will be noticed that the term "persons of color," previously defined, is not employed, the expression "persons of African descent" being used instead. A court which was so inclined would find no difficulty in extending this provision of the law to the remotest strain of African blood. The marriage relation is forever prohibited. Forever is a long time. There is a colored woman in Georgia said to be worth $300,000—an immense fortune in the poverty stricken South. With a few hundred such women in that state, possessing a fair degree of good looks, the color-line would shrivel up like a scroll in the heat of competition for their hands in marriage. The penalty for the violation of the law against intermarriage is the same sought to be imposed by the defunct Glenn Bill for violation of its provisions; i.e., a fine not to exceed one thousand dollars, and imprisonment not to exceed six months, or twelve months in the chain-gang.

CHARLES W. CHESNUTT

Whatever the wisdom or justice of these laws, there is one objection to them which is not given sufficient prominence in the consideration of the subject, even where it is discussed at all; they make mixed blood a *prima-facie* proof of illegitimacy. It is a fact that at present, in the United States, a colored man or woman whose complexion is white or nearly white is presumed, in the absence of any knowledge of his or her antecedents, to be the offspring of a union not sanctified by law. And by a curious but not uncommon process, such persons are not held in the same low estimation as white people in the same position. The sins of their fathers are not visited upon the children, in that regard at least; and their mothers' lapses from virtue are regarded either as misfortunes or as faults excusable under the circumstances. But in spite of all this, illegitimacy is not a desirable distinction, and is likely to become less so as these people of mixed blood advance in wealth and social standing. This presumption of illegitimacy was once, perhaps, true of the majority of such persons; but the times have changed. More than half of the colored people of the United States are of mixed blood; they marry and are given in marriage, and they beget children of complexions similar to their own. Whether or not, therefore, laws which stamp these children as illegitimate, and which by indirection establish a lower standard of morality for a large part of the population than the remaining part is judged by, are wise laws; and whether or not the purity of the white race could not be as well preserved by the exercise of virtue, and the operation of those natural laws which are so often quoted by Southern writers as the justification of all sorts of Southern "policies"—are questions which the good citizen may at least turn over in his mind occasionally, pending the settlement of other complications which have grown out of the presence of the Negro on this continent.

Independent, May 30, 1889

The Future American

What the Race is Likely to become in the Process of Time

THE FUTURE AMERICAN RACE IS a popular theme for essayists, and has been much discussed. Most expressions upon the subject, however, have been characterized by a conscious or unconscious evasion of some of the main elements of the problem involved in the formation of a future American race, or, to put it perhaps more correctly, a future ethnic type that shall inhabit the northern part of the western continent. Some of these obvious omissions will be touched upon in these articles; and if the writer has any preconceived opinions that would affect his judgment, they are at least not the hackneyed prejudices of the past—if they lead to false conclusions, they at least furnish a new point of view, from which, taken with other widely differing views, the judicious reader may establish a parallax that will enable him to approximate the truth.

The popular theory is that the future American race will consist of a harmonious fusion of the various European elements which now make up our heterogeneous population. The result is to be something infinitely superior to the best of the component elements. This perfection of type—no good American could for a moment doubt that it will be as perfect as everything else American—is to be brought about by a combination of all the best characteristics of the different European races, and the elimination, by some strange alchemy, of all their undesirable traits—for even a good American will admit that European races, now and then, have some undesirable traits when they first come over. It is a beautiful, a hopeful, and to the eye of faith, a thrilling prospect. The defect of the argument, however, lies in the incompleteness of the premises, and its obliviousness of certain facts of human nature and human history.

Before putting forward any theory upon the subject, it may be well enough to remark that recent scientific research has swept away many hoary anthropological fallacies. It has been demonstrated that the shape or size of the head has little or nothing to do with the civilization or average intelligence of a race; that language, so recently lauded as an infallible test of racial origin is of absolutely no value in this connection, its distribution being dependent upon other conditions than race. Even color, upon which the social structure of the United States is so largely based, has been proved no test of race. The conception of a pure Aryan, Indo-European race has been abandoned in scientific circles, and the secret of the progress of Europe has been found in racial heterogeneity, rather than in racial purity. The theory that the Jews are a pure race has been exploded, and their peculiar type explained upon a different and much more satisfactory hypothesis. To illustrate the change of opinion and the growth of liberality in scientific circles, imagine the reception which would have been accorded to this proposition, if laid down by an American writer fifty or sixty years ago: "The European

CHARLES W. CHESNUTT

races, as a whole, show signs of a secondary or derived origin; certain characteristics, especially the texture of the hair, lead us to class them as intermediate between the extreme primary types of the Asiatic and Negro races respectively." This is put forward by the author, not as a mere hypothesis, but as a proposition fairly susceptible of proof, and is supported by an elaborate argument based upon microscopical comparisons, to which numerous authorities are cited. If this fact be borne in mind it will simplify in some degree our conception of a future American ethnic type.

By modern research the unity of the human race has been proved (if it needed any proof to the careful or fair-minded observer), and the differentiation of races by selection and environment has been so stated as to prove itself. Greater emphasis has been placed upon environment as a factor in ethnic development, and what has been called "the vulgar theory of race," as accounting for progress and culture, has been relegated to the limbo of exploded dogmas. One of the most perspicuous and forceful presentations of these modern conclusions of anthropology is found in the volume above quoted, a book which owes its origin to a Boston scholar.

Proceeding then upon the firm basis laid down by science and the historic parallel, it ought to be quite clear that the future American race—the future American ethnic type—will be formed of a mingling, in a yet to be ascertained proportion, of the various racial varieties which make up the present population of the United States; or, to extend the area a little farther, of the various peoples of the northern hemisphere of the western continent; for, if certain recent tendencies are an index of the future it is not safe to fix the boundaries of the future United States anywhere short of the Arctic Ocean on the north and the Isthmus of Panama on the south. But, even with the continuance of the present political divisions, conditions of trade and ease of travel are likely to gradually assimilate to one type all the countries of the hemisphere. Assuming that the country is so well settled that no great disturbance of ratios is likely to result from immigration, or any serious conflict of races, we may safely build our theory of a future American race upon the present population of the country. I use the word "race" here in its popular sense—that of a people who look substantially alike, and are moulded by the same culture and dominated by the same ideals.

By the eleventh census, the ratios of which will probably not be changed materially by the census now under way, the total population of the United States was about 65,000,000, of which about seven million were black and colored, and something over 200,000 were of Indian blood. It is then in the three broad types—white, black and Indian—that the future American race will find the material for its formation. Any dream of a pure white race, of the Anglo-Saxon type, for the United States, may as well be abandoned as impossible, even if desirable. That such future race will be predominantly white may well be granted—unless climate in the course of time should modify existing types; that it will call itself white is reasonably sure; that it will conform closely to the white type is likely; but that it will have absorbed and assimilated the blood of the other two races mentioned is as certain as the operation of any law well can be that deals with so uncertain a quantity as the human race.

There are no natural obstacles to such an amalgamation. The unity of the race is not only conceded but demonstrated by actual crossing. Any theory of sterility due to race crossing may as well be abandoned; it is founded mainly on prejudice and cannot be proved by the facts. If it come from Northern or European sources, it is likely to be weakened by lack of knowledge; if from Southern sources, it is sure to be colored by prejudices. My own observation is that in a majority of cases people of mixed blood are very prolific and very long-lived. The admixture of races in the United States has never taken place under conditions likely to produce the best results but there have nevertheless been enough conspicuous instances to the contrary in this country, to say nothing of a long and honorable list in other lands, to disprove the theory that people of mixed blood, other things being equal, are less virile, prolific or able than those of purer strains. But whether this be true or not is apart from this argument. Admitting that races may mix, and that they are thrown together under conditions which permit their admixture, the controlling motive will be not abstract considerations with regard to a remote posterity, but present interest and inclination.

The Indian element in the United States proper is so small proportionally—about one in three hundred—and the conditions for its amalgamation so favorable, that it would of itself require scarcely any consideration in this argument. There is no prejudice against the Indian blood, in solution. A half or quarter-breed, removed from the tribal environment, is freely received among white people. After the second or third remove he may even boast of his Indian descent;

it gives him a sort of distinction, and involves no social disability. The distribution of the Indian race, however, tends to make the question largely a local one, and the survival of tribal relation may postpone the results for some little time. It will be, however, the fault of the United States Indian himself if he be not speedily amalgamated with the white population.

The Indian element, however, looms up larger when we include Mexico and Central America in our fields of discussion. By the census of Mexico just completed, over eighty per cent of the population is composed of mixed and Indian races. The remainder is presumably of pure Spanish, or European blood, with a dash of Negro along the coast. The population is something over twelve millions, thus adding nine millions of Indians and Mestizos to be taken into account. Add several millions of similar descent in Central America, a million in Porto Rico, who are said to have an aboriginal strain, and it may safely be figured that the Indian element will be quite considerable in the future American race. Its amalgamation will involve no great difficulty, however; it has been going on peacefully in the countries south of us for several centuries, and is likely to continue along similar lines. The peculiar disposition of the American to overlook mixed blood in a foreigner will simplify the gradual absorption of these Southern races.

The real problem, then, the only hard problem in connection with the future American race, lies in the Negro element of our population. As I have said before, I believe it is destined to play its part in the formation of this new type. The process by which this will take place will be no sudden and wholesale amalgamation—a thing certainly not to be expected, and hardly to be desired. If it were held desirable, and one could imagine a government sufficiently autocratic to enforce its behests, it would be no great task to mix the races mechanically, leaving to time merely the fixing of the resultant type.

Let us for curiosity outline the process. To start with, the Negroes are already considerably mixed—many of them in large proportion, and most of them in some degree—and the white people, as I shall endeavor to show later on, are many of them slightly mixed with the Negro. But we will assume, for the sake of the argument, that the two races are absolutely pure. We will assume, too, that the laws of the whole country were as favorable to this amalgamation as the laws of most Southern States are at present against it; i.e., that it were made a misdemeanor for two white or two colored persons to marry, so long as it was possible to obtain a mate of the other race—this would be even more favorable than the Southern rule, which makes no such exception. Taking the population as one-eighth Negro, this eighth, married to an equal number of whites, would give in the next generation a population of which one-fourth would be mulattoes. Mating these in turn with white persons, the next generation would be composed one-half of quadroons, or persons one-fourth Negro. In the third generation, applying the same rule, the entire population would be composed of octoroons, or persons only one-eighth Negro, who would probably call themselves white, if by this time there remained any particular advantage in being so considered. Thus in three generations the pure whites would be entirely eliminated, and there would be no perceptible trace of the blacks left.

The mechanical mixture would be complete; as it would probably be put, the white race would have absorbed the black. There would be no inferior race to domineer over; there would be no superior race to oppress those who differed from them in racial externals. The inevitable social struggle, which in one form or another, seems to be one of the conditions of progress, would proceed along other lines than those of race. If now and then, for a few generations, an occasional trace of the black ancestor should crop out, no one would care, for all would be tarred with the same stick. This is already the case in South America, parts of Mexico and to a large extent in the West Indies. From a Negroid nation, which ours is already, we would have become a composite and homogeneous people, and the elements of racial discord which have troubled our civil life so gravely and still threaten our free institutions, would have been entirely eliminated.

But this will never happen. The same result will be brought about slowly and obscurely, and, if the processes of nature are not too violently interrupted by the hand of man, in such a manner as to produce the best results with the least disturbance of natural laws. In another article I shall endeavor to show that this process has been taking place with greater rapidity than is generally supposed, and that the results have been such as to encourage the belief that the formation of a uniform type out of our present racial elements will take place within a measurably near period.

Boston Evening Transcript, August 18, 1900

CHARLES W. CHESNUTT

A Stream of Dark Blood in the Veins of the Southern Whites

I HAVE SAID THAT THE formation of the new American race type will take place slowly and obscurely for some time to come, after the manner of all healthy changes in nature. I may go further and say that this process has already been going on ever since the various races in the Western world have been brought into juxtaposition. Slavery was a rich soil for the production of a mixed race, and one need only read the literature and laws of the past two generations to see how steadily, albeit slowly and insidiously, the stream of dark blood has insinuated itself into the veins of the dominant, or, as a Southern critic recently described it in a paragraph that came under my eye, the "domineering" race. The Creole stories of Mr. Cable and other writers were not mere figments of the imagination; the beautiful octoroon was a corporeal fact; it is more than likely that she had brothers of the same complexion, though curiously enough the male octoroon has cut no figure in fiction, except in the case of the melancholy Honoré Grandissime, f.m.c; and that she and her brothers often crossed the invisible but rigid color line was an historical fact that only an ostrich-like prejudice could deny.

Grace King's "Story of New Orleans" makes the significant statement that the quadroon women of that city preferred white fathers for their children, in order that these latter might become white and thereby be qualified to enter the world of opportunity. More than one of the best families of Louisiana has a dark ancestral strain. A conspicuous American family of Southwestern extraction, which recently contributed a party to a brilliant international marriage, is known, by the well-informed, to be just exactly five generations removed from a Negro ancestor. One member of this family, a distinguished society leader, has been known, upon occasion, when some question of the rights or privileges of the colored race came up, to show a very noble sympathy for her distant kinsmen. If American prejudice permitted her and others to speak freely of her pedigree, what a tower of strength her name and influence would be to a despised and struggling race!

A distinguished American man of letters, now resident in Europe, who spent many years in North Carolina, has said to the writer that he had noted, in the course of a long life, at least a thousand instances of white persons known or suspected to possess a strain of Negro blood. An amusing instance of this sort occurred a year or two ago. It was announced through the newspapers, whose omniscience of course no one would question, that a certain great merchant of Chicago was a mulatto. This gentleman had a large dry goods trade in the South, notably in Texas. Shortly after the publication of the item reflecting on the immaculateness of the merchant's descent, there appeared in the Texas newspapers, among the advertising matter, a statement from the Chicago merchant characterizing the rumor as a malicious falsehood, concocted by his rivals in business, and incidentally calling attention to the excellent bargains offered to retailers and jobbers at his great emporium. A counter-illustration is found in the case of a certain bishop, recently elected, of the African Methodist Episcopal Church, who is accused of being a white man. A colored editor who possesses the saving grace of humor, along with other talents of a high order, gravely observed, in discussing this rumor, that "the poor man could not help it, even if he were white, and that a fact for which he was in no wise responsible should not be allowed to stand in the way of his advancement."

During a residence in North Carolina in my youth and early manhood I noted many curious phases of the race problem. I have in mind a family of three sisters so aggressively white that the old popular Southern legend that they were the unacknowledged children of white parents was current concerning them. There was absolutely not the slightest earmark of the Negro about them. It may be stated here, as another race fallacy, that the "telltale dark mark at the root of the nails," supposed to be an infallible test of Negro blood, is a delusion and a snare, and of no value whatever as a test of race. It belongs with the grewsome superstition that a woman apparently white may give birth to a coal-black child by a white father. Another instance that came under my eye was that of a very beautiful girl with soft, wavy brown hair, who is now living in a Far Western State as the wife of a white husband. A typical case was that of a family in which the tradition of Negro origin had persisted long after all trace of it had disappeared. The family took its origin from a white ancestress, and had consequently been free for several generations. The father of the first colored child, counting the family in the female line— the only way it could be counted—was a mulatto. A second infusion of white blood, this time on the paternal side, resulted in offspring not distinguishable from pure white. One child of this generation emigrated to what was then the Far West, married a white woman and reared a large family, whose descendants, now in the fourth or fifth remove from the Negro, are in all probability wholly unaware of their origin. A sister

CHARLES W. CHESNUTT

of this pioneer emigrant remained in the place of her birth and formed an irregular union with a white man of means, with whom she lived for many years and for whom she bore a large number of children, who became about evenly divided between white and colored, fixing their status by the marriages they made. One of the daughters, for instance, married a white man and reared in a neighboring county a family of white children, who, in all probability, were as active as any one else in the recent ferocious red-shirt campaign to disfranchise the Negroes.

In this same town there was stationed once, before the war, at the Federal arsenal there located, an officer who fell in love with a "white Negro" girl, as our Southern friends impartially dub them. This officer subsequently left the army, and carried away with him to the North the whole family of his inamorata. He married the woman, and their descendants, who live in a large Western city, are not known at all as persons of color, and show no trace of their dark origin.

Two notable bishops of the Roman Catholic communion in the United States are known to be the sons of a slave mother and a white father, who, departing from the usual American rule, gave his sons freedom, education and a chance in life, instead of sending them to the auction block. Colonel T.W. Higginson, in his *Cheerful Yesterdays*, relates the story of a white colored woman whom he assisted in her escape from slavery or its consequences, who married a white man in the vicinity of Boston and lost her identity with the colored race. How many others there must be who know of similar instances! Grace King, in her "Story of New Orleans," to which I have referred, in speaking of a Louisiana law which required the public records, when dealing with persons of color, always to specify the fact of color, in order, so far had the admixture of races gone, to distinguish them from whites, says: "But the officers of the law could be bribed, and the qualification once dropped acted, inversely, as a patent of pure blood."

A certain well-known Shakspearean actress has a strain of Negro blood, and a popular leading man under a well-known manager is similarly gifted. It would be interesting to give their names, but would probably only injure them. If they could themselves speak of their origin, without any unpleasant consequences, it would be a handsome thing for the colored race. That they do not is no reproach to them; they are white to all intents and purposes, even by the curious laws of the curious States from which they derived their origin, and are in all conscience entitled to any advantage accompanying this status.

Anyone at all familiar with the hopes and aspirations of the colored race, as expressed, for instance, in their prolific newspaper literature, must have perceived the wonderful inspiration which they have drawn from the career of a few distinguished Europeans of partial Negro ancestry, who have felt no call, by way of social prejudice, to deny or conceal their origin, or to refuse their sympathy to those who need it so much. Pushkin, the Russian Shakspeare, had a black ancestor. One of the chief editors of the London *Times*, who died a few years ago, was a West Indian colored man, who had no interest in concealing the fact. One of the generals of the British army is similarly favored, although the fact is not often referred to. General Alfred Dodds, the ranking general of the French army, now in command in China, is a quadroon. The poet, Robert Browning, was of West Indian origin, and some of his intimate personal friends maintained and proved to their own satisfaction that he was partly of Negro descent. Mr. Browning always said that he did not know; that there was no family tradition to that effect; but if it could be demonstrated he would admit it freely enough, if it would reflect any credit upon a race who needed it so badly.

The most conspicuous of the Eurafricans (to coin a word) were the Dumas family, who were distinguished for three generations. The mulatto, General Dumas, won distinction in the wars under the Revolution. His son, the famous Alexandre Dumas *père*, has delighted several generations with his novels, and founded a school of fiction. His son, Alexandre *fils*, novelist and dramatist, was as supreme in his own line as his father had been in his. Old Alexandre gives his pedigree in detail in his memoirs; and the Negro origin of the family is set out in every encyclopaedia. Nevertheless, in a literary magazine of recent date, published in New York, it was gravely stated by a writer that "there was a rumor, probably not well founded, that the author of Monte-Cristo had a very distant strain of Negro blood." If this had been written with reference to some living American of obscure origin, its point might be appreciated; but such extreme delicacy in stating so widely known a fact appeals to one's sense of humor.

These European gentlemen could be outspoken about their origin, because it carried with it no social stigma or disability whatever. When such a state of public opinion exists in the United States, there may be a surprising revision of pedigrees!

A little incident that occurred not long ago near Boston will illustrate the complexity of these race relations. Three light-colored

CHARLES W. CHESNUTT

men, brothers, by the name, we will say, of Green, living in a Boston suburb, married respectively a white, a brown and a black woman. The children with the white mother became known as white, and associated with white people. The others were frankly colored. By a not unlikely coincidence, in the course of time the children of the three families found themselves in the same public school. Curiously enough, one afternoon the three sets of Green children—the white Greens, the brown Greens and the black Greens—were detained after school, and were all directed to report to a certain schoolroom, where they were assigned certain tasks at the blackboards about the large room. Still more curiously, most of the teachers of the school happened to have business in this particular room on that particular afternoon, and all of them seemed greatly interested in the Green children.

"Well, well, did you ever! Just think of it! And they are all first cousins!" was remarked audibly.

The children were small, but they lived in Boston, and were, of course, as became Boston children, preternaturally intelligent for their years. They reported to their parents the incident and a number of remarks of a similar tenor to the one above quoted. The result was a complaint to the school authorities, and a reprimand to several teachers. A curious feature of the affair lay in the source from which the complaint emanated. One might suppose it to have come from the white Greens; but no, they were willing that the incident should pass unnoticed and be promptly forgotten; publicity would only advertise a fact which would work to their social injury. The dark Greens rather enjoyed the affair; they had nothing to lose; they had no objections to being known as the cousins of the others, and experienced a certain not unnatural pleasure in their discomfiture. The complaint came from the brown Greens. The reader can figure out the psychology of it for himself.

A more certain proof of the fact that Negro blood is widely distributed among the white people may be found in the laws and judicial decisions of the various States. Laws, as a rule, are not made until demanded by a sufficient number of specific cases to call for a general rule; and judicial decisions of course are never announced except as the result of litigation over contested facts. There is no better index of the character and genius of a people than their laws.

In North Carolina, marriage between white persons and free persons of color was lawful until 1830. By the Missouri code of 1855, the color line was drawn at one-fourth of Negro blood, and persons of only one-eighth were legally white. The same rule was laid down by the Mississippi code of 1880. Under the old code noir of Louisiana, the descendant of a white and a quadroon was white. Under these laws many persons currently known as "colored," or, more recently as "Negro," would be legally white if they chose to claim and exercise the privilege. In Ohio, before the Civil War, a person more than half-white was legally entitled to all the rights of a white man. In South Carolina, the line of cleavage was left somewhat indefinite; the color line was drawn tentatively at one-fourth of Negro blood, but this was not held conclusive.

"The term 'mulatto'," said the Supreme Court of that State in a reported case, "is not invariably applicable to every admixture of African blood with the European, nor is one having all the features of a white to be ranked with the degraded class designated by the laws of the State as persons of color, because of some remote taint of the Negro race. . . The question whether persons are colored or white, where color or feature is doubtful, is for the jury to determine by reputation, by reception into society, and by their exercises of the privileges of a white man, as well as by admixture of blood."

It is well known that this liberality of view grew out of widespread conditions in the State, which these decisions in their turn tended to emphasize. They were probably due to the large preponderance of colored people in the State, which rendered the whites the more willing to augment their own number. There are many interesting color-line decisions in the reports of the Southern courts, which space will not permit the mention of.

In another article I shall consider certain conditions which retard the development of the future American race type which I have suggested, as well as certain other tendencies which are likely to promote it.

Boston Evening Transcript, August 25, 1900

A Complete Race-Amalgamation Likely to Occur

I HAVE ENDEAVORED IN TWO former letters to set out the reasons why it seems likely that the future American ethnic type will be formed by a fusion of all the various races now peopling this continent, and to show that this process has been under way, slowly but surely, like all evolutionary movements, for several hundred years. I wish now to

CHARLES W. CHESNUTT

consider some of the conditions which will retard this fusion, as well as certain other facts which tend to promote it.

The Indian phase of the problem, so far at least as the United States is concerned, has been practically disposed of in what has already been said. The absorption of the Indians will be delayed so long as the tribal relations continue, and so long as the Indians are treated as wards of the Government, instead of being given their rights once for all, and placed upon the footing of other citizens. It is presumed that this will come about as the wilder Indians are educated and by the development of the country brought into closer contact with civilization, which must happen before a very great while. As has been stated, there is no very strong prejudice against the Indian blood; a well-stocked farm or a comfortable fortune will secure a white husband for a comely Indian girl any day, with some latitude, and there is no evidence of any such strong race instinct or organization as will make the Indians of the future wish to perpetuate themselves as a small and insignificant class in a great population, thus emphasizing distinctions which would be overlooked in the case of the individual.

The Indian will fade into the white population as soon as he chooses, and in the United States proper the slender Indian strain will ere long leave no trace discoverable by anyone but the anthropological expert. In New Mexico and Central America, on the contrary, the chances seem to be that the Indian will first absorb the non-indigenous elements, unless, which is not unlikely, European immigration shall increase the white contingent.

The Negro element remains, then, the only one which seems likely to present any difficulty of assimilation. The main obstacle that retards the absorption of the Negro into the general population is the apparently intense prejudice against color which prevails in the United States. This prejudice loses much of its importance, however, when it is borne in mind that it is almost purely local and does not exist in quite the same form anywhere else in the world, except among the Boers of South Africa, where it prevails in an even more aggravated form; and, as I shall endeavor to show, this prejudice in the United States is more apparent than real, and is a caste prejudice which is merely accentuated by differences of race. At present, however, I wish to consider it merely as a deterrent to amalgamation.

This prejudice finds forcible expression in the laws which prevail in all the Southern States, without exception, forbidding the intermarriage of white persons and persons of color—these last being generally defined within certain degrees. While it is evident that such laws alone will not prevent the intermingling of races, which goes merrily on in spite of them, it is equally apparent that this placing of mixed marriages beyond the pale of the law is a powerful deterrent to any honest or dignified amalgamation. Add to this legal restriction, which is enforced by severe penalties, the social odium accruing to the white party to such a union, and it may safely be predicted that so long as present conditions prevail in the South, there will be little marrying or giving in marriage between persons of different race. So ferocious is this sentiment against intermarriage, that in a recent Missouri case, where a colored man ran away with and married a young white woman, the man was pursued by a "posse"—a word which is rapidly being debased from its proper meaning by its use in the attempt to dignify the character of lawless Southern mobs—and shot to death; the woman was tried and convicted of the "crime" of "miscegenation"—another honest word which the South degrades along with the Negro.

Another obstacle to race fusion lies in the drastic and increasing proscriptive legislation by which the South attempts to keep the white and colored races apart in every place where their joint presence might be taken to imply equality; or, to put it more directly, the persistent effort to degrade the Negro to a distinctly and permanently inferior caste. This is undertaken by means of separate schools, separate railroad and street cars, political disfranchisement, debasing and abhorrent prison systems, and an unflagging campaign of calumny, by which the vices and shortcomings of the Negroes are grossly magnified and their virtues practically lost sight of. The popular argument that the Negro ought to develop his own civilization, and has no right to share in that of the white race, unless by favor, comes with poor grace from those who are forcing their civilization upon others at the cannon's mouth; it is, moreover, uncandid and unfair. The white people of the present generation did not make their civilization; they inherited it ready-made, and much of the wealth which is so strong a factor in their power was created by the unpaid labor of the colored people. The present generation has, however, brought to a high state of development one distinctively American institution, for which it is entitled to such credit as it may wish to claim; I refer to the custom of lynching, with its attendant horrors.

The principal deterrent to race admixture, however, is the low industrial and social efficiency of the colored race. If it be conceded that

CHARLES W. CHESNUTT

these are the result of environment, then their cause is not far to seek, and the cure is also in sight. Their poverty, their ignorance and their servile estate render them as yet largely ineligible for social fusion with a race whose pride is fed not only by the record of its achievements but by a constant comparison with a less developed and less fortunate race, which it has held so long in subjection.

The forces that tend to the future absorption of the black race are, however, vastly stronger than those arrayed against it. As experience has demonstrated, slavery was favorable to the mixing of races. The growth, under healthy civil conditions, of a large and self-respecting colored citizenship would doubtless tend to lessen the clandestine association of the two races; but the effort to degrade the Negro may result, if successful, in a partial restoration of the old status. But, assuming that the present anti-Negro legislation is but a temporary reaction, then the steady progress of the colored race in wealth and culture and social efficiency will, in the course of time, materially soften the asperities of racial prejudice and permit them to approach the whites more closely, until, in time, the prejudice against intermarriage shall have been overcome by other considerations.

It is safe to say that the possession of a million dollars, with the ability to use it to the best advantage, would throw such a golden glow over a dark complexion as to override anything but a very obdurate prejudice. Mr. Spahr, in his well-studied and impartial book on *America's Working People*, states as his conclusion, after a careful study of conditions in the South, that the most advanced third of the Negroes of that section has already, in one generation of limited opportunity, passed in the race of life the least advanced third of the whites. To pass the next third will prove a more difficult task, no doubt, but the Negroes will have the impetus of their forward movement to push them ahead.

The outbreaks of race prejudice in recent years are the surest evidence of the Negro's progress. No effort is required to keep down a race which manifests no desire nor ability to rise; but with each new forward movement of the colored race it is brought into contact with the whites at some fresh point, which evokes a new manifestation of prejudice until custom has adjusted things to the new condition. When all Negroes were poor and ignorant they could be denied their rights with impunity. As they grow in knowledge and in wealth they become more self-assertive, and make it correspondingly troublesome for those who would ignore their claims. It is much easier, by a supreme effort, as recently attempted with temporary success in North Carolina, to knock the race down and rob it of its rights once for all, than to repeat the process from day to day and with each individual; it saves wear and tear on the conscience, and makes it easy to maintain a superiority which it might in the course of a short time require some little effort to keep up.

This very proscription, however, political and civil at the South, social all over the country, varying somewhat in degree, will, unless very soon relaxed, prove a powerful factor in the mixture of the races. If it is only by becoming white that colored people and their children are to enjoy the rights and dignities of citizenship, they will have every incentive to "lighten the breed," to use a current phrase, that they may claim the white man's privileges as soon as possible. That this motive is already at work may be seen in the enormous extent to which certain "face bleachers" and "hair straighteners" are advertised in the newspapers printed for circulation among the colored people. The most powerful factor in achieving any result is the wish to bring it about. The only thing that ever succeeded in keeping two races separated when living on the same soil—the only true ground of caste—is religion, and as has been alluded to in the case of the Jews, this is only superficially successful. The colored people are the same as the whites in religion; they have the same standards and mediums of culture, the same ideals, and the presence of the successful white race as a constant incentive to their ambition. The ultimate result is not difficult to foresee. The races will be quite as effectively amalgamated by lightening the Negroes as they would be by darkening the whites. It is only a social fiction, indeed, which makes of a person seven-eighths white a Negro; he is really much more a white man.

The hope of the Negro, so far as the field of moral sympathy and support in his aspirations is concerned, lies, as always, chiefly in the North. There the forces which tend to his elevation are, in the main, allowed their natural operation. The exaggerated zeal with which the South is rushing to degrade the Negro is likely to result, as in the case of slavery, in making more friends for him at the North; and if the North shall not see fit to interfere forcibly with Southern legislation, it may at least feel disposed to emphasize, by its own liberality, its disapproval of Southern injustice and barbarity.

An interesting instance of the difference between the North and the South in regard to colored people, may be found in two cases which only last year came up for trial in two adjoining border States. A colored man living in Maryland went over to Washington and married a white woman. The marriage was legal in Washington. When they returned to their Maryland home they were arrested for the crime of "miscegenation"—perhaps it is only a misdemeanor in Maryland—and sentenced to fine and imprisonment, the penalty of extra-judicial death not extending so far North. The same month a couple, one white and one colored, were arrested in New Jersey for living in adultery. They were found guilty by the court, but punishment was withheld upon a promise that they would marry immediately; or, as some cynic would undoubtedly say, the punishment was commuted from imprisonment to matrimony.

The adding to our territories of large areas populated by dark races, some of them already liberally dowered with Negro blood, will enhance the relative importance of the non-Caucasian elements of the population, and largely increase the flow of dark blood toward the white race, until the time shall come when distinctions of color shall lose their importance, which will be but the prelude to a complete racial fusion.

The formation of this future American race is not a pressing problem. Because of the conditions under which it must take place, it is likely to be extremely slow—much slower, indeed, in our temperate climate and highly organized society, than in the American tropics and sub-tropics, where it is already well under way, if not a *fait accompli*. That it must come in the United States, sooner or later, seems to be a foregone conclusion, as the result of natural law—*lex dura, sed tamen lex*—a hard pill, but one which must be swallowed. There can manifestly be no such thing as a peaceful and progressive civilization in a nation divided by two warring races, and homogeneity of type, at least in externals, is a necessary condition of harmonious social progress.

If this, then, must come, the development and progress of all the constituent elements of the future American race is of the utmost importance as bearing upon the quality of the resultant type. The white race is still susceptible of some improvement; and if, in time, the more objectionable Negro traits are eliminated, and his better qualities correspondingly developed, his part in the future American race may well be an important and valuable one.

Boston Evening Transcript, September 1, 1900

THE RIGHT OF AMERICAN CITIZENS of African descent, commonly called Negroes, to vote upon the same terms as other citizens of the United States, is plainly declared and firmly fixed by the Constitution. No such person is called upon to present reasons why he should possess this right: that question is foreclosed by the Constitution. The object of the elective franchise is to give representation. So long as the Constitution retains its present form, any State Constitution, or statute, which seeks, by juggling the ballot, to deny the colored race fair representation, is a clear violation of the fundamental law of the land, and a corresponding injustice to those thus deprived of this right.

For thirty-five years this has been the law. As long as it was measurably respected, the colored people made rapid strides in education, wealth, character and self-respect. This the census proves, all statements to the contrary notwithstanding. A generation has grown to manhood and womanhood under the great, inspiring freedom conferred by the Constitution and protected by the right of suffrage—protected in large degree by the mere naked right, even when its exercise was hindered or denied by unlawful means. They have developed, in every Southern community, good citizens, who, if sustained and encouraged by just laws and liberal institutions, would greatly augment their number with the passing years, and soon wipe out the reproach of ignorance, unthrift, low morals and social inefficiency, thrown at them indiscriminately and therefore unjustly, and made the excuse for the equally undiscriminating contempt of their persons and their rights. They have reduced their illiteracy nearly 50 per cent. Excluded from the institutions of higher learning in their own States, their young men hold their own, and occasionally carry away honors, in the universities of the North. They have accumulated three hundred million dollars worth of real and personal property. Individuals among them have acquired substantial wealth, and several have attained to something like national distinction in art, letters and educational leadership. They are numerously represented in the learned professions. Heavily handicapped, they have made such rapid progress that the suspicion is justified that their advancement, rather than any stagnation or retrogression, is the true secret of the virulent Southern hostility to their rights, which has so influenced Northern opinion that it stands mute, and leaves the colored people, upon whom the North conferred liberty, to the tender mercies of those who have always denied their fitness for it.

It may be said, in passing, that the word "Negro," where used in this paper, is used solely for convenience. By the census of 1890 there were 1,000,000 colored people in the country who were half, or more than half, white, and logically there must be, as in fact there are, so many who share the white blood in some degree, as to justify the assertion that the race problem in the United States concerns the welfare and the status of a mixed race. Their rights are not one whit the more sacred because of this fact; but in an argument where injustice is sought to be excused because of fundamental differences of race, it is well enough to bear in mind that the race whose rights and liberties are endangered all over this country by disfranchisement at the South, are the colored people who live in the United States to-day, and not the lowbrowed, man-eating savage whom the Southern white likes to set upon a block and contrast with Shakespeare and Newton and Washington and Lincoln.

Despite and in defiance of the Federal Constitution, to-day in the six Southern States of Mississippi, Louisiana, Alabama, North Carolina, South Carolina and Virginia, containing an aggregate colored population of about 6,000,000, these have been, to all intents and purposes, denied, so far as the States can effect it, the right to vote. This disfranchisement is accomplished by various methods, devised with much transparent ingenuity, the effort being in each instance to violate the spirit of the Federal Constitution by disfranchising the Negro, while seeming to respect its letter by avoiding the mention of race or color.

These restrictions fall into three groups. The first comprises a property qualification—the ownership of $300 worth or more of real or personal property (Alabama, Louisiana, Virginia and South Carolina); the payment of a poll tax (Mississippi, North Carolina, Virginia); an educational qualification—the ability to read and write (Alabama, Louisiana, North Carolina). Thus far, those who believe in a restricted suffrage everywhere, could perhaps find no reasonable fault with any one of these qualifications, applied either separately or together.

But the Negro has made such progress that these restrictions alone would perhaps not deprive him of effective representation. Hence the second group. This comprises an "understanding" clause—the applicant must be able "to read, or understand when read to him, any clause in the Constitution" (Mississippi), or to read and explain, or to understand and explain when read to him, any section of the Constitution (Virginia); an employment qualification—the voter must be regularly employed in some lawful occupation (Alabama); a character qualification—the voter must be a person of good character and who "understands the duties and obligations of citizens under a republican [!] form of government" (Alabama). The qualifications under the first group it will be seen, are capable of exact demonstration; those under the second group are left to the discretion and judgment of the registering officer—for in most instances these are all requirements for registration, which must precede voting.

But the first group, by its own force, and the second group, under imaginable conditions, might exclude not only the Negro vote, but a large part of the white vote. Hence, the third group, which comprises: a military service qualification—any man who went to war, willingly or unwillingly, in a good cause or a bad, is entitled to register (Ala., Va.); a prescriptive qualification, under which are included all male persons who were entitled to vote on January 1, 1867, at which date the Negro had not yet been given the right to vote; a hereditary qualification (the so-called "grandfather" clause), whereby any son (Va.), or descendant (Ala.), of a soldier, and (N.C.) the descendant of any person who had the right to vote on January 1, 1867, inherits that right. If the voter wish to take advantage of these last provisions, which are in the nature of exceptions to a general rule, he must register within a stated time, whereupon he becomes a member of a privileged class of permanently enrolled voters not subject to any of the other restrictions.

It will be seen that these restrictions are variously combined in the different States, and it is apparent that if combined to their declared end, practically every Negro may, under color of law, be denied the right to vote, and practically every white man accorded that right. The effectiveness of these provisions to exclude the Negro vote is proved by the Alabama registration under the new State Constitution. Out of a total, by the census of 1900, of 181,471 Negro "males of voting age," less than 3,000 are registered; in Montgomery county alone, the seat of the State capital, where there are 7,000 Negro males of voting age, only 47 have been allowed to register, while in several counties not one single Negro is permitted to exercise the franchise.

These methods of disfranchisement have stood such tests as the United States Courts, including the Supreme Court, have thus far seen fit to apply, in such cases as have been before them for adjudication.

CHARLES W. CHESNUTT

These include a case based upon the "understanding" clause of the Mississippi Constitution, in which the Supreme Court held, in effect, that since there was no ambiguity in the language employed and the Negro was not directly named, the Court would not go behind the wording of the Constitution to find a meaning which discriminated against the colored voter; and the recent case of Jackson vs. Giles, brought by a colored citizen of Montgomery, Alabama, in which the Supreme Court confesses itself impotent to provide a remedy for what, by inference, it acknowledges may be a "great political wrong," carefully avoiding, however, to state that it is a wrong, although the vital prayer of the petition was for a decision upon this very point.

Now, what is the effect of this wholesale disfranchisement of colored men, upon their citizenship? The value of food to the human organism is not measured by the pains of an occasional surfeit, but by the effect of its entire deprivation. Whether a class of citizens should vote, even if not always wisely—what class does?—may best be determined by considering their condition when they are without the right to vote.

The colored people are left, in the States where they have been disfranchised, absolutely without representation, direct or indirect, in any law-making body, in any court of justice, in any branch of government— for the feeble remnant of voters left by law is so inconsiderable as to be without a shadow of power. Constituting one-eighth of the population of the whole country, two-fifths of the whole Southern people, and a majority in several States, they are not able, because disfranchised where most numerous, to send one representative to the Congress, which, by the decision in the Alabama case, is held by the Supreme Court to be the only body, outside of the State itself, competent to give relief from a great political wrong. By former decisions of the same tribunal, even Congress is impotent to protect their civil rights, the Fourteenth Amendment having long since, by the consent of the same Court, been in many respects as completely nullified as the Fifteenth Amendment is now sought to be. They have no direct representation in any Southern legislature, and no voice in determining the choice of white men who might be friendly to their rights. Nor are they able to influence the election of judges or other public officials, to whom are entrusted the protection of their lives, their liberties and their property. No judge is rendered careful, no sheriff diligent, for fear that he may offend a black constituency; the contrary is most lamentably true; day after day the catalogue of lynchings and anti-Negro riots upon every imaginable pretext, grows longer and more appalling. The country stands face to face with the revival of slavery; at the moment of this writing a federal grand jury in Alabama is uncovering a system of peonage established under cover of law.

Under the Southern program it is sought to exclude colored men from every grade of the public service; not only from the higher administrative functions, to which few of them would in any event, for a long time aspire, but from the lowest as well. A Negro may not be a constable or a policeman. He is subjected by law to many degrading discriminations. He is required to be separated from white people on railroads and street cars, and, by custom, debarred from inns and places of public entertainment. His equal right to a free public education is constantly threatened and is nowhere equitably recognized. In Georgia, as has been shown by Dr. Du Bois, where the law provides for a pro rata distribution of the public school fund between the races, and where the colored school population is 48 per cent, of the total, the amount of the fund devoted to their schools is only 20 per cent. In New Orleans, with an immense colored population, many of whom are persons of means and culture, all colored public schools above the fifth grade have been abolished.

The Negro is subjected to taxation without representation, which the forefathers of this Republic made the basis of a bloody revolution.

Flushed with their local success, and encouraged by the timidity of the Courts and the indifference of public opinion, the Southern whites have carried their campaign into the national government, with an ominous degree of success. If they shall have their way, no Negro can fill any federal office, or occupy, in the public service, any position that is not menial. This is not an inference, but the openly, passionately avowed sentiment of the white South. The right to employment in the public service is an exceedingly valuable one, for which white men have struggled and fought. A vast army of men are employed in the administration of public affairs. Many avenues of employment are closed to colored men by popular prejudice. If their right to public employment is recognized, and the way to it open through the civil service, or the appointing power, or the suffrages of the people, it will prove, as it has already, a strong incentive to effort and a powerful lever for advancement. Its value to the Negro, like that of the right to vote, may be judged by the eagerness of the whites to deprive him of it.

Not only is the Negro taxed without representation in the States

CHARLES W. CHESNUTT

referred to, but he pays, through the tariff and internal revenue, a tax to a National government whose supreme judicial tribunal declares that it cannot, through the executive arm, enforce its own decrees, and, therefore, refuses to pass upon a question, squarely before it, involving a basic right of citizenship. For the decision of the Supreme Court in the Giles case, if it foreshadows the attitude which the Court will take upon other cases to the same general end which will soon come before it, is scarcely less than a reaffirmation of the Dred Scott decision; it certainly amounts to this—that in spite of the Fifteenth Amendment, colored men in the United States have no political rights which the States are bound to respect. To say this much is to say that all privileges and immunities which Negroes henceforth enjoy, must be by favor of the whites; they are not *rights*. The whites have so declared; they proclaim that the country is theirs, that the Negro should be thankful that he has so much, when so much more might be withheld from him. He stands upon a lower footing than any alien; he has no government to which he may look for protection.

Moreover, the white South sends to Congress, on a basis including the Negro population, a delegation nearly twice as large as it is justly entitled to, and one which may always safely be relied upon to oppose in Congress every measure which seeks to protect the equality, or to enlarge the rights of colored citizens. The grossness of this injustice is all the more apparent since the Supreme Court, in the Alabama case referred to, has declared the legislative and political department of the government to be the only power which can right a political wrong. Under this decision still further attacks upon the liberties of the citizen may be confidently expected. Armed with the Negro's sole weapon of defense, the white South stands ready to smite down his rights. The ballot was first given to the Negro to defend him against this very thing. He needs it now far more than then, and for even stronger reasons. The 9,000,000 free colored people of to day have vastly more to defend than the 3,000,000 hapless blacks who had just emerged from slavery. If there be those who maintain that it was a mistake to give the Negro the ballot at the time and in the manner in which it was given, let them take to heart this reflection: that to deprive him of it to-day, or to so restrict it as to leave him utterly defenseless against the present relentless attitude of the South toward his rights, will prove to be a mistake so much greater than the first, as to be no less than a crime, from which not alone the Southern Negro must suffer, but for which the nation will as surely pay the penalty as it paid for the crime of slavery. Contempt for law is death to a republic, and this one has developed alarming symptoms of the disease.

And now, having thus robbed the Negro of every political and civil *right*, the white South, in palliation of its course, makes a great show of magnanimity in leaving him, as the sole remnant of what he acquired through the Civil War, a very inadequate public school education, which, by the present program, is to be directed mainly towards making him a better agricultural laborer. Even this is put forward as a favor, although the Negro's property is taxed to pay for it, and his labor as well. For it is a well settled principle of political economy, that land and machinery of themselves produce nothing, and that labor indirectly pays its fair proportion of the tax upon the public's wealth. The white South seems to stand to the Negro at present as one, who, having been reluctantly compelled to release another from bondage, sees him stumbling forward and upward, neglected by his friends and scarcely yet conscious of his own strength; seizes him, binds him, and having bereft him of speech, of sight and of manhood, "yokes him with the mule" and exclaims, with a show of virtue which ought to deceive no one: "Behold how good a friend I am of yours! Have I not left you a stomach and a pair of arms, and will I not generously permit you to work for me with the one, that you may thereby gain enough to fill the other? A brain you do not need. We will relieve you of any responsibility that might seem to demand such an organ."

The argument of peace-loving Northern white men and Negro opportunists that the political power of the Negro having long ago been suppressed by unlawful means, his right to vote is a mere paper right, of no real value, and therefore to be lightly yielded for the sake of a hypothetical harmony, is fatally short-sighted. It is precisely the attitude and essentially the argument which would have surrendered to the South in the sixties, and would have left this country to rot in slavery for another generation. White men do not thus argue concerning their own rights. They know too well the value of ideals. Southern white men see too clearly the latent power of these unexercised rights. If the political power of the Negro was a nullity because of his ignorance and lack of leadership, why were they not content to leave it so, with the pleasing assurance that if it ever became effective, it would be because the Negroes had grown fit for its exercise? On the contrary, they have not rested until the possibility of its revival was apparently headed off by new State constitutions. Nor are they satisfied with this. There is no doubt that an effort will be made to secure the repeal of the Fifteenth Amendment, and thus forestall the development of the wealthy and educated Negro, whom the South seems to anticipate as a greater menace than the ignorant ex-slave. However improbable this repeal may seem, it is not a subject to be lightly dismissed; for it is within the power of the white people of the nation to do whatever they wish in the premises—they did it once; they can do it again. The Negro and his friends should see to it that the white majority shall never wish to do anything to his hurt. There still stands, before the Negro-hating whites of the South, the specter of a Supreme Court which will interpret the Constitution to mean what it says, and what those who enacted it meant, and what the nation, which ratified it, understood, and which will find power, in a nation which goes beyond seas to administer the affairs of distant peoples, to enforce its own fundamental laws; the specter, too, of an aroused public opinion which will compel Congress and the Courts to preserve the liberties of the Republic, which are the liberties of the people. To wilfully neglect the suffrage, to hold it lightly, is to tamper with a sacred right; to yield it for anything else whatever is simply suicidal. Dropping the element of race, disfranchisement is no more than to say to the poor and poorly taught, that they must relinquish the right to defend themselves against oppression until they shall have become rich and learned, in competition with those already thus favored and possessing the ballot in addition. This is not the philosophy of history. The growth of liberty has been the constant struggle of the poor against the privileged classes; and the goal of that struggle has ever been the equality of all men before the law. The Negro who would yield this right, deserves to be a slave; he has the servile spirit. The rich and the educated can, by virtue of their influence, command many votes; can find other means of protection; the poor man has but one, he should guard it as a sacred treasure. Long ago, by fair treatment, the white leaders of the South might have bound the Negro to themselves with hoops of steel. They have not chosen to take this course, but by assuming from the beginning an attitude hostile to his rights, have never gained his confidence, and now seek by foul means to destroy where they have never sought by fair means to control.

I have spoken of the effect of disfranchisement upon the colored race; it is to the race as a whole, that the argument of the problem is generally directed. But the unit of society in a republic is the individual, and not the race, the failure to recognize this fact being the fundamental error which has beclouded the whole discussion. The effect of disfranchisement upon the individual is scarcely less disastrous. I do not speak of the moral effect of injustice upon those who suffer from it; I refer rather to the practical consequences which may be appreciated by any mind. No country is free in which the way upward is not open for every man to try, and for every properly qualified man to attain whatever of good the community life may offer. Such a condition does not exist, at the South, even in theory, for any man of color. In no career can such a man compete with white men upon equal terms. He must not only meet the prejudice of the individual, not only the united prejudice of the white community; but lest some one should wish to treat him fairly, he is met at every turn with some legal prohibition which says, "Thou shalt not," or "Thus far shalt thou go and no farther." But the Negro race is viable; it adapts itself readily to circumstances; and being thus adaptable, there is always the temptation to

> "Crook the pregnant hinges of the knee,
> Where thrift may follow fawning."

He who can most skillfully balance himself upon the advancing or receding wave of white opinion concerning his race, is surest of such measure of prosperity as is permitted to men of dark skins. There are Negro teachers in the South—the privilege of teaching in their own schools is the one respectable branch of the public service still left open to them—who, for a grudging appropriation from a Southern legislature, will decry their own race, approve their own degradation, and laud their oppressors. Deprived of the right to vote, and, therefore, of any power to demand what is their due, they feel impelled to buy the tolerance of the whites at any sacrifice. If to live is the first duty of man, as perhaps it is the first instinct, then those who thus stoop to conquer may be right. But is it needful to stoop so low, and if so, where lies the ultimate responsibility for this abasement?

I shall say nothing about the moral effect of disfranchisement upon the white people, or upon the State itself. What slavery made of the Southern whites is a matter of history. The abolition of slavery gave the South an opportunity to emerge from barbarism. Present conditions indicate that the spirit which dominated slavery still curses the fair section over which that institution spread its blight.

CHARLES W. CHESNUTT

And now, is the situation remediless? If not so, where lies the remedy? First let us take up those remedies suggested by the men who approve of disfranchisement, though they may sometimes deplore the method, or regret the necessity.

Time, we are told, heals all diseases, rights all wrongs, and is the only cure for this one. It is a cowardly argument. These people are entitled to their rights to-day, while they are yet alive to enjoy them; and it is poor statesmanship and worse morals to nurse a present evil and thrust it forward upon a future generation for correction. The nation can no more honestly do this than it could thrust back upon a past generation the responsibility for slavery. It had to meet that responsibility; it ought to meet this one.

Education has been put forward as the great corrective—preferably industrial education. The intellect of the whites is to be educated to the point where they will so appreciate the blessings of liberty and equality, as of their own motion to enlarge and defend the Negro's rights. The Negroes, on the other hand, are to be so trained as to make them, not equal with the whites in any way—God save the mark!—this would be unthinkable!—but so useful to the community that the whites will protect them rather than lose their valuable services. Some few enthusiasts go so far as to maintain that by virtue of education the Negro will, in time, become strong enough to protect himself against any aggression of the whites; this, it may be said, is a strictly Northern view.

It is not quite clearly apparent how education alone, in the ordinary meaning of the word, is to solve, in any appreciable time, the problem of the relations of Southern white and black people. The need of education of all kinds for both races is wofully apparent. But men and nations have been free without being learned, and there have been educated slaves. Liberty has been known to languish where culture had reached a very high development. Nations do not first become rich and learned and then free, but the lesson of history has been that they first become free and then rich and learned, and oftentimes fall back into slavery again because of too great wealth, and the resulting luxury and carelessness of civic virtues. The process of education has been going on rapidly in the Southern States since the Civil War, and yet, if we take superficial indications, the rights of the Negroes are at a lower ebb than at any time during the thirty-five years of their freedom, and the race prejudice more intense and uncompromising. It is not apparent that educated Southerners are less rancorous than others in their speech concerning the Negro, or less hostile in their attitude toward his rights. It is their voice alone that we have heard in this discussion; and if, as they state, they are liberal in their views as compared with the more ignorant whites, then God save the Negro!

I was told, in so many words, two years ago, by the Superintendent of Public Schools of a Southern city that "there was no place in the modern world for the Negro, except under the ground." If gentlemen holding such opinions are to instruct the white youth of the South, would it be at all surprising if these, later on, should devote a portion of their leisure to the improvement of civilization by putting under the ground as many of this superfluous race as possible?

The sole excuse made in the South for the prevalent injustice to the Negro is the difference in race, and the inequalities and antipathies resulting therefrom. It has nowhere been declared as a part of the Southern program that the Negro, when educated, is to be given a fair representation in government or an equal opportunity in life; the contrary has been strenuously asserted; education can never make of him anything but a Negro, and, therefore, essentially inferior, and not to be safely trusted with any degree of power. A system of education which would tend to soften the asperities and lessen the inequalities between the races would be of inestimable value. An education which by a rigid separation of the races from the kindergarten to the university, fosters this racial antipathy, and is directed toward emphasizing the superiority of one class and the inferiority of another, might easily have disastrous, rather than beneficial results. It would render the oppressing class more powerful to injure, the oppressed quicker to perceive and keener to resent the injury, without proportionate power of defense. The same assimilative education which is given at the North to all children alike, whereby native and foreign, black and white, are taught side by side in every grade of instruction, and are compelled by the exigencies of discipline to keep their prejudices in abeyance, and are given the opportunity to learn and appreciate one another's good qualities, and to establish friendly relations which may exist throughout life, is absent from the Southern system of education, both of the past and as proposed for the future. Education is in a broad sense a remedy for all social ills; but the disease we have to deal with now is not only constitutional but acute. A wise physician does not simply give a tonic for a diseased limb, or a high fever; the patient might be dead before the constitutional remedy could become effective. The evils of slavery,

CHARLES W. CHESNUTT

its injury to whites and blacks, and to the body politic, were clearly perceived and acknowledged by the educated leaders of the South as far back as the Revolutionary War and the Constitutional Convention, and yet they made no effort to abolish it. Their remedy was the same— time, education, social and economic development;—and yet a bloody war was necessary to destroy slavery and put its spirit temporarily to sleep. When the South and its friends are ready to propose a system of education which will recognize and teach the equality of all men before the law, the potency of education alone to settle the race problem will be more clearly apparent.

At present even good Northern men, who wish to educate the Negroes, feel impelled to buy this privilege from the none too eager white South, by conceding away the civil and political rights of those whom they would benefit. They have, indeed, gone farther than the Southerners themselves in approving the disfranchisement of the colored race. Most Southern men, now that they have carried their point and disfranchised the Negro, are willing to admit, in the language of a recent number of the Charleston *Evening Post*, that "the attitude of the Southern white man toward the Negro is incompatible with the fundamental ideas of the republic." It remained for our Clevelands and Abbotts and Parkhursts to assure them that their unlawful course was right and justifiable, and for the most distinguished Negro leader to declare that "every revised Constitution throughout the Southern States has put a premium upon intelligence, ownership of property, thrift and character." So does every penitentiary sentence put a premium upon good conduct; but it is poor consolation to the one unjustly condemned, to be told that he may shorten his sentence somewhat by good behavior. Dr. Booker T. Washington, whose language is quoted above, has, by his eminent services in the cause of education, won deserved renown. If he has seemed, at times, to those jealous of the best things for their race, to decry the higher education, it can easily be borne in mind that his career is bound up in the success of an industrial school; hence any undue stress which he may put upon that branch of education may safely be ascribed to the natural zeal of the promoter, without detracting in any degree from the essential value of his teachings in favor of manual training, thrift and character-building. But Mr. Washington's prominence as an educational leader, among a race whose prominent leaders are so few, has at times forced him, perhaps reluctantly, to express himself in regard to the political condition of his people, and here his utterances have not always been so wise nor so happy. He has declared himself in favor of a restricted suffrage, which at present means, for his own people, nothing less than complete loss of representation—indeed it is only in that connection that the question has been seriously mooted; and he has advised them to go slow in seeking to enforce their civil and political rights, which, in effect, means silent submission to injustice. Southern white men may applaud this advice as wise, because it fits in with their purposes; but Senator McEnery of Louisiana, in a recent article in the *Independent*, voices the Southern white opinion of such acquiescence when he says: "What other race would have submitted so many years to slavery without complaint? *What other race would have submitted so quietly to disfranchisement?* These facts stamp his [the Negro's] inferiority to the white race." The time to philosophize about the good there is in evil, is not while its correction is still possible, but, if at all, after all hope of correction is past. Until then it calls for nothing but rigorous condemnation. To try to read any good thing into these fraudulent Southern constitutions, or to accept them as an accomplished fact, is to condone a crime against one's race. Those who commit crime should bear the odium. It is not a pleasing spectacle to see the robbed applaud the robber. Silence were better.

It has become fashionable to question the wisdom of the Fifteenth Amendment. I believe it to have been an act of the highest statesmanship, based upon the fundamental idea of this Republic, entirely justified by conditions; experimental in its nature, perhaps, as every new thing must be, but just in principle; a choice between methods, of which it seemed to the great statesmen of that epoch the wisest and the best, and essentially the most just, bearing in mind the interests of the freedmen and the Nation, as well as the feelings of the Southern whites; never fairly tried, and therefore, not yet to be justly condemned. Not one of those who condemn it, has been able, even in the light of subsequent events, to suggest a better method by which the liberty and civil rights of the freedmen and their descendants could have been protected. Its abandonment, as I have shown, leaves this liberty and these rights frankly without any guaranteed protection. All the education which philanthropy or the State could offer as a *substitute* for equality of rights, would be a poor exchange; there is no defensible reason why they should not go hand in hand, each encouraging and strengthening the other. The education which one can demand as a right is likely to do more good than the education for which one must sue as a favor.

The chief argument against Negro suffrage, the insistently proclaimed argument, worn threadbare in Congress, on the platform, in the pulpit, in the press, in poetry, in fiction, in impassioned rhetoric, is the reconstruction period. And yet the evils of that period were due far more to the venality and indifference of white men than to the incapacity of black voters. The revised Southern constitutions adopted under reconstruction reveal a higher statesmanship than any which preceded or have followed them, and prove that the freed voters could as easily have been led into the paths of civic righteousness as into those of misgovernment. Certain it is that under reconstruction the civil and political rights of all men were more secure in those States than they have ever been since. We will hear less of the evils of reconstruction, now that the bugaboo has served its purpose by disfranchising the Negro. It will be laid aside for a time while the nation discusses the political corruption of great cities; the scandalous conditions in Rhode Island; the evils attending reconstruction in the Philippines, and the scandals in the postoffice department—for none of which, by the way, is the Negro charged with any responsibility, and for none of which is the restriction of the suffrage a remedy seriously proposed. Rhode Island is indeed the only Northern State which has a property qualification for the franchise!

There are three tribunals to which the colored people may justly appeal for the protection of their rights: the United States Courts, Congress and public opinion. At present all three seem mainly indifferent to any question of human rights under the Constitution. Indeed, Congress and the Courts merely follow public opinion, seldom lead it. Congress never enacts a measure which is believed to oppose public opinion;—your Congressman keeps his ear to the ground. The high, serene atmosphere of the Courts is not impervious to its voice; they rarely enforce a law contrary to public opinion, even the Supreme Court being able, as Charles Sumner once put it, to find a reason for every decision it may wish to render; or, as experience has shown, a method to evade any question which it cannot decently decide in accordance with public opinion. The art of straddling is not confined to the political arena. The Southern situation has been well described by a colored editor in Richmond: "When we seek relief at the hands of Congress, we are informed that our plea involves a legal question, and we are referred to the Courts. When we appeal to the Courts, we are gravely told that the question is a political one, and that we must go to

Congress. When Congress enacts remedial legislation, our enemies take it to the Supreme Court, which promptly declares it unconstitutional." The Negro might chase his rights round and round this circle until the end of time, without finding any relief.

Yet the Constitution is clear and unequivocal in its terms, and no Supreme Court can indefinitely continue to construe it as meaning anything but what it says. This Court should be bombarded with suits until it makes some definite pronouncement, one way or the other, on the broad question of the constitutionality of the disfranchising Constitutions of the Southern States. The Negro and his friends will then have a clean-cut issue to take to the forum of public opinion, and a distinct ground upon which to demand legislation for the enforcement of the Federal Constitution. The case from Alabama was carried to the Supreme Court expressly to determine the constitutionality of the Alabama Constitution. The Court declared itself without jurisdiction, and in the same breath went into the merits of the case far enough to deny relief, without passing upon the real issue. Had it said, as it might with absolute justice and perfect propriety, that the Alabama Constitution is a bold and impudent violation of the Fifteenth Amendment, the purpose of the lawsuit would have been accomplished and a righteous cause vastly strengthened. But public opinion cannot remain permanently indifferent to so vital a question. The agitation is already on. It is at present largely academic, but is slowly and resistlessly, forcing itself into politics, which is the medium through which republics settle such questions. It cannot much longer be contemptuously or indifferently elbowed aside. The South itself seems bent upon forcing the question to an issue, as, by its arrogant assumptions, it brought on the Civil War. From that section, too, there come now and then, side by side with tales of Southern outrage, excusing voices, which at the same time are accusing voices; which admit that the white South is dealing with the Negro unjustly and unwisely; that the Golden Rule has been forgotten; that the interests of white men alone have been taken into account, and that their true interests as well are being sacrificed. There is a silent white South, uneasy in conscience, darkened in counsel, groping for the light, and willing to do the right. They are as yet a feeble folk, their voices scarcely audible above the clamor of the mob. May their convictions ripen into wisdom, and may their numbers and their courage increase! If the class of Southern white men of whom Judge Jones of Alabama, is so noble a representative, are supported and

CHARLES W. CHESNUTT

encouraged by a righteous public opinion at the North, they may, in time, become the dominant white South, and we may then look for wisdom and justice in the place where, so far as the Negro is concerned, they now seem well-nigh strangers. But even these gentlemen will do well to bear in mind that so long as they discriminate in any way against the Negro's equality of right, so long do they set class against class and open the door to every sort of discrimination, there can be no middle ground between justice and injustice, between the citizen and the serf.

It is not likely that the North, upon the sober second thought, will permit the dearly-bought results of the Civil War to be nullified by any change in the Constitution. So long as the Fifteenth Amendment stands, the *rights* of colored citizens are ultimately secure. There were would-be despots in England after the granting of Magna Charta; but it outlived them all, and the liberties of the English people are secure. There was slavery in this land after the Declaration of Independence, yet the faces of those who love liberty have ever turned to that immortal document. So will the Constitution and its principles outlive the prejudices which would seek to overthrow it.

What colored men of the South can do to secure their citizenship to-day, or in the immediate future, is not very clear. Their utterances on political questions, unless they be to concede away the political rights of their race, or to soothe the consciences of white men by suggesting that the problem is insoluble except by some slow remedial process which will become effectual only in the distant future, are received with scant respect—could scarcely, indeed, be otherwise received, without a voting constituency to back them up,—and must be cautiously made, lest they meet an actively hostile reception. But there are many colored men at the North, where their civil and political rights in the main are respected. There every honest man has a vote, which he may freely cast, and which is reasonably sure to be fairly counted. When this race develops a sufficient power of combination, under adequate leadership,—and there are signs already that this time is near at hand,— the Northern vote can be wielded irresistibly for the defense of the rights of their Southern brethren.

In the meantime the Northern colored men have the right of free speech, and they should never cease to demand their rights, to clamor for them, to guard them jealously, and insistently to invoke law and public sentiment to maintain them. He who would be free must learn to protect his freedom.

Eternal vigilance is the price of liberty. He who would be respected must respect himself. The best friend of the Negro is he who would rather see, within the borders of this republic one million free citizens of that race, equal before the law, than ten million cringing serfs existing by a contemptuous sufferance. A race that is willing to survive upon any other terms is scarcely worthy of consideration.

The direct remedy for the disfranchisement of the Negro lies through political action. One scarcely sees the philosophy of distinguishing between a civil and a political right. But the Supreme Court has recognized this distinction and has designated Congress as the power to right a political wrong. The Fifteenth Amendment gives Congress power to enforce its provisions. The power would seem to be inherent in government itself; but anticipating that the enforcement of the Amendment might involve difficulty, they made the supererogatory declaration. Moreover, they went further, and passed laws by which they provided for such enforcement. These the Supreme Court has so far declared insufficient. It is for Congress to make more laws. It is for colored men and for white men who are not content to see the blood-bought results of the Civil War nullified, to urge and direct public opinion to the point where it will demand stringent legislation to enforce the Fourteenth and Fifteenth Amendments. This demand will rest in law, in morals and in true statesmanship; no difficulties attending it could be worse than the present ignoble attitude of the Nation toward its own laws and its own ideals—without courage to enforce them, without conscience to change them, the United States presents the spectacle of a Nation drifting aimlessly, so far as this vital, National problem is concerned, upon the sea of irresolution, toward the maelstrom of anarchy.

The right of Congress, under the Fourteenth Amendment, to reduce Southern representation can hardly be disputed. But Congress has a simpler and more direct method to accomplish the same end. It is the sole judge of the qualifications of its own members, and the sole judge of whether any member presenting his credentials has met those qualifications. It can refuse to seat any member who comes from a district where voters have been disfranchised; it can judge for itself whether this has been done, and there is no appeal from its decision.

If, when it has passed a law, any Court shall refuse to obey its behests, it can impeach the judges. If any president refuse to lend the executive arm of the government to the enforcement of the law, it can impeach

CHARLES W. CHESNUTT

the president. No such extreme measures are likely to be necessary for the enforcement of the Fourteenth and Fifteenth Amendments—and the Thirteenth, which is also threatened—but they are mentioned as showing that Congress is supreme; and Congress proceeds, the House directly, the Senate indirectly, from the people and is governed by public opinion. If the reduction of Southern representation were to be regarded in the light of a bargain by which the Fifteenth Amendment was surrendered, then it might prove fatal to liberty. If it be inflicted as a punishment and a warning, to be followed by more drastic measures if not sufficient, it would serve a useful purpose. The Fifteenth Amendment declares that the right to vote *shall not* be denied or abridged on account of color; and any measure adopted by Congress should look to that end. Only as the power to injure the Negro in Congress is reduced thereby, would a reduction of representation protect the Negro; without other measures it would still leave him in the hands of the Southern whites, who could safely be trusted to make him pay for their humiliation.

Finally, there is, somewhere in the Universe a "Power that works for righteousness," and that leads men to do justice to one another. To this power, working upon the hearts and consciences of men, the Negro can always appeal. He has the right upon his side, and in the end the right will prevail. The Negro will, in time, attain to full manhood and citizenship throughout the United States. No better guaranty of this is needed than a comparison of his present with his past. Toward this he must do his part, as lies within his power and his opportunity. But it will be, after all, largely a white man's conflict, fought out in the forum of the public conscience. The Negro, though eager enough when opportunity offered, had comparatively little to do with the abolition of slavery, which was a vastly more formidable task than will be the enforcement of the Fifteenth Amendment.

The Negro Problem, 1903

A Note About the Author

Charles W. Chesnutt (1858–1932) was an African-American author, lawyer, and political activist. Born in Cleveland to a family of "free persons of color" from North Carolina, Chesnutt spent his youth in Ohio before returning to the South after the Civil War. As a teenager, he worked as a teacher at a local school for Black students and eventually became principal at a college established in Fayetteville for the purpose of training Black teachers. Chesnutt married Susan Perry—with whom he had four daughters—in 1878 and moved to New York City for a short time before settling in Cleveland, where he studied law and passed the bar exam in 1887. His story "The Goophered Grapevine," published the same year, was the first story by an African American to appear in *The Atlantic*. Back in Ohio, Chesnutt started the court stenography business that would earn him the financial stability to pursue a career as a writer. He wrote several collections of short stories, including *The Conjure Woman* (1899) and *The Wife of His Youth and Other Stories of the Color-Line* (1899), both of which explore themes of race in America and African-American identity as well as employ African-American Vernacular English. Chesnutt was also an active member of the NAACP throughout his life, writing for its magazine *The Crisis*, serving on its General Committee, and working with such figures as W.E.B. Du Bois and Booker T. Washington.

A Note from the Publisher

Spanning many genres, from non-fiction essays to literature classics to children's books and lyric poetry, Mint Edition books showcase the master works of our time in a modern new package. The text is freshly typeset, is clean and easy to read, and features a new note about the author in each volume. Many books also include exclusive new introductory material. Every book boasts a striking new cover, which makes it as appropriate for collecting as it is for gift giving. Mint Edition books are only printed when a reader orders them, so natural resources are not wasted. We're proud that our books are never manufactured in excess and exist only in the exact quantity they need to be read and enjoyed.

Discover more of your favorite classics with Bookfinity™.

- Track your reading with custom book lists.
- Get great book recommendations for your personalized Reader Type.
- Add reviews for your favorite books.
- AND MUCH MORE!

Visit **bookfinity.com** and take the fun Reader Type quiz to get started.

Enjoy our classic and modern companion pairings!

Printed in the USA
CPSIA information can be obtained
at www.ICGtesting.com
JSHW022338140824
68134JS00019B/1552